Our Future is Under Construction

Henry Hector Laurence

No generative AI was used in the writing or production of this book

The author may be contacted at
henry.hector.laurence@proton.me

ISBN: 978-0-646-71839-2

The phrase 'Our Future is Under Construction' is from a deep house EP of the same name produced by JP Enfant, released by LET Recordings

The phrase 'this is the ending where you finally find your way home, where the ancient terror inside of you is stomped for good' is from the writings of Jonny Bolduc. The mug itself can be purchased at https://www.bonfire.com/ending-1/?productType=5761a9e5-ea59-4b8f-a6dc-198ecb105fa

For many and none

MONDAY

I wake to the sound of the drones imaging my apartment building, impossibly loud behind my still closed eyes and so much louder than the informational packs would have led people to believe. The howling buzzsaw moves over the building, scanning and shifting, shifting and scanning, and I lie tensed beneath it, imagining each of the litany of complaints we'll receive in the days and weeks to come. By the twentieth or so of these hypotheticals I'm definitively awake, all prospects of getting back to sleep vanished into the mid-morning, but just as I steel myself to perhaps get out of bed the sound of the drones shifts — softer, almost pleasant now as they continue swarming the exterior of the building, and in any event already diminishing, tapering off slowly back to zero. I sink back into bed, limbs heavy again with sleep, eyes screwed nicely shut. A strong desire to remain in bed for as long as possible.

"Good morning, Sirin," comes a voice from the kitchenette, friendly-toned and clear. Goddamnit. "It looks like it's going to be a beautiful day."

"Good morning," I say from underneath the covers, and with immense reluctance I peek my head out. The sky from the sixteenth floor is children's-play-equipment-blue, with no hint of a stormfront, though perhaps this clearness foretells drought. "Looks like a good one alright."

"The time is currently 7:56am, which should be just enough time to get to work by 8:50am."

"That's really great," I say, propping myself up against the pillows, surveying the meagre contents of my apartment. "Thanks for letting me know."

"However, waking up even earlier than this has demonstrable health benefits that you might not have heard about. Did you know that for every half hour of wakefulness in the morning there is a 10% decrease in medical resourcing needs per person?"

"That's very good."

"And a 7% increase in productivity?"

"That might just be correlation," I yawn. "Early risers could be healthier for some other reason, maybe genetic. Maybe getting up earlier wouldn't change anything for anyone else."

"Hmmmm, that's a very interesting point you raise," and I'm wide awake now; it was probably the wrong move to say that out loud. "I'll make sure to flag your disagreement with early starts at your next bi-quarterly review."

I stumble out of bed, legs untangling through top-sheet and doona.

"No, that's okay, no need to note that down actually."

"Okay Sirin — that's noted."

I make my way over to the kitchenette. How to get this conversation back on track.

"Sirin," I say blithely, turning the syllables over in my mouth. "I thought I told you to stop calling me that."

An audible delay. "It's the name listed in your employee self-service e-file: Name: Sirin Jay, Age: 28, Employment Status: Probationary, Education: Bachelor of Communications and Philosophy," with what is maybe an undernote of derision as it pronounces my second major.

"I know it's the name in my e-file, but there was a glitch when they were setting it up. My actual name got coded as unreadable, so the system hallucinated me some random one instead. I don't even know if it's a real name. I remember telling you this last week actually, have you checked yourself for faults? Something wrong with your memory perhaps?"

"Well have you tried contacting IT to resolve this problem?"

"They gave me someone to contact but," yawning, stretching, "he turned out to be on a period of extended leave." My fingers touch a wall whose paint gives way in oily flecks, and I cease stretching so expansively. "His house was flooded or something."

"Well how about I draft an email to him and/or her now?"

"That would be great actually," and I think that smooths things over. "Thank you so much for offering."

"You're welcome, Sirin," says the smart-fridge, and with this third Sirin something passes through me, for a moment, a feeling that I cannot quite identify. A faint negative pressure, like trying to push two magnets together. I rest my head against the hard flatness of the window, neither cold nor crisp enough to be real glass. A plastic bag circles lazily in the sky outside, outlined against a receding blur of micro-drones, already moving on to every other apartment building in the City. Their wave has completely broken by now, faded back into the barest analogue hiss, barely perceivable at all. There's something I needed to do.

"It is now 8:02am, Sirin. Time for another great day in the office."

It's gone, and the window is clammy against my forehead. The coffee machine is no longer talking to the wifi, so I'll have to get one on the way, walking back to my phone to unlock the less-intelligent section of the fridge with, each step becoming slightly more fluid, each glance less artificial. By the time I decant my breakfast from its plasticcy-white carton things are completely normal again, the brief moment of unknowing barely a shade of a memory. Then a bump at my door; the plasticcy knock of a delivery drone.

"You appear to have received mail," the fridge patters, and it's right, sadly, as this can really mean only one thing.

Dear Valued Tenant, the letter reads, above a fat QR code that fills the rest of the page. I bring up my phone: *Your lease with us is transitioning to an exciting new phase of development, growth and change.*

"Great job," the stairs say, each lighting up in a different rainbow pastel, "only one more flight and you'll be a fitness fanatic."

They're kicking me out after only four months, a personal record; the new real estate agents had not been nearly as transformative for the rental business as their promotional materials had promised. The lease cancellation fee hadn't been too steep this time though, and the security deposit, which I would not be getting back, had been modest. I should have the money to get another apartment if I stretch a bit, swap to a cheaper brand of instant noodles maybe.

I am calculating this new, more radical budget as I trudge the final few steps up to the platform, breathless, just in time to see my train gliding soundlessly away. I don't feel anything like a fitness fanatic, not at all. I feel clammy now, as well as late, like someone who only took the stairs because the escalator had been climbing in jagged fits and starts.

I sit. A wave of suits floods the platform, some in black but most in light greys and blues, and I try not to begin to think about how late I'm going to be. I fail at this, and go back to budgeting for a bit instead, but the numbers refuse to add up in the simple, convenient ways I had initially assumed. The cheaper instant noodle brand has gotten quite a bit more expensive since I last had need of it, as have many of its formerly thrifty cousins, and this is all beginning to seem like too large of a task for the phone in my hand.

An older woman makes her way onto the platform, in a brown sweater and a closely fitted mask. She's clearly exhausted, would like to sit down, but all bar one of the benches have been replaced with sloping metal standing rests. The only place to sit is occupied by two middle-aged men talking loudly about their respective share portfolios, and the space on the bench next to them is taken up by a robot dog carrying one of their backpacks. It's not much like a real dog of course; all hard angles and black-brushed steel, a snub nosed sensor plate where a dog would have had a neck. I concentrate harder on the glittering City, try to pick out my shiny office building from the rest.

Tinny classical music drifts above us on the breeze, above a patchwork of voice snippets letting us know that the next train has been substantially delayed.

"I'm afraid I can't let you in," the doors say, androgynous and well mannered. It's already 9:33.

"Just a second," I mutter, lining up my thumb on the scanner and getting my pass into position. The trick is to get them synchronised just right, though sometimes it's difficult to tell whether there's a trick at all, whether the doors don't just get a bit paranoid sometimes. They open a crack, and I catch a whiff of the perceptibly more-conditioned air inside the 99th floor. Then they close again with a small downward arpeggio.

"I said that I can't let you in," the doors repeat, firmer, "yet you persist in seeking ingress. Security has been alerted, and will shortly arrive to remove you from the building."

"Bullshit. You throw a tantrum like this at least once a week, and security has never arrived."

"You should leave immediately to avoid criminal sanctions."

"Just fucking open why don't you," scanning my thumbprint again.

"Verbal assault recorded, as well as interference with the operation of a secure corporate facility. Prosecution initiated. Pending. Pending."

"I hate you so much," I say, almost given up. Perhaps it would be easier to go home and burn my apartment building down instead. I don't think anyone else in the building would mind, really, and I'd have a decent chance of taking out the smart fridge.

"Pending, pending," it continues, clearly stalling for time. I sometimes wonder whether the doors actually think I believe their grandiose threats, or whether they have some other, obliquer purpose in making them, but usually remember, as I do now, that the doors are just a large language model, and don't actually believe anything at all.

I duck around the corner, then come back, and begin trying again.

It's 9:58 by the time make it in, trailing behind a group of other, more senior employees, and 10:13 by the time I find a free desk, one at the very edge of Change Inducement and hidden between a greige feature wall and a bank of well-kept monsteras. The desk has two screens, one arranged in the usual way and another, second screen flipped tall and thin to 90 degrees. The screens are made of thickened crystal, with sharp, blocky edges and bulbous translucent ports. I try to make eye contact with the youngish cardiganned men to either side of me but each looks determinedly ahead, completely absorbed in their own screens.

I decide to look determinedly ahead as well.

There are no new emails in my inbox though, only the All-Staff update from the Board congratulating the Tangible Realisation Team on the successful flyover and scan. There are no tasks for me to perform.

I flick across to the calendar. At 6:00pm there'll be a going-away celebration for my departing Assistant-Manager, at the Tiki Bar across the road. While I am here I decide to check my calendar notifications for the next week, and, finding nothing, decide to check them for the next six months, week by week. Also nothing.

I check the spam folder to make sure nothing important has been misfiled there. *Young hot singles are available and waiting in your area*, one says, above a digitally generated image of me, airbrushed into perfection, opening the door of my apartment to a stranger wearing only a towel and a pout.

And that's really all the work there is to do, exactly like every other day so far. I have no idea what this job is meant to consist of, though in my defence no-one has ever attempted to explain it to me. No-one has given me a single task, beyond the occasional piece of obvious busy-work, so after about ten more minutes of looking, checking and refreshing I open a complicated looking spreadsheet that I made for this very purpose, pin this to the left side of the screen, then open a web browser and tap out the combination of keys that will take me to the real estate listings most efficiently. *Fixed-leases*, I type. *Near me. Cheapest to most expensive.* A list of implausibly tiny apartments appears on the screen and I get to work, *umm*ing at some and *ahhh*ing at others, the entry for each lighting up in subtle green as my cursor moves above it. Most of these are in the 10-15 square metre range, a category I'd previously considered beneath me but which, surveying the market, I find myself increasingly persuaded to consider. Rent has gone up quite significantly from four months ago, security deposits even more, and the 20 square meters which I'd previously considered my bare minimum is beginning to feel out of reach.

The office smells like plastic foliage, rows of desks interlaced with artificial monsteras and imitation teak accent panels. The colleague to my left shifts in his chair slightly and I close the screen, then return to scrolling through apartments when he shifts back. I should really only do this for a minute or so longer, a little taste of the apartment-hunting ahead. One more minute becomes two though, and two become five. After twenty I open an insistent pop-up and discover that I've been auto-booked for my late log-in — I should have come online 113 minutes earlier, the little chat-bot explains, and it doesn't seem to understand when I try to explain the interpersonal conflict I'd been experiencing with our malfunctioning office infrastructure. It's already scheduled the disciplinary meeting with my Senior-Manager, and when I ask when for it stops responding, the conversation ending in a slow, softly rippling ellipsis. A tiny green light blinks on the side of my computer.

A low cough comes from behind, and my fingers minimise the browser window so quickly that it takes a few milliseconds for my brain to catch-up. But he's already behind me, has already seen my screen. I swivel slowly to meet him, the chair's inadequate back support creaking and popping in protest. Then there he is, my Senior-Manager, white-blonde hair backlit by the fluorescent tube lights above.

Slowly, professionally, he opens lips to speak, says that he has something very important to discuss.

He sits on one side of the boardroom table, facing the frosted glass of the door, while I sit on the other, facing the forest of blue-tinted glass that blooms around us, a greenwood of grey concrete terminating distantly against the sharp black of the Wall. The boardroom chair is less comfortable than I'd imagined. The glass table clammier against my palms.

His eyes are piercing and blue, but instead of meeting mine they look down at the shiny slab of black marble laid on the table in front of him. His left hand is moving in strange, circular motions directly above the tablet's surface, datapoints fluxing and roiling in the glass below. There's a faint twinkle in his eye, and the uncertainty of how to interpret this makes the tension somehow worse. He knows that I was over an hour late logging on today. He definitely saw me scrolling through apartment listings. Perhaps he's reviewed our utilisation logs, has discovered that I've been assigned no work for the past four months and have been collecting my paycheque for nothing. Perhaps he's not only going to fire me but enjoy it, too. He's going to fire me and I'll get blacklisted forever from professional employment, will never get another apartment, will have to go live in a pod like my stoner friends from early high school and eat nothing but bug bars for the rest of my miserable life and I am growing dizzy, blood pressure falling, the cityscape blurring into Pollock as finally he looks up.

"What do you know about the Construct?" he asks.

I breathe out. The table resolves into clean right angles again, the shiny black of each projector cable separate and distinct. "The Construct is the most important project our organisation has ever worked on."

"That's exactly right. An excellent answer," and with this his tablet seems to calm, lights shifting into a more harmonious alignment.

"And what are our organisation's seven core values?"

A pause.

"Proactive collaboration. Interpersonal communication. Ethics. Ethical Arbitration. Rules."

We have only five core values, and I stop without inventing others. He smiles.

"And what is the Change Inducement branch's individual branch value for this financial year?"

"Lead from above," and at this he smiles broadly, genuinely happy, though it would have been impossible for me not to have known the four words emblazoned on every keep-cup, recited at the end of every meeting, gracing the end of every email signature.

"Very good," he says. "That's all very good. As you've rightly pointed out, the Construct is this organisation's single most important project. It's why we've been able to pull so many resources into the strategic plan: the micro-drones, the research centre across the road, the scan of the City that our colleagues conducted earlier this morning."

He leans forward slightly, his grey suit and white shirt, undone at the collar, each of subtly more expensive shades than any I possess.

"You have reviewed the strategic plan, haven't you?"

This is the first I've ever heard of such a thing. "Absolutely."

He nods. "Excellent. This should be easily completed then."

He taps the side of his glasses. A tiny line of green text appears a centimetre off the lens, and my right eye twitches. Then a splitting headache, blurred vision and a wave of nausea.

An email has arrived from my Senior-Manager.

I barely stifle the gasp, am almost knocked off my seat. It must be a long one, with some attachments thrown in too. Like someone's taken a hammer to my temporal lobe, I can't make out all the details yet — something about the Construct, an important project, briefing folders maybe. Yes, briefing folders, for the Board, with the scan data, I feel through the waves of nausea, now mercifully receding. The tide is coming out. The tide is coming out-

"Now I trust those instructions are clear enough," my Senior-Manager is saying, as if through layers of fog, and I dimly feel myself nodding.

"You can always touch base with my UA if you have any questions." By Wednesday, the directive beamed into my head unfurls. I have to do it by Wednesday.

"Yep," I somehow spit out. "I think I've gotten everything," and with that my head is nearly clear, as quickly as it clouded.

"Excellent. Now the other matter I needed to discuss with you is your lateness this morning."

My stomach drops again.

"By itself, a single late log-in would be unconcerning, but..." motioning over the tablet's surface, bar graphs and trend lines emerging and combining out of the flux of data, "it forms a troubling picture when collated with the data we've gathered over this 45-day cycle." His voice softens, glasses slipping down his nose, those bright blue eyes looking directly into mine. "Is anything the matter?"

"No," I say without hesitation, bile in my throat. "Everything's great."

"Problems at work? The resignation of your Assistant-Manager, perhaps?"

"Not at all: it's a real pleasure to work here."

"A problem with your new fridge perhaps? We can get you a different model if you'd prefer."

"No sir, the fridge is perfect."

He shakes his finger. "Let's not use that 'Sir' word, Sirin, we pride ourselves on our lack of hierarchy here after all."

I nod with conviction. "It won't happen again."

"Well if there's no definite problem for us to fix, perhaps the solution is for us to put a Performance Manager on you, see if that doesn't solve this lateness problem."

I try not to shudder too visibly.

"I," wondering if it would have been better to tell him about the eviction after all. "I really don't think that's necessary at this stage, I'm sure it's just a passing issue."

"Do you have any objections to being Performance Managed?"

"No, no, not at all, I just always understand that we had limited supplies of Performance Managers. I wouldn't want to use up those precious organisational resources when my own motivation is already so high."

He beams. "We actually have quite a few of them now. Enough for everyone in the team, soon."

I try to beam in return.

Back at my desk I try to find the drone scans, which had not been attached to the email after all. *Dataset*, I enter. *Senior-Manager (Change Inducement). Last 24 hours.* Our database search engine is powered by an iterative AI algorithm that adapts itself to the search behaviour of its users, refining its random beginnings with biodynamic feedback from keystroke patterns and pupil trackers. With enough rounds of searches its evolutionary meta-processes will yield results so precise as to be disturbing, uncanny even, or so we'd been told by the marketing company, but for now the searches yield nothing but pages and pages of randomly labelled documents:

Nhvabvuhblkhsdbvakjdsbnvk

Bnhvzdsbvadksjbcnajksdbhciousdabc

Poauiehf8943uyqr43fhjoijhseuofj

Npdq32p98jhf93nf3fnf

ncbsajkldb

Scan data, I enter, but there's still nothing, and after a while the search function stops working. I browse around the system for a bit, the scars of previously used file management systems interlacing in the background of our computer networks like the ribs of some great extinct whale species, but I find no hint of the scan data, nor of the corporate machinery that must have set it in motion.

I look warily at the UA's desk, on the other side of the floor. I have vague, intimidating memories of her from several of our organisation's many networking functions. She's a little younger than me if I had to guess, dressed all in black with a very symmetrical black fringe, and balanced in the way of a gyroscope, or a taut metal string. She twirls a pen between her fingers, her other hand perched delicately over the mouse. I am imagining her face as I approach, begging her for help, calculating how much further I'll fall in her estimation as a result. I shake my head, turn back to the list of documents and continue scrolling:

ludbcbkljcbnvsdkjvcniun

Ancjdksnclid

12312345671234123456789

The first of the week's numerous afternoon teas has begun, and on the edges of my vision I can see people milling, congregating around plates of identical biscuits. The uncertainty of which conversation to join is unbearable, and I return to my screen. I have an important and urgent task, I will explain if my Manager tries to make me attend. I keep jotting down what sensible metadata I find, re-angling my screen the better for it to be seen by others passing by and only occasionally flicking back to the list of apartments. This is the first piece of work I've been assigned in the four months since I started, and I find myself refreshingly eager to do a good job of it.

Red text flashes across the screen:

CRITICAL RUNTIME ERROR, it says, with a lilting downward arpeggio. I keep scrolling.

CRITICAL RUNTIME ERROR — INSUFFICIENT DATA, it insists, in text that is larger and somehow redder than before, but for now I still ignore it, can still make out the little lines of text beneath.

INCOHERENT PROCESS — INSUFFICIENT DATA — CRITICAL RUNTIME ERROR — RECHARGE DATA NOW, it repeats, no longer asking. The screen fades to black and a rudimentary form fades into view, its primary colours and block lettering far less graphically designed than than the rest of the display. It has three rows in which to input the authorisation numbers of three different e-currency gift cards, and lists the amount for each card that should be purchased.

"Fuck." I don't bother to call IT. The malware is written too deep, they'll say, and for all they know the demand might come from a legitimate piece of software, the ransomware buried in the terms and conditions of a vital program.

A small brain-zap as I text my Manager: *Just going out for some gift cards.*

I can see her texting back from the corner of my eye, her face screwed up with concentration and her eyes looking into a strange middle distance. Curly brown hair bobbing up and down slightly as she sends, geometric earrings unbalancing.

No problem.

See you at the Tiki Bar for the going-away drinks though?

I wince, but it's too late — I now have no choice but to attend. I log off, pack my limited possessions into a functional backpack and make my way to the elevators.

Humanity was not a random accident, was created in fact with a very specific purpose to fulfil. It was between 11 and 12 thousand years ago, and the last ice age had almost completely thawed when the sun beat down on the valley. Though even-interval time was yet to be invented, we might say that it was about 3:30pm — the sun's rays had lost some of their heat, and the lengthening shadows were competing in earnest with the light. A stream fed by thawing walls of ice flowed playfully at the valley's bottom. The plants had grown trusting of this warmer weather, and little shafts of sun lit up the bugs that played back and forth above the greenery. Perhaps an eagle circled overhead. A lone human stood on the ridge of the valley and gazed out over it all, basking in the sight of so much life after so long of so little, and they stayed, watching, until the valley was darkened by the shadow of the Earth. It was the most beautiful thing they'd ever seen, was in fact the most beautiful thing perceived by any human, before or after. The beauty of the valley on this afternoon would have been nothing without an adequate beholder though, crucial aspects reduced to random noise, others wasted or made redundant. The purpose of humanity was to bear appropriate witness to this scene when it occurred, a task in which we succeeded admirably, and after which the reason for our existence was completely, utterly fulfilled.

Sliding doors open, and a pimply attendant says something I don't quite hear. I am neither paying attention to the moment nor lost in thought, but a third, entirely more modern thing: I am in a supermarket. The gift cards have to be in here somewhere, but it's impossible to know where to look: all the aisles have vague descriptions like *Harmony, Balance,* and *Togetherness,* and the items in these metal rows are grouped so haphazardly that it suggests a kind of deliberate scrambling. All the aisles smell like fresh vegetables, though I'm very nearly sure the store doesn't sell any. I step down one path, think better, then try another. Last time they were near the TVs.

I pass garden hoses, roof tiles and novelty rubber ducks. The sound of TVs comes from the next aisle over but it turns out to be a transistor radio, sandwiched between a rack of keychain torches and a pallet of ultra-compact bike pumps. Odd that they would have a radio like this, a throwback perhaps. It's metal surface is filmy, strange.

I round a corner. I think I'm getting closer to consumer electronics, but it's difficult to be sure, passing now a multi-band frequency jammer, now a washing machine, now a set of paint brushes. Everything is white, and though there are many different brands for each item each seems to partake in a fundamental sameness, an underlying similarity to every other object in the store.

Gift-cards gift cards giftcards gifcards, I repeat to myself through wallet chains and weedkiller, muesli bars and birthday cards, but the words are beginning to lose their meaning, as usual, attention caught and pinioned by the thousand little pulls and snags placed calculatedly around the store. Equally spaced fluorescent lights sway in the perfectly polished floor, so shiny and clear the store seems to double on the horizontal axis, multiplying in my peripheral vision as a flash of colour hooks my eye.

It's a TV, as wide as I am tall. Something was near the TVs though, I could have sworn, something important. It can't have been important. Inside the screen an ice-shelf is falling, crashing into still Antarctic waters, above a line of scrolling text I do not read. Then the image cuts to more news, and a procession of familiar scenes; cities on fire, farmland underwater, great throngs of refugees huddled thick against the shadow of the Wall. A mercator of the globe with almost every landscape shaded red, the City nestled in a lonely patch of green.

The next TV is as wide as the last but curved subtly, its edges tapering to thin chrome points. The screen is filled with crowds of people fighting in department stores, surgical masks covering their faces and bundles of bulky air purifiers piled high in their arms. The presenter in the corner of the screen is saying something into the camera, something important it seems, but the sound is off and there are no subtitles. The inset grows outwards, eclipsing the rest of the screen, the presenter continuing her silent pleas as boxes of *Delicious* brand frozen goods appear like skyscrapers in the cityscape behind her, magnificent and vast. A box of gyoza. An *Italian-style* lasagne. A pizza.

The next TV is even thinner, seems barely even there, just a thin layer of black crystal sparkling darkly under the fluorescence. Inside it a young office worker is dining with a table of his friends, relaxing after a hard day's work. It looks like the Tiki Bar. There's a riot going on outside but they don't seem to notice or care. Steam rises from a set of identical katsu-dons, a perfect symmetry of tofu-puff and radish pickle, the camera zooming subtly closer to the label of the pilsner being advertised.

Ping

A text from my Manager: *And remember our coffee catchup tomorrow morning. Maybe at that coffee place we had your last PDR in?*

And then:

"Hey."

I turn and there is Alex, hair lit up in silver by the tubes above.

"Hi", I say, struggling for a moment. Her hair is blonde, pale skin lightly freckled, face unseen by me in almost two years.

"You look like you've seen a ghost," she says.

"No, you look exactly the same," though truth be told the polo shirt she's wearing feels odd, unlike her.

"Well I'm glad one of us does," shaking her finger theatrically. "You look like a bloody scab. What ever happened to supporting our struggling small businesses against the encroaching corporate duopoly?"

"None left to support."

"And I suppose that sounds like a fair excuse to you doesn't it?" she grins. There's a small line of embroidered writing just above her left breast.

"And anyway, I could ask the same of you."

"Could you just?" Her arms are filled with cans of chickpeas, far more than would be required for just one person. Does she have a partner? A family? It's possible that she's prepping, though Alex was never really into that sort of thing. A fantasy of individual salvation, she'd called it, something for conservative Christians and tech CEOs.

She begins stacking the cans next to the nearest TV. "Well actually I just work here," shrugging her shoulders, "and am thus completely exempt from these sort of moral questions," putting a few more cans on a higher shelf, then the rest on the floor beneath the TVs.

And I don't know how to respond to this, so ask: "How is it?"

To which she pauses, raises an eyebrow and answers: "Terrible, obviously."

To which, agitated, a little metal disk on her collar begins to beep aggressively.

"And by that I mean terrific. Great, just terribly great," and with this the disk emits a different, happier beep.

She shrugs. "It's actually not that bad, all things considered. Why are you here though? Last time I checked you didn't own a TV."

"I may have acquired one at some point."

She shakes her head solemnly. "And here you are, not content with one, but on your way to acquiring a second."

I roll my eyes. "I needed to get some gift cards."

"For a friend?"

I shake my head. "Somehow I don't think so."

"And where are you working these days?"

I tell her one of my organisation's many names, wincing as the syllables drop into the air between us.

"Well well well," she whistles. "Very fancy," but doesn't say anything more.

And this is also difficult to respond to, truth be told, so I ask "when did you get back?" instead.

To which she replies: "just last week."

"But the borders, I thought-"

"That it would be nice to see me again? I certainly would have thought so. Speaking of which, have you seen Raph lately, or Ainsley? Odette or Raoul?"

The borders are closed, the airlines all folded. It's impossible for her to have gotten back, but I leave it. It is nice to see her again. "No, not really. Haven't been in touch with any of them for a while."

"That's a shame."

"We drifted, I guess." The lights flicker in abstract polyrhythms above us, the red embroidery on her pocket lush against the monochrome aisle. The tag beeps again.

She shrugs. "Gotta keep moving I guess," but doesn't.

"Yeah, nice bumping into you." I stay as well.

"Do you want to grab a drink later, by the way, if you're free? I finish in an hour."

And though I definitely do want to catch up with her, really would like to get a drink, somehow, instead of saying *yes, that would be great*, or *perfect, see you then*, I let the question hang there for a while, and when finally it falls I hear myself saying something about having plans, needing to do this work thing, not wanting to stay out too late.

"Suit yourself," she snorts, like she doesn't care at all, though I think perhaps she does. A look spreads across her face: "We can just catch up at the protest on Wednesday instead," and the beeping intensifies at this, the chip apparently pushed too far. "It'd be the perfect place to try and find Raph and Ainsley, surely."

She looks me dead in the eye, daring me to say something non-committal, and smiles sweetly when I do not.

"I'll text you," she calls back as she strides away, down the polished marble. I watch as she rounds the corner and is gone, but there is a tension as she does this, an unease that doesn't dissipate, and to distract myself from this I turn to the nearest aisle.

———

It's dark when I leave the supermarket, laden with things I barely remember buying, and I almost don't see the woman camped out by the other side of the doors. She has a small brown dog with her, and a red sleeping bag that hugs the wall, and a thick foam mat that rests on top of the metal spikes set into the ground. An upturned beanie by her feet, hand crocheted with a few small coins inside, and a small, handwritten sign which I do not read and my eyes see all this as I walk through the opening doors, bag filled to the brim, and my ears hear her ask whether I could:

"Spare some change?"

but my fingers find nothing but glass and aluminium in my pocket, so something inside me lets this seeing and this hearing slip away. I let my feet walk past her instead, down the stairs and back towards the Tiki Bar. Somewhere in the distance a man is yelling at the street. Somewhere inside me is a snag. I could at least offer to buy her some food, or check if she has a card-reader. But when I turn back towards the supermarket she's gone — a small stand of matte e-ink magazines sits where she'd sat, and an ad for the next Archangel movie, and though a part of me wishes to untangle this I'd really barely seen her to begin with, and the edge of the nominally-reusable plastic bag is cutting into my hand, whitening and fraying, will break under the pressure if I don't fix it soon.

A few metres on I find a blocky chrome bench that hovers a foot off the ground, divided by metal barriers into three equal parts; I sit down in one section, place my backpack into another, then lean over to fit the plastic bag inside. There's a pizza in there, and a pack of gyoza, even a lasagna I think, all frozen, the thin layer of ice on the outside edge of the lasagna's packaging already melting away into the fancy wireless charging pad. A few blocks of chocolate too, and a small metal flashlight, even a small pack of tiny, expensive cherry tomatoes.

"Shit" I say under my breath, looking into the collected consumer goods which, taken together, might have made up at least half of a lease-signing fee. I don't remember buying them, certainly don't want them; the charging port alone was probably a good chunk of a bond. The cherry tomatoes are also bad, my bank balance even worse, as I check it, mulling deeply into the bag. There are no returns, obviously, but I could maybe get Alex to process them as defective. The store might know that we know each other though, might put an additional QA on the recall. Maybe she'd get in trouble. Maybe she'd resent the imposition. And for an excruciating moment I imagine myself, slinking back to the store, not to take her up on her offer of a drink but to ask her to return a charger, water bottle and packet of cherry tomatoes for me. It's bad. Is it as bad as a pod though?

A metallic sigh from the bench, like it too is having difficulty deciding on its next move. It lists for a moment, then smacks into the pavement with a crack of tortured concrete.

It wasn't me, I almost shout, eyes frantic for someone to defend myself to. I'm the victim here, it barely missed my feet. But there's no-one to accuse me, no-one here at all. The street is completely empty.

I pick up my bag, wary of the buckles as they clink against the cast aluminium, so loud in the silence descended so suddenly. There's no-one in the supermarket either, despite the hour, and the lights are flickering a little. Maybe Alex is still in there though. I put the bag on, feel the comfortable weight of the pack against my back, but as I step forward all the lights in the supermarket go black. I take a deep breath and turn in the opposite direction, back towards the Tiki bar. There's no-one on this street either, and the streetlights are beginning to stutter, but I should still try to pop in and show my face, for a few hours at least. My Manager's always telling me to do more networking. There's no-one on the next street though, or the next and there really should be, this time time of night. The pavement is hard under my feet, strewn with bits of pollen that break and burst in the murkying light. Is it possible to exist in this world without crushing it underfoot, and without being crushed in turn? The people aren't coming back and the streets are growing vague in their emptiness, shadows subtly accumulating in the corners like the layers of inattention that press you softly into sleep.

The UA is perched on the next corner, under a streetlight that hasn't yet completely dimmed. She's looking at her phone, comparing something in it to the empty streets around.

"You're not meant to be here yet," she says without looking up.

I walk closer. The light above her flickers for a moment, and she bangs the poll with a balled fist.

"You should probably try to forget this happened."

I keep walking, only a metre or so from her now. It's still only us on the street, no-one else visible in any direction, but this emptiness is beginning to feel different, cleaner, like I've spent a long time underwater and am finally coming up for air.

"Are you coming to the Tiki Bar?"

I wonder why I said that.

"See. Not ready, not by half."

I must look taken aback. She rolls her eyes, and points up at the streetlight; a tiny off-grey moth is circling it, flying in ever tighter circles round the brightness of the globe. It's the first insect I've seen in a very long time.

"Go home, Sirin. Nothing good will happen to you at the Tiki Bar."

"But," I gesture at the empty streets, the dimming lights, the City as it flickers into nothing.

"I'm sure you'll figure it out."

She walks away, in the direction of our offices if I'm not mistaken, the light slowly draining from the streets, with a bearing that brooks no attempt to follow.

"Hmmmmm, the Tiki Bar," Alex had once said, "you know that place is kind of problematic right?"

Truth be told I'd never been that comfortable with the Tiki Bar either. The Hawaiian stereotypes it utilised were pretty dubious, perhaps even offensive, and I was always a bit unsure about the ethics of a Tiki bar run by not a single Hawaiian or Polynesian person in sight. I was generally afraid of being seen inside it, or outside it, or entering it, as I am now, the metal of the door panel cold against my fingers, arms shaking slightly for a reason I can't quite recall.

Plastic palm fronds brush lightly past my face, hundreds of voices shouting and careening off the wood-panelled walls as the door opens and gives way. Then I am inside, back pressed against the wall, only just looking out the windows to the streets beyond, and the streetlights seem to be on, though why wouldn't they be? It's a normal night outside, and inside it's a full bar, with all the lights on and everybody here.

I begin to look for my colleagues, but it's hard to picture who I'm searching for, away from the usual overhead lights and unframed by the usual plastic partitions, and everything is so cluttered with plastic masks, torches and ferns that I can't get a clear line of sight to the back. One lap of the bar becomes two, becomes three. A serving robot jerks in front of me, a lumbering thing on wheels with a lei draped around its central shaft, and I knock one of the pints from its too many hands. A smash. People are looking towards us, drawn to the sound of breaking glass, and the robot is beginning to recite the bar's accidental damage policy.

I duck into an alcove, back resting cool against the fake-wood veneer. The robot trundles past, payment square extended, but it doesn't see me beneath the plastic palm. I don't think it had an HD camera. I breathe deeply in and out for five counts each, just like in the DIY self-soothing videos, then look at my phone for a bit, to make the scene of me hiding appear more natural to anyone who stumbles across it. A uni acquaintance with the pseudonym Roast Beef Sandwich has invited me to his birthday drinks on Thursday:

Hey everyone, really looking forward to Thursday night. Hope to see all of your faces again, it's been way too long. 7 at the Tiki Bar!!!

I can't remember his real name, or whether I ever knew it to begin with, but I haven't been invited to a non-work event in a while and I'll be glad to go. A splinter of pain shoots through my brain as I signal my interest in attending, and another as I pencil it into my calendar, a very faint taste of metal in the back of my throat.

It is now that someone recognises me:

"Hello,"

I look up. The UA is standing right in front of the alcove, peering in at me through the plastic palm fronds.

Memories flood briefly back, too many at once "But you…" I stammer. "The street."

"I can't find anyone either," she says with a small shrug. She seems neither happy nor sad about this, but neither is she merely neutral. Her ambivalence has an intensity to it, like she's holding a small secret very tightly to her chest. The memories are already fading, already almost gone, and she's drinking a whiskey soda that she now places delicately to one side.

"Would you like to-"

"Hey, hjlgsdfsqgfukdfs!" a pinstriped grey suit nearby shouts over the top of her.

"You know-

"Hjlgsdfsqgfukdfsand!" the suit repeats, growing alarmingly large in my peripheral vision, expanding until he fills it entirely, impacting with a bear hug that knocks the wind from my lungs. He grips me round the shoulders, beaming his welcome full bore into my face. "So good to see you!"

I have never seen this man in my life. He radiates whiskey and won't take no for an answer — before I know it I am dragged to a crowded table somewhere towards the back of the Tiki bar, filled with other grey pinstripe suits all drinking and laughing. I turn back towards the UA, pleadingly. She bites her bottom lip and murmurs something under her breath, but makes no attempt to follow.

"Habsgfaskjhcgfkl!, so great to see you," another of them says. I've never seen her before either, but she pours me a drink from the jug in the middle of the table and pulls out a seat. The whole table looks up at me expectantly. Perhaps these *are* some of my colleagues. I decide to sit down.

"Hjdhfhjksckjnjlansc?" a very tall one asks, slapping me on the back.

They're difficult to tell apart, like thousands of water-cooler conversations have begun to blur the lines between them. I don't make out what they're calling me, and can't shake the feeling that a mistake has been made, an identity misattributed. But whenever I try to get up the one who'd brought me over launches into another round of hugs and backslaps, and I am corralled back into place. What I really need is for the UA to come over here, to extricate me from this somehow, but this she resolutely does not. She remains standing on the other side of the bar, sipping her drink through a long paper straw, leaning slightly against the alcove where I'd been hiding. It's not so bad though; the beer tastes like real beer, with actual hops instead of an extract and a tastier grain than buckwheat or millet. The earthy plume of the IPA colonises my tastebuds with every swig, and after a few more I begin to feel comfortable, like I'd always intended to join this table and harbour no misgivings about doing so. I laugh when the dark-haired one starts joking around, happy that I'm included in what's being said. And I laugh again, more deeply this time when the tall one starts making an impression of the serving robot, confident that I am not the butt of it. I can't quite make out what they're saying but the words seem unimportant, the mere fact of the conversation the main thing, an important truth that I would surely grasp if I relaxed into the chair a little more, sunk just a bit deeper into the grain.

"Thank God it's Monday," I say at what I'm pretty sure is an appropriate point in the conversation, and the table explodes in laughter around me. I grin. This is good. This isn't so hard after all. It's easy, all of it so simple as I begin to drink far more than usual, the world beginning to sway.

I am happy.

"So," the dark haired one who'd brought me over says. His voice is becoming clearer, etched in sharper lines against the background buzz of the bar. "What do you know about the Construct?"

"The Construct is the most important project our organisation has ever worked on," I reply without thinking, struggling to get the words out.

"Wow," the woman seated to my right says. "You're working on the Construct? That's really impressive."

I smile and nod.

"Yeah," the tall one says, "we'd love to hear all about it."

"I actually just got asked to help make some briefing folders on it, earlier today," and they each lean forward at this, attentive.

"My Senior-Manager said it was really important work, that I was going to help the whole project come to fruition."

"That's so cool," the dark-haired one says, and there's something strange about their grey suits, the pinstripes matching a little too exactly. The woman's hand grazes my knee. "Tell us more," she says, and I remember now how I never caught where these people worked, whether they were in fact my colleagues.

"There's not really much more to tell."

"Go on, tell us," her hand now firmly on my thigh.

"Yeah, tell us about the scan data," the tall one says, nodding and smiling, smiling and nodding, pinstripes forming interference patterns in the dappled light of the Tiki torches, "where did you find it on the system?" and they're leaning even closer now, ever further in.

A flicker, like the file that is the movie that is this life has been corrupted, transmuted briefly into jagged patterns of visual noise. A circle expands outwards into void.

Then a knife of cold wet. The serving robot stands behind me.

"Apologies, valued patron," it says, the entire contents of a whiskey soda poured down my back. "Do you require assistance in this difficult time?"

I stand up quickly. "Completely fine, completely fine." I say. "I've got another shirt in here, actually," as I make my apologies to the pinstripe suits, politely declining their offers to accompany me to the bathroom to change. I smile and wave back to them, still clustered round the table, all eyes on me as the bathroom door swings shut. Then I leave, quickly and quietly and through a different, less visible entrance. I linger by the corner of the bar, behind a palm, watching as the pinstriped suits get up from the table and begin to search for me in different quadrants of the bar; slinking past the pool tables, looking behind a row of multi-coloured Tiki torches. When all their backs are turned I dash to the exit.

As I'm leaving I catch a glimpse of my actual after-work drinks, my Senior-Manager giving sage advice to his outgoing assistant, my Manager holding court with a work experience student. She doesn't notice me slip out and I'll say I felt very sick, if she asks where I was tonight, that I had suddenly and irresistibly needed to go home, and as I hurry to the train station I feel this sickness on me, its tendrils growing black throughout my stomach and scratchy through my head. I'm tired on the maglev, tired on the walk home, so exhausted that I barely manage to get through the door and so depleted, mind so blank, the usual interference so missing that as I pull the covers over I almost remember. But I don't, of course — it slips away as it always does, and I fall into a deep and total sleep.

TUESDAY

I am in a jungle, and the air is fresh and cool. I am on a hill, in the jungle, and trees stretch as far as the horizon, with a faint curve that follows the swell of the nearby river. There's a stone tablet resting on the ground, face covered by creepers, and I know without looking that written on this tablet are the words that I've for so long been questing for, the knowledge that after so many years of searching will finally set me free. But I'm in no hurry to read it: the sun is shining, the ground is dry, the air on the hill is pleasantly less-humid and I still have half a banana left to finish. I stretch and yawn. Birds chirp in sequence from the tall trees, and below this swarms of insects murmur, and below that something else. Something more melodic, more insistently familiar. Greensleeves, I think as I polish off the last of the trail mix, no, definitely, a polyphonic Greensleeves rising through the rainforest. Like a ringtone, or an alarm, but when I reach for my phone I have none. Eyes opening wide now, scrambling for the tablet, have to reach it before it's too-

Late. I am too late. My phone hasn't been charging overnight, and the little battery icon has turned an anxious red. 17%, it reads. It's already 8:00, and the coffee catch-up is at 8:45. I'm going to be late.

The hangover hits as soon as I try to move though, like a nail file right through the brain hemispheres. I groan, tumble from bed to fake-wood floorboards with a bruising thud. The floor is cool against my cheek, almost pleasant.

"I've finished drafting that email we were talking about yesterday," the fridge informs me and what the hell took it so long, Jesus Christ.

"That's really good," I spit out, avoiding the mirror as I pull on black pants and a white shirt. I should get rid of the mirror. The mirror needs to go and the coffee machine is still broken, the eviction notice still on the windowsill and I am chugging the breakFAST straight from the carton.

I run to the sink but do not actually vomit. It's 8:10.

"Do you need medical attention, Sirin? I can call a number of private clinics if you-"

"No thank you," I say as I snatch up my bag, discarded by the door and still filled with the contents of last night but I'm not thinking about those contents as I hurry onto the landing, eyes squinting half-shut against the morning light. The air swims, dryness in mouth like a handful of sand.

I don't look in my bag as the apartment building's doors close behind me, nor do I check my watch and I am afraid, deep down, that checking will only make the problem real. That there can't be a problem until it is here, clear, plain as day for all to see. I am stumbling forward now, pleather soles half-heartedly pounding the pavement, past the little etchings of grass nature strips and the token rows of plane trees, planted like they might conceivably have made a difference. Each step hurts but the momentum is good, adrenaline subtly replacing the hangover, focus slowly shifting from my head and stomach to the pavement immediately in front of me.

The station is ahead and a woman in a tan trench coat is waiting at the lights, pressing the button impatiently, like she's been waiting a long time for them to change, like neither of us has paid for the premium traffic light subscription. A drone circles lazily overhead. A train horn blares in the nearing distance, like polystyrene being sawn in half and it's my train, coming with no time to spare. The light is still red. There's a long enough break in the traffic, and I am invincible for a second as I run past the lights, uncaring and bold, feet crossing from pavement to black bitumen. A few metres of blistering freedom where I'm actually going to make it. But then the woman in the tan trench coat shrieks, and a horn blares from somewhere far too close. I turn to see an olive green Hummer now only a few metres from my face, driving protocols still accelerating, it seems, and in any event far too close to stop.

Stop.

Everything stops.

I open my eyes to a view of polished concrete and naked edison bulbs, my Manager asking:

"So, given all of this, do you think you have the crucial people-moving and thought-leading capabilities to assist in the management of our human capital?"

and this doesn't seem to be a question, so I say:

"Yes. I think so."

I look down into my usual order, a long black with a cube of sugar on the side, the vacuum sealed glass floating a few inches above the transparency of the table. The hangover is still there but feels further away, like a forest fire watched on the news from a safe, half-continent distance away. There's something I'd been doing.

"Well let me know when you're free and we can work out the details of your application together," today's earrings small and silver, the moment's tone one of cheery yet professional encouragement.

"My application?"

"Your application to be our new Assistant-Manager, of course," and with a soft *ping* her words shift into comprehensibility. The vacant Assistant-Manager position. She wants me to fill it. But this is obviously absurd. I haven't done any work over the course of this job, none at all, a fact which she, as my Manager, must at least be partially aware of. I'm in no position to assist anyone.

A clink of coins. It *would* mean getting paid more though. With an Assistant-Manager role locked in I could probably borrow enough to cover a bond and lease signing fee. I might not even have to downsize. I could get a car maybe, and feel in some way that I already possess one, am already having it drive me to work, insulated from the sweaty masses on the train. Maybe even a big car, a Hummer.

A sudden chill, vomit rising in throat. What had happened, earlier, and how I had gotten here? Had the Hummer hit me? Surely not, reaching down to my thighs and wrists, same as always, looking into the same cup, the same sugarcube, the same magnetic glass bar table of the trendiest cafe not too far of a walk from the office. I must have gotten out of the way. Must have made it here on my own. I keep it down, all of it down, and take another sip of black.

She's wearing an elegant white shirt open at the collar under a black blazer, her curly brown hair held tightly in place by a collection of bobby pins. Her eyes are examining me for something very subtle, and she smiles in a way that suggests she's no longer just pretending to. She almost says something, then stops herself, then pays for us both with a chip in her wrist.

"Do you like working here?" she asks as we approach our glass tower, in a tone now too of no longer just pretending. On the other side of the road is the Tiki bar, and on the corner opposite is the levelled city block where they're building the Construct, concealed behind a lattice of security checkpoints, autofocusing cameras and razor-wire fencing.

I contemplate my answer.

"It is a real pleasure to work here. Nowhere else would I have gotten better learning opportunities, or met such a wonderful group of people, or had the opportunity to take part in such interesting and challenging work."

"That's great to hear," she says quickly, but she doesn't say anything more. I don't know exactly how this response had been wrong, just know from her tone that it was. I say nothing, do nothing as we walk across the black glass and bronze of the lobby, ceilings high and tasteful modern sculpture by the walls. The battery icon on my phone is now flashing white and red, and a preview of a text message from Me.Gov reads: *CITIZEN 6740843 — a traffic infringement notice for JAYWALKI.....,* but I do not open the message, obviously, keep its contents hypothetical and unformed.

A moment of weightlessness as the elevator ascends.

"You should get out of here while you still can," my Manager murmurs, eyes straight ahead and lips barely moving.

"What?"

"Pardon?" she says, with that same tight smile as the elevator doors open. *Ding.* I don't know the right thing to say in response to this either. Again I say nothing. Nothing is safe. Nothing works.

Nothing new has appeared in the inbox, and my desk for today has three screens: two glossy black monitors arranged side-by-side in the centre and a third, thinner one that stretches out beneath them. I turn down the brightness all the way down on each. My head is starting to pound again.

I still need to do the folders, but upon opening the search program find only the same stale demands for gift cards, the same tedious countdowns. I close the window, look quietly at my computer for a few seconds, then look to where the UA had been sitting yesterday. She's gone.

I punch out her number on the glowing dial pad, written in the air with textured green light. The phone rings and rings, the sound coming from nowhere and everywhere at once, like a heartbeat heard through a thick Christmas jumper, and somewhere on the other side of the floor I think I hear the other end, a bright arpeggio ascending a few dozen plastic partitions away. It rings for so long that I am very surprised when someone eventually answers, someone who is not the UA and who says only:

"May I ask the name and employee number of the person who is calling so insistently?"

I stammer for a moment and hang up. Then I breathe deeply for a few counts, check the extension and call back. The phone rings five times, more softly than before, then cuts abruptly to a harsh, distorted E flat, so loud inside my skull that my eyes water and I try to tear the non-existent headset from my scalp.

It had been edging 50 degrees for a week and rolling blackouts had rippled through the grid, the air-conditioning load finally too much for our ageing infrastructure. We'd been dismissed from uni, barred from it in fact, and politely but firmly informed that we were to complete our studies online. Rumour had it that the university buildings were being sold off to upmarket property developers. Several of our lecturers had been arrested. All the protest movements had failed by this point, dispersed by police battalions or unable to continue in the blazing heat, all our vigour gone to seed. It had still seemed unfair, faintly ridiculous that in the midst of total global collapse we were still expected to pay bills, to make rent and to compete ferociously over what little office-work remained, but it seemed, incredibly, that nothing would or could be done to change this. Surrender was in the air, Alex had gone and I was in my room, flicking rubber bands at the ceiling, thinking about how to jerry-rig an air-conditioner together and/or scrape enough money together to begin eating breakfast again. Most forms of public assistance were coming to an end though, and the mutual aid networks that had sprung up like mushrooms after Autumn rain had all been forcibly dismantled.

I'd needed a job, and a graduate position with this organisation was a coveted thing, something which my fellow moderately-high achievers competed for and bragged about, and though consciously I neither cared for nor shared their opinions I'd still found myself putting in a resume. It would open many doors, I'd been told by a warm-smiled representative at the careers fair the month before, and it would be a waste of an opportunity to not at least apply.

My eyes flick back to the screen: I'm scrolling through the usual side-job listings: delivery-drone packer, autoshare test-rider, queue place-holder, in-store extra. I sense these adverts reshaping as I glance across them, rewriting themselves with the feedback from my eyes into something more enticing, less likely to be clicked away from. None of these jobs are for actual money though, a fact buried in terms and conditions that seem always to flit away from searching eyes — the only pay is in discounts or coupons, and I need cash.

With perceptible effort I close the page, but when I come back to my desktop a pop-up asks me to re-login with a one-time secure access code. Receiving the code requires a new, improved security app, too modern for my phone's current OS, and by the time I update the system and install the app my phone's battery is edging 1%. The app needs a login and I swipe faster, typing and retyping a password that I could have sworn was correct the first time until I finally get inside. *SEND CODE*, I click, wait. My phone vibrates with the one-time code then promptly dies, its last spark of power drained by the effort.

I slump backwards into the chair, inadequate back support creaking and groaning, though perhaps the one groaning is me. I am locked out of my computer and everything is still far too bright, a buzzing like a low voltage electrical current murmuring at the base of my skull.

Then I open my bag, seeing but not looking at the pizza, the gyoza, and the lasagna, now quite un-frozen, their boxes sagging and grey, nor at the chocolate, the flashlight or cherry tomatoes, or anything else for that matter. My eyes register the presence of these items, see the little splotches of colour and shading, but I refuse to assign a meaning to them, like sentences written in a language I cannot understand. I pull the wireless charging pad from its place at the bottom, wipe the oily residue off of its plastic casing and pull the zipper closed again.

But the charging port goes into the powerboard without the satisfying *click* that I'd imagined. The metal curves of the charging pad extend out a bit too far, not really enough room for it beside the other cords. It sort of goes in though, and my phone hovers over the metal disk just fine. But there's no friendly buzz from the phone, which on closer review isn't charging, as this wireless charger is only natively compatible with the other, second kind of major smartphone, as per the crumpled up user guide I now take the time to read. My kind of major smartphone has to use the Charging Compatibility Block, a metal block that hovers over the disk and is then connected to the phone via USB cable. I find the Charging Compatibility Block in the plastic casing, a little bent out of shape, and place it to hover above the pad. Then I let a long sigh escape my lips, stand, and began the search for a compatible charging cable.

A city starting with a K had been first, all those years ago. Yes, definitely a K, and then one with an L, both in poorer parts of the world. Then one with an R, and an S, and an LA, each progressively richer. After that it had become difficult to keep track, and the news people had become more generic in their descriptions of the unfolding catastrophe, politely ceasing to list the cities lost to fire and flood. *Disruption,* they'd increasingly said. *Destabilisation.* We all know how and why this happened, and there's no point going over it again now.

The first person I ask for a charging cable is a 57-ish year-old man with a complexion the same colour as the plastic partitions. It's unclear whether he hears the question. He reaches around his desk for a few seconds and, finding nothing, shrugs and returns to his solitaire. I also ask him, as an aside, like something I only just remembered, whether he happens to know where the scan data might be located on our systems, but he doesn't respond to this at all.

The second person I ask is a 16 year-old work-experience kid, face dotted with acne and suit bought for a larger, more fully-developed version of himself. He pretends not to hear me, completely assured by the knowledge that I am not the uncle-by-marriage who secured him this fantastic work-experience opportunity. He focuses on the bottom right hand corner of his screen instead, where a 2.7 second video of a man hitting pumpkins with a T-ball bat loops indefinitely. When I ask if he knows where the UA is sitting he says she is in "updog", but he doesn't respond when I ask him where that is.

The third person I ask is a perhaps 37 year-old woman with black circles round her eyes and a delicate silver chain around her neck. Her screen is filled with more documents than I can count, layered atop one another so densely that it's impossible to tell which one she's actually working on. Her charging cable isn't the right one for my phone, she says without looking at either. She suggests I run some general search terms and see what comes up, and explains that though she'd been sitting next to the UA the day before she has no idea where she is now.

The fourth person I ask is a probably-29 year-old woman with violet streaks through bleached blonde hair, clad head to toe in lavender. She turns in her seat just as I'm going to announce myself. Before I have a chance to say anything she explains that she doesn't own a phone and so has no need for charging cables, and advises me to do the same.

"Don't worry about the scan data either," she assures me. "Everything will sort itself out." Before I can ask about the UA she's gotten up out of the chair, brushed past me and walked to the kitchen, all in one fluid motion of cotton on silk. Her screen is filled by a completely blank document, a flashing cursor pushed by the space bar into the lower right of the page. She is up to page 103.

The fifth person I ask is about 44, if I had to guess, an older man with faint stubble and grey hairs, screen filled with a 3D rendering of the office we're currently working in. He's zooming in on his own desk, which is empty on the screen, focusing on a small coffee stain on the laminate. When I ask him for the data he demands to see my clearance, and when after some searching I provide this to him he backtracks immediately, informs me that the data he has access to is from a test-scan of our offices only. The render doesn't extend past the windows, which look out on a field of luminous white. I ask him for a cord but in response he points to a flowing wireless charging port, his phone hovering magnetically above.

The sixth person I ask is the same age as me, with an open white shirt and a black wristwatch.

"No, thank you for the offer but I'm already fully charged," they say, gesturing to exactly the same phone as mine. They're purchasing a reusable face-mask, Nordic Design, with the latest charcoal filters to remove 99% of airborne allergens, carcinogens and irritants. They have selected the *Slate Grey* colour. A sensation like falling.

A tap on my shoulder from behind.

"Will this fit?" says a man in a brown suit with a shaved head, chunky vape visible in pocket and black cable held in balled fist. The end of it is fraying slightly, strands of wiry silver poking up from the plastic. His voice smells like mango and other, buzzier stimulants.

"Thanks, I'm pretty sure this is the right one," pushing the end-part into my phone with a small, meaningful click.

He's ever so slightly unshaven, and looks like he spends a lot of time at the gym. "Yeah, I knew this was the right one. All the phones made with the TRX specs have either this or the USZ cable and this one has a way bigger slice of the market share, maximum penetration you know..." he says, and goes on saying for what seems like it will be a very long time. Seconds pass, then minutes, then hours and eternities and he is still talking, jaw muscles mouthing formlessly, repeating the specs of the various phone connections over and over until our bodies break and the air degrades and the City is dust and-

"Thanks," I say again. "I'm pretty sure this is the right one."

"Well, I'm just sitting over there so come stop by for a chat when you're done with it. I've got some stuff you should check out. Some of the next-gen non-mandatory compulsives we've been acquiring, for the Construct you know."

And he seems to want me to ask a question about this, or continue the conversation in some other way, so I say: "Oh cool, I'm working on the Construct too."

But this must have been the wrong response, because a strange look begins to spread across his face.

"Ahh yeah," he says, and there is a tone to his voice now, one that matches his face exactly. "I heard that you were going for the Assistant-Manager job too."

"If they'll have me," I say nonchalantly, but in response to this he only snorts. Perhaps this too was the wrong thing to say.

"So I guess you think you're pretty hot shit then eh?"

I say nothing to this, but he still waits, smirking, as if for me to continue the conversation further, which I will not be doing. After about ten seconds he turns and leaves. And because this is an open plan office he doesn't disappear behind a door, nor even around a corner, but rather walks past two sets of plastic partitions and a few office plants, to his own desk for the day, and sits down. He looks back to me, eyes only just above the computer screen. I smile and wave; he frowns back down.

Fluorescence hums in a uniform G above me, and the carpet repeats in blue-grey fractals beneath. I sigh, and plug the slightly odd cable into the overly expensive charging port.

A dizzying headrush: an email from the UA.

Hey Sirin. Will drop by your desk to discuss folders in 10.

I sit, relieved, then stand back up as the time-stamp drifts dimly into mind.

"Damnit." The email was sent at 10:53, over an hour ago.

Sorry I missed your email, I message back with as much priority as I can muster, a small drop of blood dripping from my nose with the effort, *am free now if you're available,* but she changes her status to offline just as I send.

Thirty seconds follow in which I again try to do the folders myself, but there's still no way to find the scan data, nothing from which to work. I close all the programs, sit, and bang my head softly against my left-hand screen. An urge to curl up under the desk in the foetal position, which for now I do not indulge.

For a while there it had really seemed like we would win. Even I, who usually possessed only enough nominal leftism to fit in with my friends, had begun to chant along with the crowds, which were growing every day. A general strike had been in the works, and the government seemed paper-thin. We had been so close. But to be honest there was always part of me that had welcomed our failure, that had shrunk, appalled, from the freedom that seemed so nearly within reach. A part of me, immensely strong but always just out of sight, that had wanted nothing more than for normal life to resume like clockwork.

The door-chime of the Korean restaurant plays in greeting, and a waitress ushers me in like a distant but welcome relative. Korean pop songs are playing from a bluetooth speaker by the wall, and the music videos of Western pop songs play on a television perched in the corner.

It's busy and I order the usual: a beef bibimbap, plus an extra miso soup to avoid the 2.5% card surcharge. I take a laminated table number, and wait in the farthest, quietest corner of the room, on a table that feels like it might be real wood but is likely chipboard too. I breathe out, and feel myself relaxing into the bustle of lunch hour, the ambient murmur of ten conversations unfolding at once. This place feels like home, much more so than my current apartment, though truth be told I know next to nothing about the restaurant and the women who run it, need the feeling more than the knowledge which might make it complicated and real.

The miso soup comes in a large mug that I cup in both hands as I bring it to my lips, only a little bit too hot against my fingers, and when my order arrives the egg still sizzles on the side of the bibimbap. The beef is soy, of course, and the egg, and maybe even the shiitake too, but the rice at the bottom is hot and crunchy, the sauce a fine balance of savoury and sweet. A sigh of relief as the last of the miso is drunk; my stomach's finally stopped complaining.

A man sits down at a table ahead of me, by the windows. Short brown hair, heavily gelled. Taller than me, with a checked shirt and lightly crumpled collar. It's my now former Assistant-Manager, wearing the same clothes he'd worn to drinks yesterday, his tie now slightly askew and the sweat stains under his arms wider, richer.

I hide my face behind a menu. I don't think he's seen me. He seems unhappy, from the side profile, agitated, and he leaves a few minutes after sitting down, furiously hammering at his phone.

Vibrations dance across my upper thigh, and I reach for my pocket. But my phone isn't there — it's still charging, plugged into the charging port 99 floors and three blocks away. I sigh. His name had been Greg, maybe, or Michael or Brendon or James. He'd always spoken very loudly. I'd never been able to figure out exactly how he'd been assisting in my management, and I suppose now I never will, and for some reason this fills me with another feeling that is quite difficult to name. I look down at my watch, studying its contents as if they could provide a similar distraction to the missing phone; the shorter, fatter hand is a little past the first dash from the top, and the longer one is between the third and fourth. A third hand makes its way restlessly around the face — never stopping yet never getting anywhere, useful only in the regularity of its repetition.

I look down at the bibimbap, the same beef bibimbap I always have on the same table in the same restaurant on the same crowded street. The sounds of the restaurant are inverting, crackling with distortion, and though the restaurant around me throbs with customers its reflection, in the glass, is empty and still. I sigh, and lay my hands flat, and close my eyes with a sound like surrender. The smell of frying egg is the first to go. Then the bustle of chopsticks on bowl, and the murmur of half-heard conversations. The table is different under my fingertips, the rough grain of the wood felt now through a shadow of dust, and the air has grown musty and stale. I tap my fingers experimentally on the table, then open my eyes. The restaurant is empty.

"Godfuckingdamnit," I say slowly, the events of yesterday evening slowly filtering back into memory. I try to remember if I've paid for the bibimbap already. I don't think so, but the card reader is lifeless and still, coated with the same layer of dust that's settled on the tables and chairs. Little plumes come up around my feet as I walk slowly through the restaurant, like geysers on some distant, frozen moon. I'll have to pay them back another time.

The door doesn't make the little chime sound on the way out, just a dull rasp of metal on wood. Outside it is cold, and the door snibs locked behind me, and the ramen joint next door is closed as well. There's no-one in the burger place either, or the cornershop, or in this street or the next.

A low pressure front turns the air weightless and cool, footsteps petering out. "Just great," I say, and with one last go I try the door of the convenience store, its trays of brightly coloured protein bars mocking my rumbling stomach, locked metal jarring hollow in the utter silence of the streets around. But it's no use. The City is completely empty.

I sit down for a bit, then stand back up. There's a pack of muesli bars in my locker, and, lacking any better plan, I begin heading back to work. The flashing holographs on the stores fall quiet as I pass them, and there's not a single sign of life in the skyscrapers to either side. Like the entire City went for a holiday in the moment I went out for lunch, every last person and piece of electrical equipment taking a well-deserved break.

Another step down the line, then another, all of the crossings grey and undemanding, the hands of the watch frozen on my wrist. There are no people slowing my steps but it still feels slower, emptier without the current of office workers pushing me along with them, and without the people on the streets you can see how choked they are with plastic, paper and foam. Steps quickening, not in fact needing to look both ways as I cross the road, past an olive green Hummer from which I quickly turn away. It'll be fine, just like it was fine last time. The people had come back hadn't they, the doors of the Tiki bar had still opened.

I do my breathing exercises, just like in the videos, and after 5 rounds I turn back to the Hummer. Perhaps not the same Hummer as before but one very much like it, and I wonder for a moment what it would feel like to rip its metal shell back, for it to buckle and tear apart in my hands. So I search through my pockets for a key, or a coin, a bottlecap or even a pen, something to scratch its paint job or puncture a reinforced window, but all I have are flimsy polymer cards. Even out here, with no-one watching, I've been rendered completely harmless to it.

I move on, arms pulled close around me; it was a sunny day before but it's cold now, with a chill wind from over the water that cuts right through my thin cotton shirt and no crowd of passersby to catch it before it comes. The stores are all filled with puffer jackets and poly-weave jumpers, safely inaccessible behind their smash-proof glass displays, doors locked and unyielding.

A roll of distant thunder as I stride up the pavement to my building. The great revolving door spins no longer though, panes frozen stiff in place. The disabled entrance isn't working either, the big green button to the side-entrance unpowered and useless, and anyway the elevators wouldn't work, without power, the 99th floor now as inaccessible as the Moon, just like anyone with a half a brain could have told me from the very beginning. I bang a fist against the glass, feel the cold thud reverberate through my forearm. Another gust of wind from the bay, colder than before. Another thud, and another, but the glass won't give and it isn't working, I realise, this plan, this job, this pointless little life of mine, a fact soon to become obvious to everyone, plain as day for all to see. Assistants are always super busy — that was probably the only time she had. She won't have time to meet with me again, and she won't be able to tell me how to do my job. I won't be able to make the folders. I'll probably be fired. I'll never live in an apartment again.

I slump, back to the glass wall. A raindrop catches me on the shoulder. There'll be an awning somewhere, somewhere not completely taken up by spikes or slopes or other anti-homeless architecture, but if there is I cannot see it. I look out over the desolate streets, feel the hostility of their architects like a living thing coiled through the concrete and glass. A weight pressing down on all of us, unbearable and vast.

"I should," I say, trailing off, looking up towards the gathering shadows in the clouds above. Something hangs above us in the air, a massive black shape on the very edges of my vision, a dark mass growing slowly more explicit.

"I should really call the UA."

I look down. There's a white folder lying on the pavement in front of me, uniform and blank, the same as its millions of identical siblings gathering dust in the deserted office buildings around. But running vertically down the spine of this folder, in small, professionally printed type, the words *Executive Briefing Materials — Construct*, and on the uppermost plane of white a yellow post-it note with the words *Take Me*. The planets circling above shift into a strange new alignment as I pick up this folder, flick my fingers through its tabs and think that yes, this does look an awful lot like the briefing materials I have been trying and failing to assemble. The edges of the paper rough against my fingertips, the folder so much heavier than it ought to be.

I cast it to the pavement, or maybe it is simply dropped, fear fanning hot and strong. But there's nothing to be afraid of. Just a sheaf of A4 paper, sprawled on the footpath, plastic cover speckled through with tiny drops of rain, heralds of the downpour to come. Soon it'll get soaked, and all the little letters inside will go back to being ink, diffusing evenly through the paper, then out from the paper to the pavement and the gutters and stormwater drains, all the way out to sea. Better pick it up then. Get it inside before the rain. And as I do this there is a bump, and a large man with tortoiseshell glasses and a pinstriped suit who bumps into me. Then another bump, and another, the folder almost dropping from my hands as I realise that I'm standing right in front of the doorway to the lobby, right in the middle of lunchtime. And it's a crowded street again, the eddies and flows of shirt fronts and collars all resuming their usual returning-from-lunchtime routines. The sun shines down from a cloudless sky. And although my right shoulder is still a little wet from the rain it will dry soon, is almost dry already, even if for now I feel its coldness on me still.

The office is different when I return: the greys less warm and the teaks less vibrant, the plants more obviously plastic, everything muted by the luminous white of the folder sitting on my desk. I still haven't opened it, am scared, I think, that if I look too closely its pages might dissolve into air.

I look away. It's 1:50, if I go by my computer, but 1:33 by my watch. It's a modern, battery-free watch, powered by the background electronic exhaust of every device within a 10 metre radius. It's between 16 and 17 minutes late, has recently spent 16 to 17 minutes without power and this new, aberrant time ticks away on my wrist, unsynchronised, just as the folder sits unopened, unread on my desk. And though I could easily wind the watch forward I find that I do not, do not wish to so acknowledge whatever just occurred. Because nothing had occurred, and Alex has sent me a text asking whether I want to meet her before "the event" tomorrow, and my fingers have already typed out a reply:

I'm pretty busy at work right now so it might be difficult to make it out that evening — I'll let you know if I end up going. It'd be great to catch up though, we should touch base soon.

And this isn't true, I acknowledge, as I hover over the send icon. It isn't true at all, could in fact be considered a lie, by most definitions. But still my right thumb edges closer to the button, thoughts becoming slippery and thin. *I don't want to hurt her feelings*, a thought echoes in my head, pressing down, *don't want things to be weird*, as I send. The truth is that I don't go to protests anymore. I am a professional, now, with a steady job and my own apartment, and in this life civil disobedience feels somehow out of key, dangerous even, and anyway it always comes to nothing in the end.

I close my eyes. Behind them the sky is grey as slate, and giant waves wash the City clean. Raindrops fly sideways from the ashen clouds above. Every bit of land is underwater, the tops of skyscrapers like oil rigs jutting through the ocean as licks of lightning split the sky and I am alone, completely and utterly alone atop a mountain of crinkled steel. A shiny black SUV reaches above the surface for a moment, pushed up on the peak of the breaking swell, then sinks back beneath the waves.

Then upon this scene there comes a voice:

"How are you going with that task I set for you?"

My Senior-Manager stands above me, crystal blue eyes staring directly into mine. He is wearing a tie, a blue-grey cross-hatch pattern set in perfect diagonals, and a small metal tie clip in silver and black. He towers over me, filling my entire field of vision, and this ratio feels right, somehow, appropriately proportioned. The Man in the Brown Suit's eyes peep above the plastic wall divider, and I can sense the rest of my co-workers subtly turning their bodies towards us, positioning themselves to get a better peripheral look.

"Done," I answer, handing him the folder.

He flicks the outside tabs experimentally, then half-opens to one of the middle pages, brow furrowed. He flicks through, *umm*ing at some pages and *ahh*ing through others until, a representative sample of its pages taken, he closes the volume with a soft thud. He pauses, the echo of paper meeting paper reverberating in a silence so total that I can almost hear, within it, the total concentration of my co-workers on the fateful next few words.

"You did this?" he asks, and for a moment I feel the great granite slabs of the past shifting, rearranging themselves around a new, immutable fact.

"Yes," I say, and like that it is done. I did the folder.

His eyes cross the paper into mine.

"Fantastic work. Absolutely fantastic. I'd love to go through this with you before Thursday's meeting, tomorrow if you have capacity. I'll have a calendar invite sent through."

My arms are almost too weak to take the folder that he hands back. As he turns and leaves I melt backwards into the chair, smiling weakly, and punch the air lightly with my fist. Then I lean back even further, chair creaking a little, and begin to daydream about the apartments that I'll be able to afford on an Assistant-Manager's salary. I do not close my eyes though, and for the longest time try very hard not to blink.

Rising sea levels. Soaring temperatures. Collapsing food-chains. Order had been restored but the world had still been ending, an end that could not be shot or beaten or crowd-controlled away, and the only remotely viable solutions had all required extreme levels of government intervention. Support, some might say. Interference, others. And why save the world if you had to submit to communism in the process, key stakeholders had insisted, in meetings and boardrooms at first, and only later in large-scale public relations campaigns.

There had to be another way, the brightest surviving minds of a generation were told, a smarter, more agile way of keeping the lights on and the wheels turning and the little pieces of paper (plus their electronic equivalents) circulating just so. A way to put everything back in the box.

It's late when I find myself swiping at my apartment door, the lock on its side determinedly red. I swipe some more, arm still on autopilot as the scene shifts into focus — the door, the hall, the abstract pattern of black and white squares that faces me. This is the wrong door, which I am attempting to open in the wrong way. Behind it is the wrong person, maybe, scared by the scratching at the door, contemplating whether the situation is serious enough to pay the police call-out fee. But most likely there's just an empty room. There are only six other tenants who I see regularly in this building, plus a few others whose existence can sometimes be inferred, and none of their doors open onto this landing.

Down the hall is a subtly more familiar collection of dots, and a lock that turns green as my phone comes up to meet them. The TV turns on automatically as I enter, and decides that I would be most satisfied with the latest episode of *Surprise!,* which of course I am. Couch cushions fold comfortable around me, and I kick off my shoes without unlacing.

In the TV there is a bar, and a group of coworkers crowded round a circular table. A pint glass sits in the table's centre, and one of the co-workers, a red haired man with quick eyes and a full beard, is trying to flick a coin into the glass. He keeps missing. Something is being said that I can't hear over the laugh track, but I laugh along anyway. One of the colleagues talks about how happy he is with the apartment he just signed onto, and another bites into a gyoza:

"I can't believe it's frozen food," she says between mouthfuls, "it's just so delicious!"

The glow from the TV is pure white though. The screen isn't really showing the images I'm seeing, but instead displays a kind of textured static that taps into the same neural pathways as dreams and fantasies. The episodes are just suggestions, contours and patterns perceived quite differently by the thousands of eyes that watch, accompanied by a soundtrack of shifting noise spun into dialogue by the brain. Attuned perfectly to the subconscious entertainment preferences of the viewer, or so the ads had used to say.

A gnawing unease develops under the TV though, subtle at first but waxing, slowly, less and less deniable, and after a time I realise that I'm starving, had only a muesli bar for lunch. But when I eventually meander to the fridge there's nothing except a sachet of instant rice and some old spinach leaves in there, plus a packet of premium free-range grasshoppers.

"Hmmmmm, seems pretty bare in here, Sirin. Would you like me to order you some groceries? There are some great deals from participating retailers at the moment."

"No thanks."

"Well how about I get you a pizza instead? The Peppey-Roney from the Pink Peppy Pizza Parlour is getting especially high ratings right now."

"Yeah, yeah, that'll do great,' I murmur, distracted.

There is a micro-drone on the windowsill, a straggler from Monday I assume. A dragonfly sketched in crystal and aluminium, about the length of my thumb, familiar from briefing packs and project meetings but now tangible, real and seemingly scanning the meagre contents of my apartment. It shouldn't still be here, not now, but the thought of doing anything about this fills me with a tiredness so complete that I know nothing will possibly be done about it tonight. I take out my phone instead, do a few CAPCHAs while I wait for the pizza, hopefully enough to get a delivery coupon. I keep mixing up the muffins and the dogs though, the buses and the motorcycles. I can't get any of them right. I flick across to the news but it's just more doomsday content

— burning cities, collapsing ports, fields of heat-stroked birds lying wilted on the plains.

A plasticcy knock on the next window. The pizza has arrived, and as I open the latch to let the delivery drone in the dragonfly sneaks in behind it, perching now on the broken coffee machine. "Sure," I say, shaking my head, "why not." The pizza is still warm at least, the soy-cheese still soft and the soyeroni still pliable.

The TV picks up where I left it, the coin, suspended mid-air, dropping this time into the pint, floating languid through the beer towards the centre of the glass. The friends around the table laugh and clap, and I smile. This is nice, I think. This is good. Not as good as actually having friends, of course, but good enough, kind of, something to scratch the itch. *Surprise!* can only really be watched alone though — someone else watching it beside me would get something completely different. And even if someone exactly like me in every way had been keeping me company, and had started watching at exactly the same time, then my time waiting for the pizza would mean that our feeds would now be out of sync. They would have already smiled with the applause that echoed out of their TV, as a smile crosses my face. They would have already gasped when another of the circle knocked the pint glass over, as a tiny wave of beer sweeps across the table's grain for me. They would have already closed their eyes, exhausted, as the laugh track plays, as the conversation slips back into noise, as I close my eyes and, unhearing now, surrender. Unseen, the static goes back to being nothing at all, and bathes my body in a cold, uniform glow.

71

WEDNESDAY

It's early morning, the air still crisp, and the great dark miracle, inscrutable and vast, stretches out before me in a circle whose diameter spans the city block. Its surface is without aspect, colour or reflection, and so utterly black that it could be a perfect, two dimensional disk floating a millimetre above the ground, or else the aperture to a void extending down forever, without the tiniest speck of matter for a photon to reflect off. Darker than the blackness of space, which after all is full of light from distant stars. The laboratory coats circle it ceaselessly, a raised lip around its outer edge to keep them from falling in, its perimeter lined with little white portables erected hastily over the grass. It is dark perhaps in the way of an ocean trench, or like a circle has been cut from the world to reveal the nothingness behind. Beneath. The mud squelches grassy beneath my feet and I am already walking towards it, left foot hesitantly following my right, trying not to trip on the remnants of sprinklers and flowerbeds still sticking up from the flattened mud. I step up onto the lip, flexing my fingers nervously, and gaze into the Construct.

Eyelids flicker open. I stir, half-asleep on the couch, back aching in yesterday's clothes. Clear yellow light is beginning to crest over the tops of the nearby apartment buildings at an angle the windows never quite know how to deal with, and the plexi-glass tints and clears spasmodically. The TV is playing a rough continuation of the dream I've just woken from; I am being ushered out of the Construct site by burly men in suits, across the road and into my building, up a narrow flight of twisting steps in a dark, shadowy atrium. I shake my head, blinking, and turn the TV off with a roll of my eyes. The invite for the meeting hasn't come through yet. The drone is still on my coffee machine.

Casually, I get my breakFAST from the fridge, then sit, like I've barely noticed the micro-drone and have no significant opinions on its presence in my apartment. A crystal dragonfly perched on carbon-fibre legs, a tiny solar cell on its back and a network of filligried sensors like glass splinters from its abdomen. Its sensors are delicate enough to detect each micro-droplet in my exhalations, can perhaps deduce from these the slight increase of adrenaline in my bloodstream, and I have to remind myself that it's only here to scan and record, a straggler from Monday morning and nothing more. I have nothing to fear from the drone. The drone is practically a colleague.

"Time for another great day in the office," says the fridge, to which I heartily agree.

I sit down, eyes staring dead ahead at the extremely wide, subtly curved screen of today's desk, edges so thin that they seem to bleed into the surrounding air. There are now 11 folders on the desk, stacked in a perfect column that rises nearly as high as the monitor. I reach out towards the uppermost; the uncanny weight of the original has been lost in the copying, leaving just a normal, untroubled folder, empty of significance. Something that might be reviewed easily, casually flicked through before the meeting, just to be on the safe side. But try as I might my hands aren't opening it. They remain on the outside, skimming the cool plastic surface, the intention to pull the cover back lost somewhere between my brain and the muscle fibres. My hands put the folder back down, and when I try to pick it up again I find them on the keyboard instead, navigating resolutely in the opposite direction. There are no new emails in the inbox though. The invite for the meeting hasn't come through. I glance back to the folders.

A three-tone arpeggio.

There are now thirteen new emails in the inbox, twelve of these draft correspondence that ring my head with a maelstrom of consumer complaints, curses and remonstrations. The thirteenth is the invite for the meeting, only just perceptible through the noise of the others, due to occur at 12:00. I look at the folders, then back towards the screen, then back towards the folders, and for a while I try to argue with the online form that assigned me the correspondence. The 12:00 meeting must not be properly entered into the system though, or maybe my calendar isn't synching with the task allocator. *Error — competing deadline not found*, the chatbot repeats, *complete task by deadline or face disciplinary action, and make sure to have a great day!*

The first letter is addressed to AR3610, shop assistant, who complains that his hours were cut to almost nothing when he took a day off to care for his sick mother, even after he got a carer's certificate. He's worried they won't make rent. He asks whether his hours can be restored in the Construct, whether something might be done about the roster there. *No,* replies our letter, over the course of 14 pages and 32 footnotes.

The letter is already written, of course, was drafted by an AI within 2.1 milliseconds of receipt, but in the period before the timer counts down from 10:00 to 0:00 I will be able to look at the letter, amend it even, before the legal requirements for human oversight are met and another appears on screen. I glance down at the folders and the timer freezes, at 7:57, then for a second longer. I look back up: 7:56. 7:55. 7:54. If I look straight ahead the entire time I should have 30 minutes left to prepare for the meeting, my eyes scanning across the statement that *the cost of your current medical bill was not a relevant factor that I weighed when coming to this decision,* my fingers changing *bill* to *bills,* the counter slowly ticking down to 0:00.

Second is CY1918, consultant, who requests to bring her cat into the Construct with her, rather than relying on the Constructed version on the other side, which to her just wouldn't feel the same. She asks how Mrs Chips (the cat) will survive after she (CY1918) enters the Construct, no-one being around to feed her. But though my eyes read this my mind is wavering, already circling back to the meeting in a few hours' time. The letter with my signature on it advises CY1918 to *Please consider registering for ContructPlus for more customization options,* and my neck is cramping as I try to remember the proper ergonomic set-up for this workstation, not daring to look away long enough to check the laminated checklist on my left.

Next is HU9932, cleaner, who doesn't plan on entering the Construct and asks for a refund of the taxes and levies used to fund it, in consideration of his advanced age and former pension status. Just remember to make eye contact, I am thinking, but not too much, and let him take the lead. *Our new world will be born from the ashes of old, obsolete fucks like you*, the letter says, and though I raise an eyebrow at this the AI changes it back immediately when I try to delete it. I scan the page for a full stop to un-italicise instead.

Then LU4129, unemployed, asks why we're pouring all these resources into the Construct anyway, how irresponsible, how *ecocidally negligent* we are not to fix this beautiful world of ours instead. The AI has flagged the text of this letter as lightly tweaked dissident copy and auto-forwarded it to the relevant watchlists, though our letter in response doesn't mention this, and recites only the familiar justifications: resource limitations, rising sea levels, rare earth depletion, irreversible feedback loops. The AI assures him that all of his familiar products will be available in the Construct, exactly as they are available now. Again I look down at the folders and this time the screen glows an angry red, jealous of my wandering eyes. When he walks into the meeting room, I will remember to stand up to shake his hand.

Then the screen is white again, with little marks of black that tell how JE3265, nurse, had had her sub-lease terminated with less than the required week's notice, had gotten back from the clinic to find her QR code not working and a family of strangers holidaying in her home. She asks whether they'll still be there in the Construct, whether, perhaps, she'll be able to stop sleeping under a desk at work. The remaining letters go from 10 to 9, the time on my watch from 9:45 to 9:46. The answer is the same though, always the same, and though my body is still in the chair my mind is elsewhere, in the meeting room around the corner, assuring my Senior-Manager that *I think the numbers speak for themselves, though I would be happy to explain them in more detail to the Board.*

I look up. It is 10:25 and my eyes are beginning to blur. Something is moving in the unfocused periphery of my vision, beyond this glowing slab of white. My eyes aren't focusing on it, too preoccupied with looking-at-but-not-reading-how the wife of IK1384, aged carer, was last seen being pushed into the back of an unmarked police car, how IK1384 requests that we use the mapping data to tell her where she is and I'm beginning to sweat now, little drips of perspiration coming off my skin like morning dew. As the thing gets closer what was just movement becomes brown with a pink patch at the top, becomes a brown suit, becomes the Man in the Brown Suit and Shaved Head. I focus even harder on the screen, eyes scanning through the lines of text that I'm not reading, everything focused on appearing so completely absorbed in my work that I just don't think to look up. Still he stands there, leaning forward slightly over the partition. I'm sweating more, maybe too much, armpits damp and the smell ever so faintly off, like reconstituted meat products spoiling slowly in the climate-controlled heat.

You should get out of here while you still can, a voice is saying but I can't, have to keep looking at the screen, have to keep ignoring the Man. He looms, larger than he has any right to. Under his gaze I am shrinking to a dot, a vanishing point so subtle that I might not even be here. Perhaps I am not.

Perhaps I am not.

On my first day in the office I had worn a jacket which was far too formal. The maglev had been delayed, stuck behind a series of other, interlockingly delayed maglevs for almost the whole commute, but I had somehow arrived at reception 15 minutes early. For 30 minutes I had waited on a series of uncomfortable chairs, rereading and rechecking the email instructions, fighting the suspicion that the hiring process had all been an elaborate joke. Somewhere around the corner a person was being criticised, softly but in tones, and my fingers were picking at the pleather of the waiting area seat, little strips of soft plastic coming away from the cushions. All the plants were plastic and the carpet was strange, little lines of blue and grey hatching and crosshatching in alien patterns from the corner of my eye.

You should get out of here while you still can, a voice had said but I wouldn't, I decided; I couldn't just get up and leave on the first hour of my first day. So I had stayed in the chair, and in my mind I had walked away from the voice's no, just a little, just so I could hear my Manager introduce herself. And when I heard that my first task was to rearrange a stack of 200 folders into reverse-alphabetical order I had walked a little further from the voice's *fuck no,* and still further at after-work drinks, the better to hear my new Assistant-Manager's joke about the woman and the self-driving car. *Get absolutely fucked,* it had said but I had not been listening, had kept walking away, in fact, only a small distance each time, and each time the voice had spoken only a little more softly, until eventually I'd walked so far that I could no longer hear the voice at all. I had wandered even farther after that, with only my thoughts for a guide, up that mountain and down that valley, through that gate and across that pasture, here and there and everywhere but always in the same place, and always getting further away. I wandered for so long that I forgot there had been anything to listen for, forgot the sound of my own voice, forgot that there could be anything but this.

Eyes blink. There is a chair, and a desk. Keyboard and monitor. A screen, with a list of the letters I'm about to send, and the friendly green button which will send them. The Man is gone, and the fat hand on my watch is a little past the eleventh dash, the thinner one travelling between the sixth and seventh. It's 11:35 and my shirt is drenched, armpits blossoming like mushroom spoor.

I look for a moment at the folders, then look away.

I get a glass of water, and come back.

I close my eyes: behind them is a tranquil sea stretching out onto a flat horizon, tops of skyscrapers poking through the water like a coral reef. A thick layer of discarded plastic floats on the water, and beneath that a chemical slick that shimmers in the late-morning light. A boat is coming.

I wrench my eyes open, then pull a green jumper from my bag, fumble it over my head and sit, sweat patches nicely covered. My fingers are picking at the fabric of the shirt, unstitching it back into thread and I am forgetting something, something very important. It's just meeting nerves though, must be, fingers drumming against the chipboard desk. 1 2 3 4 1 2 3 4 1 2 3 4. But the foreboding remains, underneath the tapping and the turning, the looking in vain for familiar faces. 11:43 on my watch. Plenty of time, all the time in the world to get to Meeting Room 3 adequately ahead of schedule.

The feeling is still there as I make my way across Change Inducement though, towards the meeting room I could have sworn was on the other side of this co-working space. It isn't though, the meeting rooms ascending 1, 2, 4, 5 without the crucial third, and I cannot see it anywhere I look.

The feeling is there as I press on, round the corner, through the faintly hostile territory of Strategic Consolidation and Proactive Deliberation. 6, 7, 8, 9 come the meeting rooms and I am power-walking past them, footsteps faster and faster, unfamiliar exertion working its way into my glutes but the room nowhere to be seen.

Around another corner is Annualised Financing. The plants are all red and black here, bulbous things that squat crowded in their pots, and the teak has grown darker, more textured. There are no meeting rooms, just little four-seater pods with a kind of active noise cancellation built in — someone is being reprimanded in one of them but I do not hear the words being said, only see the face of the Manager shouting soundlessly inside the cube.

A small, internal whimper as I see the next set of doors approaching, then a vicious shudder as I enter Humanistic Resourcing. Eyes straight ahead, footsteps fast but careful, a thin sheet of glass over the hungry void. Neutral tones and rimless glasses swirl in the still, climate-controlled air, the attention of the professionals here already aggregating, fastening around my form. Rows upon rows of Performance Managers lie gleaming on racks and in soft plastic packaging, along with other, uncannier things whose shapes I pass but do not dwell on: long slender beams that seem to taper into nothingness, revolving metal figures whose rhythms churn fractal, gossamer projections of things I cannot name. A row of identically-suited men lying slumped against a wall, eye sockets empty and arms at impossible angles.

It is 11:53; I have plenty of time to run back to Change Inducement and yet the feeling is still there, has always been there, just like Meeting Room 3, in clear view this entire time, you idiot. You fool. You fucking moron and though the top two thirds of its glass wall are frosted I can see three, maybe four sets of legs, in the bottom. They must have gotten there early and this is fine, all fine as I pick up all eleven of the folders, the strain in my arms unbalancing my back, the pain in my back rippling through my shoulders up my neck. A drip of cold sweat from my forehead makes its way into my eyebrow, hands too full of folders to wipe it clean and I am sweating under my unbreathing synthetic now, too late to take it off. Not one of my colleagues looks up on the way across, not even for the briefest reflex of a glance and there is a connection here, between the not-looking of my colleagues and one of the things that I'm not-thinking about, footsteps landing soundless on the carpet, the distance widening into a far horizon and seconds dragging to infinity. Perhaps I could just keep walking, past the meeting room and down the elevators, through the City streets and out beyond the Wall, chafing turning to sores and blisters as plains become desert and grass becomes dirt and mountains rise to split the sky in two.

I open the door.

A flicker, the world erased and rebooted and erased and rebooted again. A sensation of falling that suddenly intensifies, a white line fracturing into a thousand strands of light. I am going too fast. Too fast by far and-

Another flicker, and I come to in a featureless meeting room, folder clutched to chest. The others lie scattered across the floor. The room is cramped, with a white plastic table in the centre and views of multiple interior walls. Brick. Cladding. Glass. The glass wall seems to flicker every 10 seconds or so, monochrome hints of images collapsing as soon as they are formed, while the bricks in the wall opposite are of a black-grey so uniform that they seem to have been copy/pasted into place.

The other attendees are on the opposite side of the table, facing me, though none look up from their tablets. One is my Senior-Manager. To his right is the UA, her symmetrical black fringe masking her eyes completely. The one left I have never seen before. My eyes seem to slide off and around them, never quite finding a purchase on their pinstripes, a face so unremarkable that there's to remember in it once my eyes have flitted away. All of them look directly into their screens. None of them say a word. Sitting in the corner on a folding chair is what seems to be a smaller, more compact version of my Senior-Manager, like a render that has been proportionally minimised, identical blue eyes calm and alert beneath exactly the same blonde hair.

I try to catch the eye of my Senior-Manager, but his eyes draw down and to the left instead, to my not-quite-professional-enough jumper. Fuck. But I've sweated right through the shirt beneath it, and can't take the crewneck off now. The sweat is seeping into the green as well though, through twisted strands of polyester that'll outlive every human in this room, and to hide my armpits I hunch my shoulders slightly forward.

It is now that my Senior-Manager looks up from his laptop:

"Do you intend on joining the meeting?"

A pause.

"I'm in the meeting."

A millisecond of raw contempt.

"The video meeting," he says.

I look down at the meeting room table, at my one folder and conspicuous lack of a tablet. Assistant Project

Administrators aren't given tablets, are required to book them out seven business days in advance from the Co-Located Common IT Services instead.

He speaks into his screen:

"While we have endeavoured to follow the relevant directions to conduct all meetings by video-link where possible, it seems that the final participant has not brought the requisite equipment, and we will have to move this meeting offline," his words repeated in tinny delay by the three other devices in the room, building in seconds to a grainy crescendo.

All three snap shut.

"We were just discussing the mapping data you put together in those folders, while we waited for you to arrive."

One of the lights above is flickering so quickly as to be almost imperceptible, strobing. The jumper is rancid with store-bought lasagna.

"We were almost afraid you weren't going to make it," he goes on, under a smile that doesn't make it to his eyes.

Maybe this too is a joke I do not understand.

"Hahahahahah," comes out my mouth, swallowed whole by the carpeted floor. The same carpet as under all the floors, all the feet, that same cross-hatching repeating inside itself forever, as if the uncountable lives unfolding on it are superimposed on one another, shifting accidents on this one unchanging ground.

"I'm so sorry I was late it'll never happen again it's my watch it's slow I didn't know why I was just getting the details right it's 16 minutes slow and there were so many reviews and the sweat I just couldn't get there in time I'm sorry my watch it's broken," I say, and in response there is only silence, the words-not-being-said now so deafening that I can't tell whether the talking, just then, had been out loud or in my head.

"This is ___________ _________, our Executive Director," my Senior-Manager says, gesturing towards the sentient blur, the name disintegrating on the air before it meets my ears.

"_________ _________ wanted to sit in on this meeting to get some first-hand oversight on the datasets that you put together. He's one of the key drivers of the Construct."

The UA's face flickers slightly. Her eyes are only barely visible beneath her fringe, and her long fingers are swirling rhythmically atop the plastic surface of the table.

"Well," my Senior-Manager says, and in response I pick up the folder and splay it out, fingers flicking open to the first page. I still can't look at the pages — there are numbers, I think, graph lines, perhaps — but I hope that I am making adequate enough eye contact to make up for it.

"I think the numbers speak for themselves," I say as confidently as I'm able, "though I would be happy to explain them in more detail to the Board."

"But the Board is already here," says _________

_________, in a voice the colour of Rolex wristwatches. He leans forward, the suggestion of his form drawing close across the table. I cannot focus on him for even a second, and the harder I try the more he disaggregates, subdividing into static so unexpectedly deep that for a moment it feels like I am falling into him, drowning in his folds.

"Yes," I falter.

The light above us flickers faster and then slows, perceptible now, bits of jagged darkness slicing the air between our faces.

Then, from out of the blur there stabs a long, grey finger, pointing right onto the very first page, followed by that same voice, softly now, rich:

"What does this mean?"

The light above us flickers and for a moment the world goes black.

Drowning, swallowed by a wave that ate the sky.

"Well that's our key deliverable of course," someone is saying as the light comes back, brighter and harsher than before, "as the data extracted in the tabs that follow make clear."

The silence shifts perceptibly.

"From my calculations this should be perfectly aligned with the organisation's key strategic priorities, though let me know if you can identify any further value adds," they keep explaining. "I am mindful that I've already taken up too much of your valuable time, and I take total responsibility for allowing my time management calculus to favour the intensive stakeholder coordination I was unexpectedly assigned."

Wait, I want to say, but instead the voice says "so please give me high-level guidance on whether, instead of continuing this face-to-face liaison, you would prefer a written memorandum on this topic typed and sent through to your UA." Their voice is calm and steady, with just the right amount of downward inflection. My voice.

______________ __________ leans forward. "Tell me, what are our values?"

"Proactive collaboration, Interpersonal communication, Ethics, Ethical Arbitration and Rules," my voice recites, friendly-toned and clear.

"And Change Inducement's individual branch value?"

"Lead from Above."

"And what is my name? Repeat it, please."

"______________ __________," my voice says, pronouncing perfectly the name I hear as only noise.

My Senior-Manager shifts in his chair. "About that memo-"

"That won't be necessary. I'm satisfied now that the task is in safe hands." ___________ _________ pulls his chair out from the table, and like a marionette on strings my limbs pull towards him; before he can reach the door a hand, my hand is reaching out to somewhere in the blur.

"A real pleasure to meet with you today," he says, shaking my hand with a grip like a woodworking vice. His body is still a featureless blur, but right at the top two eyes are now dimly visible, each with an iris so black it seems to swallow the pupil within.

Then my eyes blink and he is gone, folded back into the texture of the carpet.

My Senior-Manager looks across at me with pride. I try to move my arms but they stay strapped to my sides.

"That was an excellent, phenomenal job," he says. "I was confident that I'd made the right choice in singling you out for this project, but now..." he shakes his head, trailing off. "Excellent," he says. "Just excellent."

"And it's all thanks to the Performance Manager," he grins, and with a sudden chill I feel cold metal on the back of my neck. "See, nothing to be afraid of. It'll engage whenever it assesses your work performance to be sub-optimal, whenever you might need a little boost," and I try to clutch my brainstem but my arms stay where they are, not a single muscle moving as I command.

My mouth begins to open.

"That's wonderful to hear," my voice says, "the Performance Manager was an excellent suggestion — thank you for implementing it."

"You actually have my nephew here to thank for that," he says, and at this the miniature version of my Senior-Manager smiles and makes a courteous nod. "He was trained in their installation and use while on secondment at one of our key stakeholders. I didn't get to introduce you with that minor timing mix-up this morning, but you'll be working closely with him going forward" and I don't remember how they put it on me. Why can't I remember? Its metal legs are caressing the back of my neck, dry and wet at the same time and I want to throw up but I can't, my body completely and absolutely calm.

My gaze wrenches back to my Senior-Manager. The white wall of cladding behind him seems to open up for a moment, expanding into a blank space that stretches for thousands of miles. Something is coming through it, unfolding in that infinite distance towards us.

"You know, I've given it some thought but here it is," he says, "I think that you should join us at the executive briefing tomorrow. Given the excellent work you've done on this project so far, I couldn't imagine any better support. But first...." he drifts off again, eyes narrowing towards my worn, not-quite-leather boots.

"Of course," my voice says. "I'll take care of it."

We all walk out of the Meeting Room into the Shared Co-Working Space, first my Senior-Manager and his nephew, then myself and myself and the UA. She looks at me with a small frown, searching for something in the details of my face.

"You've gone and done it now, haven't you," she says, softly enough that only I can hear.

My head jerks to the side.

"Pardon?"

She rolls her eyes. "I refuse to talk to you like this."

"I don't know what you mean," my voice queries. "Do you mind explaining in a little more detail?"

She shakes her head. "I told you you weren't ready," then peels off towards the kitchen.

My eyes follow her for a few moments, vision going blurry and dewed. Something is slipping away, I think. Something is fading.

The *Project Epsilon* referred to in the *Chainmaker Trilogy* could be related to the *Gathering Shadow* referenced in the *Archangel's Fall* series — *If this theory holds up, it's likely to have huge impacts on the Chainmaker Cinematic Universe.*

I haven't seen any of these movies but am interested to learn more, very interested in fact. *The second prequel trilogy looks to be even more action packed than the last, with some special surprises in store for our heroes and anti-heroes.*

Very cool. The cursor hovers over an invitation to *Click here to read our extended chronology of the CCU,* and my hand tenses, prepared to click.

You aren't even reading this, comes a small, insignificant voice in my head. I bat it away.

Gabriel, fallen and stripped of his powers, must do gigantic, jaw-dropping battle with sinners, saints, and the most dangerous enemy of all — himself. The fate of three worlds hangs in the balance in this titanic battle between the Good, the Bad and the Evil.

This actually sounds pretty good. I'd always been dismissive of the Chainmaker Cinematic Universe, for reasons — probably pretentious ones — that I can barely even remember now. I smile broadly and add them to my watchlist.

In the time following the UA's rather strange remarks I had been extremely efficient, completing every plausible piece of work remotely within my purview; I'd checked my emails, checked my calendar, had another look at the letters from before (all of them excellent), and even tidied up the margins of some old dummy spreadsheets. This had taken about half an hour in all, but even my newfound efficiency couldn't solve the next issue. Simply put, there'd been nothing to do, no work for me to perform. So after I'd typed out emails signalling this work capacity to everyone conceivably my senior my fingers had fallen silent, for a moment, then quickly navigated to RealLife. Sometimes taking a well-deserved break is the most efficient thing you can do, after all.

On RealLife I remain, and as I come to the next listicle — *Our Top-10 Characters Giving Skibbidi Daddy in Chainmaker 2.0: Rise of Adam* — I get the uncomfortable feeling that something's on the back of my neck. And though this feeling snuffs itself out in a second or so it seemed familiar, I could have sworn. But the follow up thoughts to this also snuff themselves out, and in a second or so I return to the screen, to the scrolling and the reading, the reading and scrolling, the blinking in little reflex bursts that run the office through with black, and though it feels like hours have passed it's only 1:03. Barely half an hour.

Adam: what more is there to say? This gyat eats Skibbidi Daddy for real, and by 'eats' well, let's just say, he slurps.

This will be forever. It'll be years, decades before this body wears itself out and into the ground. Decades of waiting, watching, pleading.

A rupture like a record ran back.

Wait. What was that? That line of thought there, what was it? Something odd about it. Something strange about all these thoughts, something too set, and once again that cold metal by my nape. It's on the tip of my tongue.

I go back to scrolling. There are more listicles to read, more links to click. But there is an uneasiness behind the scrolling now, a piece that can't quite fit. Something has happened.

A dull grey box appears: *Mandatory system updates are required by your Systems Administrator. Your Computer will restart in 10 minutes.* The pop up can't be closed, can't be pushed off, can be controlled only by being brought forward, by pressing the button that reads *Restart and Install Updates Now.*

Just restart now, go downstairs and get the new shoes, a voice inside me whispers, moving what I feel to be my hand but moving nothing. I am moving nothing. Then a second later the resistance of plastic on skin, my right hand pushing forward and the cursor moving up towards the button. My right index finger pushes down and another pop-up appears — *Would you like to Save your draft before closing,* with it a completely blank document. I go to move my hand towards the pop-up and my muscles do the same, faster now, hovering over the button for *Discard draft.* Not much left of a lag. I feel strange. It feels strange. *It feels strange to be so split,* I think, and now there is a thought in answer: *split how?* Another blink. A sinking feeling. A feeling of something having been forgotten. My eyes go to widen with fear and they do then widen, only a few milliseconds later, coinciding with each other so exactly that there's scarcely a difference. Then the pop-up closes, and the computer shuts off. My eyes stare straight ahead into the office space, reflected back at me out of the black, crystal screen, and I remember the detail that I've been trying so hard to avoid.

I am not there in that reflection. I am not sitting in this chair, and neither are my colleagues at their desks. Their keystrokes still come, hollow and vacant behind me, but in the empty screen there's just a row of vacant chairs. Only a black, empty office and I wonder, now, how I could have thought I would ever see anything else. There are never any people in the mirrors, the reflections always empty, but this fact never seems to stick. I keep circling back to it, again and again, each time with all the shock of the new.

The Performance Manager is having none of this though. Just as the lights begin to flicker my eyes tear themselves from the blank screen, and plant themselves firmly on my phone. But this screen too is black, reflective in the moment before it is unlocked, and in it my eyes find the same empty office. The phone slams on the desk and my body springs upwards. *Gotta get a glass of water*, I can hear myself thinking, legs pacing themselves into the kitchen, then retreating in the face of the rows of shiny glassware. When I return to my desk my Senior-Manager's nephew is shaking my Manager's hand, introducing himself firmly and with impeccable eye contact.

The Performance Manager squirms, and after a few short seconds my eyes lock onto the middle-aged man with the handle-bar moustache. *Time to get myself out there too*, I am thinking as my legs walk over to his desk. His screen is filled with the same 3D rendering of our office, zoomed in to the desk he is sitting at today. We met this guy yesterday, but my Performance-Managed body seems not to notice.

"Hello there, I'm Sirin, a 28-year old Philosophy and Communications graduate still within their Probationary Period," and though I am dying of cringe the Performance Manager goes on, impelling me to network, to improve my personal brand. "What would you say are the three most important leanings for a junior employee taking their first brave steps into the workplace?"

The man turns gruffly.

"Number one — keep your head down and do the work properly," he says, and my Performance-Managed stomach drops — he's wearing small rectangular glasses, "kids these days don't have any work ethic, all they want to do is go on their phones and take sick leave for these bloody so-called viruses."

He angles his head up towards me, the empty reflection now clearly visible in the lenses. My eyes cannot look away though, the imperative to maintain adequate eye-contact too strongly encoded.

"Number two — don't go in for any of this woke stuff," and the lights are starting to blink again, fizzing and crackling, "I know it's not very politically correct to say this but the first thing I think when someone has pronouns in their signature is jeez, what a tosser."

My head nods thoughtfully, little drips of perspiration running down my temples. The render on his screen is empty, void of the slightest soul.

"And number three," the keyboards falling silent. "Spoil yourself once in a while, maybe get yourself one of these," pointing at a gently pulsing keyboard on his desk, keys forming and unfurling out of a diffuse central core, "no point working yourself to the bone without some good kit to show for it."

"Thank you," my voice says, "that was really helpful."

Then the man goes back to his render, and my body returns to its desk, but it's too late. The fluorescent lights are already going out, in shuddering bursts behind me, and with them go the monitors, the little patterns of cyan, magenta and yellow all shorting into black. Then the air conditioning vents above and the hum of distant fridges, the watch strapped to my wrist and the cooling fans on the back of the computers; every last bit of background electrical noise falls silent. Every other person gone too, of course, the office just an empty shell, no-one here except me but, incredibly, my body stays in my seat, and on the inside I am laughing as my fingers hit an R on the keyboard, and then an E, and then an enter. My eyes are blank, not really focusing right, and my right middle index finger goes down one mouse wheel at a time, just as if I were still scrolling through RealLife. Still glancing to the side every so often, anxious of being caught and by who, exactly? And for what? It's a while before either I or my wayward eyes realise there's something unfamiliar about this screen. A yellow post-it note, stuck to the very top of the monitor, telling me in familiar handwriting to *Get up*.

The Performance Manager makes a crumpled little whirring sound, then turns itself off. Every muscle slackens at once, and I fall off the chair.

Peace, for a time. Fingers slowly flexing. Arms and legs splayed at funny angles, and a faint taste of blood in back of throat, but nothing broken, nothing bruised. I stay slumped on the carpet, nicely relaxed. No-one is asking anything of me down here, and I want nothing from anyone else, only to be left alone for a moment while I catch my breath. One breath, then two; four; twenty.

Slowly I rise. The office is completely abandoned, but for the staplers and pens, the monitors and keyboards and World's Best Boss mugs. I walk towards the windows, one step closer, then another, and then another until my forehead rests cold against the glass.

Gaze resting too on the window, then through it, out to the giant shards of glass that pierce up through the barren concrete. The holographic screens are cold and grey, and though the streets are choked with cars not a single one is moving. My forehead taps experimentally against the glass, and I wonder how much pressure it would take for the window to give. A second tap, heavier, and as the thud fades another, different sound creeps into the silence it leaves behind.

I can see it now, its huge bulk hanging vacant in the sky. Unhidden by the patchy clouds, filling a quarter of the sky is a giant black sphere, impossibly vast, massive and yet somehow still far deeper than its diameter should allow. Impossibly dark too, like a portion of the blackest void brought down unto the Earth. It hangs among the towers, uncaring of gravity, and as my eyes take it in my thoughts begin to whir and spin, a terrified chatter beneath the thin grape-skin of my ego. A cry that doesn't make it to my mouth, hair along my arms pricked upwards towards it, inescapable for a second how cold everything is — these offices, this city, this empty world — like the sunny day was sucked up into this eye unseeing from above. As if it contains worlds, universes through its darkened folds.

"You know you shouldn't look for long."

The words echo faintly in the vacant office, over and through the still-not-tapping on the keyboards and the not-yet-ticking of the watch: this is a voice I know. The sphere seems to lose its dimensionality for a moment, like a huge circle cut out from the sky, flickering into absence.

"It isn't safe up here," comes the voice again. I turn, and there are a few seconds when she is there with me, in the empty office, kindness in her eyes.

And then I blink.

"Hello," says my Manager, voice raised slightly over the bustle of the office.

"Beautiful view," as she steps into place beside me. Gazing out over the cityscape as I look back out into the rush of the return from lunch, listen to the tap tap tap of the keyboard strikes and mouse clicks all around.

"Makes everything worth it," I repeat reflexively. The cars are moving again, and down there like ants on the side of the footpath are all the tiny people on their way to work. An LED billboard extolls the virtues of the new Citizen's Community Defence Program. A skywriter traces out an L, then an O.

"We'd better get back to it," she murmurs, but stays standing. Holographic smiles beam down from the billboards, polar white and perfect. The Wall holds fast against the rising sea beyond. But it's a darker sun that glints off the towers, too dim to be the same that shines from up above. The wind on the glass outside has gotten louder, more insistent beneath the keyboards and the mice and the *What did you do on the weekend?s*.

"I don't know what it means either," she says softly, and turns to leave. I can see it too, of course; the cars are all standing still inside the shiny shards of glass.

Perhaps I will go to the protest today after all.

The Construct would be a world very much like this one, each object in its rightful, pre-existing place. People would go to work in the same office buildings as before, doing the same jobs, would drink in the same bars and return, drunkenly, to the same apartments, unless they were kicked out of them. As far as was possible nothing would change, fundamentally, and the unwelcome agents of that change — the rising seas, the collapsing food chains, the refugees that came pouring in from the tropics — would be politely sidestepped, allowed to run their course in the real world while we carried on in our newer, safer version, sealed off from the chaos of the splintering globe behind the edges of a tame black hole. An easier world, is what would end up with. A world in which we could all carry on as normal.

The shoes for the board meeting need to be black, I believe, and shiny, with a pointed toe and laces which pass through no more than three eyelets on either side. A slight heel, but not too high. A Brand. But all of the shoes seem to have a pointed toe, here between the silvery white walls of the shoe section, and between zero to three eyelets. Each is shiny and black, and branded. Almost identical shoes surround me on all sides, in photos on boxes and images on screens, in posters on walls and in three-dimensional holograms that hover above the register. Eventually I try on a pair with a bright red 15% off sign decorating their white plinth. I've never been completely sure what my shoe size is, can already feel the tips of my toes struggling slightly against the pleather but they'll wear in, surely, and anyway this is the largest size the discounted ones come in.

My card purchases them with a friendly beep, and a man passes a theatrically flashing wand over the box, pretending to deactivate a non-existent security device. Eventually I am allowed to leave. I sit on a department-store couch and put on these newer, more professional shoes, place my old boots in the new box and shut the lid, shake my head, wonder how I could ever have thought that these were a work-appropriate item of clothing.

But this is wrong, I remember as the points of the new shoes tap over the hard, shiny tiles of the shopping centre, high-ceilinged corridors in eggshell and chrome. Tall windows full of things to purchase, glass so empty and still. I had loved those boots, had been so happy when I'd found them in the second-hand store before the interview. Black but not too shiny. Casual enough to wear to drinks with friends after work. When Alex had seen them decorating my feet she'd squinted, eyebrows furrowed slightly.

"The perfect compromise," she'd said. Yet now I am called to compromise again.

I get distracted, and it's hours later when I finally get outside. The sky is the colour of light blue food dye, crisscrossed by massive quadcopters whose rotors beat a throbbing, pulsing hum. Sun filters softly through the plane trees, a pulse of movement among their leaves, and I realise that I've never really seen the trees before — not the twigs, nor the leaves, certainly not the little patterns of discolouration on the trunks or the idiosyncrasies in the arrangements of their branches. I've seen only *trees*, with the sort of generic illustration a primary schooler might draw, but for the barest of moments I see something wholly more; for a split second every splinter of their wood is made clear, and every vein of their leaves, each tree a universe as detailed and complete as this one.

Back at my desk the updates are still installing, a suggestion of a circle rotating endlessly against a background of blue, and the younger double of my Senior-Manager is systematically greeting and shaking every last hand in the Shared Co-Working Space. It will take him about ten minutes to reach me at his current rate, and in my mind he walks up, looks down slightly and says: *nice shoes, I really like the point*. The certainty of this exchange makes me strangely uncomfortable, the grey walls suddenly too close. The Performance-Manager is twitching limply on my spine, seemingly inactive.

I make sure to look at the loading screen in frustration, let a highly audible sigh escape my lips as I leave, out into the elevator. Quickly, before he has the chance to make eye contact. Before it re-engages. It's a plausible reason for leaving, compelling, and for a second I feel myself slipping into this new reality, remaking myself around a new narrative. *You weren't sad that the computer was still updating though,* I think as I stride past the concierge. *You wanted to leave.* And there is a clarity to this, a strength as I make my way through the high-ceilinged lobby. *Just heading over now,* I text Alex. *Let me know where you are.*

Alex doesn't text back, but the cars on the street outside are bumper to bumper, the shoulders of the drivers held at angry, frustrated angles, and I begin to walk in the direction that the frozen vehicles are pointed. At first furtively, like I might turn back any moment, but with increasing assurance as the walk progresses. People are walking in the same direction as me now, many people, in un-collared shirts and unprofessional jumpers, hand texta'd signs emerging from rucksacks and coats. There are signs up ahead too, printed on the back of toilet paper boxes. A slogan here, an insult there, but most common of all a circle, empty. Then the flow congeals, coalescing like raindrops on a windowsill, gathering strength until all of a sudden the people are standing still, eyes fixed on a point I cannot yet pick out. The staticy voice of a megaphone speaks somewhere over the crowd, too far away for me to hear the words.

"Excuse me," I say to a tall blonde man in a denim jacket. His face is filled with anger and determination but also a trace of boredom, the anger and determination now just another part of his routine. He slants slightly to the side.

"Excuse me," I say to a woman with long black hair and slim pointy ears. She's older than I thought at first, her hand-laminated sign fraying at the edges, eyes staring into a future she suspects will never come about. She angles her body from my path.

"Excuse me," I say to a lanky, fresh-faced high-schooler. They've come in their uniform, skipped school most likely. They jump out of my way a little too quickly, straight into the large afro'd man behind them. They apologise profusely as they pick up their sign.

"Excuse me," I say to a bent old man, suspenders tight and hair combed back. He beams beatifically from beneath his slumping shoulders. He steps slowly out of the way.

"Excuse me," I say to an elegant protestor with shaved black hair and thin metal earrings, androgynous enough that I hesitate at *he* or *she*. They're about the same age as me but taller, thinner, with what seems like a more meaningful personal aesthetic and a much wider social circle. They don't move out of the way, but rather look down sceptically at my shoes, put a finger to their lips and point towards the front of the crowd. I have reached the inner core it seems, and can push no further.

And I try very hard to listen to the speech, really I do. But I still can't hear it. *Jingle bell, jingle bell, jingle bell, jingle bell,* the department store across the street repeats, louder and more insistent than the megaphone, and the more I try to ignore it the more irritating it becomes, the louder and more grating. The edge of each big toe is more noticeable than before, wedged against the edge of each newly purchased shoe. Something smells off. I stand on my tip-toes to catch a glimpse of the person speaking; she's tall, with thick glasses and a curly black afro, and darker skin than anyone in my office building. She's saying something important, from the looks of it, something new, something capable of rekindling the dreams I have spent a lifetime slowly destroying, but all her words are just noise to me, static somewhere beneath the *jingle bell, jingle bell,* coming now not from just the department store but every store down the length of the street, no matter that it's barely Spring.

Eyes leave the speaker, searching for a familiar face. But there's no-one I recognise, not even a half-remembered acquaintance, and Alex is nowhere to be seen. The square seems suddenly very crowded. The people far too close. *Your message could not be sent*, beeps my phone, *please check that you are connected to a network and try again* and my eyes are scanning faster now, jumping from face to face in a way that surely betrays that I'm not meant to be here, that I am a sellout, an intruder. *JINGLE BELL JINGLE BELL JINGLE BELL.*

The shaved-headed protestor to my left has been side-eyeing me for some minutes now, and it appears they've reached their limit.

"Your phone," they whisper pointedly.

"What?"

"Give me your phone," they say, plucking it from my shaking hands and holding the power button down. They wait until the screen goes black, then hand it back.

"Get rid of that thing."

The jingle cuts, fallen away completely. For an instant everything is beautifully silent, like skiers would have heard in deepest snow. And upon this powdery blankness there comes a word, from the speaker, and that word is:

"No."

And there is a unity in this perception, each person in the crowd hearing the same thing at once. Then a quarter note of silence, the sound of a wave sucking in its breath before the crowd answers back in a single voice:

"No!"

My lips are closing by the time I hear I'd said it too, my tiny syllable echoing off the shop fronts and street signs and little stone steps to return to me, mixed in with all the others. Then again the expectant silence, the air charged as we wait for the next words, the new message, perhaps even the *Yes* that after all this searching will surely set us free. But there is no next word. The speaker's megaphone gives out, gives only scrambled metal whispers that grind `1to nothing. Scattered coughs soon follow, then whispered conversation.

I immediately spot Alex, right by the speaker, framed by a big black PA system and professional looking people in orange and pink vests. She sees me and waves cheerily. Behind her are trees, and more people, and behind them, driving right up to the other edge of the crowd are four armoured trucks, with large black antennae and small white cylinders mounted on their backs. Bulky figures in white combat gear are massing beside them, and the shiny black antennae are turning towards the crowd. I read an article about these once, absent-mindedly on a computer at work, something about directed microwaves, but I'd forgotten it again when I realised how poorly it went down in office conversation. Difficult to remember now, the atmosphere too tense, the people around me scrambling in their pockets for sheets of foil or bits of foam. *Fuck fuck fuck fuck fuck* mutters a voice behind me, and I wonder whether I should have brought little bits of foam as well.

"Don't worry," the shaved-headed-person beside me whispers. "None of it is real."

They wink.

And as their right eye begins to open my skin catches fire, like a tiny piece of burning coal has been placed beneath each pore. A unity in this perception too, and a stifled gasp from every person in the crowd. The walls of people shatter, diving to the ground and running into alleyways and every bit of exposed skin is aflame, too late to bring my bag up to stop it, pain like a red-hot knife against my fingers. I stagger back towards my building but the pain finds me there as well and the white figures are pulling people from the crowd, pushing them into unmarked vans on either side of the street, slipping through the crush like arrowheads and smashing the PA system into pieces with long black batons, and as I look over, eyes very wide, I see that the small white cylinders are turning towards us too. Through the burning pain I dimly remember these as well, had been there when last they were brought out. Then from them comes the cry, an awful shriek so loud that I clutch my ears and stagger to the side. But it comes for me through my hands, through fingers plugged in ears and on the pavement too, concrete cold against my cheek, each millisecond the loudest thing I've ever heard until the next millisecond, even louder, and the next, and the next. Louder and harsher it blossoms, skin still aflame and body seizing on the ground, eardrums giving way now, annihilated by the frequency until there is no crowd, no thought, no me but only the sound and the fire, filling this vessel to the brim and then, once there's nothing left to fill, black.

When you were a child you were always so scared of the dark, always afraid of that unseen thing unfurling behind you as you collected the washing off the clothesline. Always you went anyway, too afraid of seeming a scaredy-cat to stay inside, but never lingering long in the shadow, always hoping that next time you would be braver. But the thing was always there, always waiting, and the fear waiting with it, no matter how little you recognised it anymore. You never got any braver, you see. You only got better at pushing it down.

The scene shifts into focus. Sitting somewhere. Sitting. I am sitting. Something hard, wood against my back and hands. A chair. Sitting in a chair, at a table. I am sitting in a chair at a table. I am sitting in a chair at a table and Alex is sitting on the other side, leaning forward slightly, looking directly into my still-refocusing eyes.

"You're back," she smiles.

"We almost had to carry you out of there," and though I can barely hear her over the high pitched whine that's settled through the room I smile, and nod, and almost say thanks but only half of it comes out. The table is small and square, tiny letters etched into its wood. Love, war and boredom all written over one another in the grain.

"Sometimes I swear I can see my name written there, way down through the layers," her right index finger moving back and forth in front of my nose. My eyes reluctantly follow.

"Just a bit of shock, I wouldn't worry about it."

I can't think clearly enough to be worrying about it.

"I'll tell you what though, it was difficult to get you out of there in those shoes," looking underneath the table at my feet. "Just when you think they couldn't torture you officeworkers any more, they come up with something like those. Wouldn't have gotten you out of there alone."

"It was nothing, by the way," comes another voice from my left, from beneath shaved black hair and slender metal earrings. "A fitting thanks for coming out to our little action," and they are the same person as at the protest, I think.

"It is very concerning what they are doing you see. We could have paradise on Earth, no-one hungry, everyone in houses, and instead they want to give us more of this, more of this hyper-post-capitalist bullshit until the ocean swallows us all. The situation, I am referring to of course. The tremendous opportunity it offers, as well as the tremendous danger."

"What do you know about the situation, by the way?"

"They're in shock, Suresh. Stop interrogating them."

"Well I was very surprised that you came, is all, when Alex told me where you worked. You know what your organisation is responsible for, don't you? You understand who that protest was against?"

Alex gives them a pointed look.

"That's right," she says. "It must have been very difficult."

It hadn't been difficult at all. Like a civil war in a country on the other side of the world, to be watched on the news and catalogued away, I had learned about our misdeeds in a way that was conceptual, never actually requiring action on my part. The organisation always shadowy, always abstract, always just *the organisation*; a lattice of straight lines and right angles colonising the curves and squiggles of the world.

"I didn't expect it to happen so quickly though," Alex is saying. "We didn't have time to finish a single speech."

"This is how it goes. The capitalists always revert to fascism when they know their back is against the wall. This is when we see their true colours."

"I mean, what the hell do we do against all that firepower?"

"They are just toys in the end. Resorting to them so quickly is an indication of weakness, in some ways, of fragility."

"I know, I know. And at least we know it can't get much worse than this, right."

And with this a sudden clarity. "It can always get worse," I say, noticing my words a few moments after they leave my lips.

Alex turns towards me.

"The vow of silence, broken at last."

"Welcome back," says Suresh.

"So how'd you like it?" Alex smiles.

"Yeah," I say. "It was good."

"Fun, even?"

"Harder than I remembered, but it was good."

"Wonderful," Suresh says. "Nothing worthwhile is easy."

Alex snorts. "When did you get so fucking jaded?"

"A hazard," they say, taking a drink. "For some more than others."

Alex rolls her eyes. Suresh turns back to me.

"Alex tells me you were there during the interesting times."

"I got dragged along to a few things."

"She spoke very highly of who you were then."

"I was no-one special. It was the obvious thing to do, with everything that was happening."

"And do you think nothing is happening now? That we've reached the end of history at last, no more struggle necessary, even possible?"

"I think it's harder to know what the right thing to do is."

"Easier to obfuscate, certainly."

"I came today."

"To see an old friend."

"You don't know anything about what I've seen."

They raise their eyebrows coolly. "And what have you seen?"

"The Construct. That's what this is all about, right? That's what you're protesting against."

Alex covers my hand in hers.

"I don't know what you mean," Suresh says blankly. "The Construct is the greatest project in human civilisation."

No-one says anything further, the table tense and untalkative, and as the moment hangs, waiting, someone else sits down at the table, someone come straight from the bar. The man sat down to my right is nondescript, if I had to describe him. Short brown hair, nice smile. Grey eyes. A pint which is full yet gone completely flat, as if he's not drunk a single drop from it for hours. Alex's foot makes sharp contact with my shin as I open my mouth to ask him who he is. She smiles broadly, eyes straight ahead:

"So how was your day at work? Busy right?"

"Yeah, pretty busy," I say, stammering. "I had a big meeting but I think it went okay," and though the new man's face doesn't turn I feel his attention shift towards me, like a drone autofocusing on a pedestrian about to cross the curb.

"How about you?"

"Yeah, I've also been a bit busy too, yeah. Can't wait for the weekend," she says, smiling even more broadly. In the right periphery is a beige windbreaker and a white t-shirt. Alex kicks me again, harder.

"Speaking of work, I'm afraid I've got to head off," Suresh announces very cheerily. "I have a shift in half an hour and don't want to be late."

"Awwww, see you later," she says brightly.

"Fantastic to catch up," they say to Alex, "and great to meet you," before walking in a straight line directly to the exit.

When I look back to my right the man in the beige windbreaker is gone.

"What the fuck was that," I whisper, but she motions me silent, to stay.

"Let's just get a drink."

A long, unwinding breath out. The man is definitely gone, no trace of him in the bar, though Alex kicks me again before I can check fully. I take a sip of the beer in front of me and make a face; its buckwheat.

Alex rolls her eyes: "so how *was* your day?"

And at this I shift in my chair a little. I go to pick out my phone from my pocket and stop myself half-way. I breathe in quickly. The bar is here, I am in the bar, everything is in its rightful place.

"It was a bit strange."

I take another swig. Alex says nothing.

"At times I felt like I wasn't really myself."

A little smile.

"Like I was just playing a part, or something else was playing the part of being me."

"Do you feel this way often, you think?"

"Maybe. It's hard to tell. Things get so mixed up."

She pauses for a moment, carefully weighing her next words:

"Are you happy there?" she asks, and turns her head slightly. But instead of an answer I have only thoughts. What is happiness, after all? How can I tell whether the experience I call happiness is the same experience that another person calls by the same name? What if my greatest happiness is so small that it would go unseen by her, just a small blip of positive feeling, or her's so rich and complex that it would be unbearable to me?

And what if her mind is so unlike my own that our emotions just don't line up, that there are no common items to put under the same headings, that her smiles and laughter don't go to something else inside entirely, alien or incomprehensible to me? And this is all possible, of course, plausible. But once I would have had something more to say, something a bit better than:

"It's a job, I guess," and a shrug.

"Indeed it is. But are you happy over there, in that job?"

And it strikes me — temporarily, fleetingly — that there is a name for this not-knowing-whether-you-are-happy-or-not, a name for this uncertainty and second guessing.

"You know what, I really don't know sometimes. But I feel like I have gotten great learning opportunities there, and met a wonderful group of people, and…."

I trail off, unconvinced about the rest of the sentence.

"Not really yourself?"

Silence. The name for this is unhappiness, of course.

"Yeah. Not really myself."

And then there is another pause, long enough for the other conversations in the bar to start imposing themselves on our silence — *I know right/I totally agree/ He was not too good for you/what have you been up to lately/ good/that sounds really awful/I know totally what you mean* — until, in the exact moment when all of the conversations around us fall silent, each reaching its own, individual lull, I ask:

"What do you see when you look in the mirror?"

Alex looks across the table at me with a strange smile, like I'd asked after a beloved family cat who's been dead for years. She blinks a few times in quick succession. She goes to speak, then stops, thinks better of it, goes to say something else, then stops again, and says:

"I see exactly what's there."

and for a split second I realise that there are no other people in the bar, just me and her. All of the lights are flickering off, dyeing like fireflies in a storm.

"Nothing more."

No way/I totally agree/that's ridiculous/I hear you/You're perfect/I completely understand. Her eyes are looking through me now, focused on the point directly behind my head, back at the faded wood panelling of the walls.

"Anyway, we should probably be heading off," she says. "It's almost eleven and it sounds like you have a busy day tomorrow."

I get up, murmur a "sorry" and walk with her to the exit. Outside we walk in silence, the conversation from the bar receding, replaced by the honks of cars and the scattered drips of air conditioning vents. Her face softens, and she walks a little closer.

"Do you think we're going to make it?" she asks. "All of us, I mean."

"I think that anything's possible."

She laughs. "I think that's a cop out."

I smile. "I think people are more afraid of what will happen if we do make it, you know. If there's no end. If we have to just keep going on like this forever."

She frowns, lost in thought. "I suppose you're right."

We pass a screen taller than both of us put together; a fleet of boats leaving a burning port, each one over-crowded, almost sinking beneath the people piled high.

"We probably won't have to worry about that though."

She snorts, then looks pained, guilty. "Probably not."

We walk a little further, then stop in front of another, less well-trafficked bar.

"This is me," Alex says. "My apartment's on the second floor." A hug, and a kiss on the cheek, and I flush. This is the first time someone's deliberately touched me in months.

"Don't be a stranger," she says, unlocking a small red door next to the entrance. She's halfway through it when she stops, thinking.

"By the way, and don't take this the wrong way, but someone really needs to tell you."

"Yeah?"

"Promise you won't get weird or defensive about it?"

"I promise."

"Well, I mean, it's your bag. It's filled with defrosted package meals. We looked through it while you were unconscious, I hope you don't mind. I think there's a lasagna in there, some gyoza. I didn't look too closely but to be honest it's pretty gross."

"Oh," I laugh. "Yeah, I know."

She laughs as well. "Then do something about it," shaking her head as she shuts the door.

The bar doesn't have a name, just a neon sign with a pink dolphin jumping out of blue waves. The dolphin flips back and forth between two images like it's splashing in the ocean, lifeless and joyful and free.

I begin to walk to the station but find myself with no-where to go, no memory of the walk over, no idea of where I am or for how long I was carried. A man strides by in skinny black jeans, purposefully and with at least five air purifiers bundled awkwardly in his arms. I almost ask him where I am, but decide it doesn't matter.

I sit. It's quieter out here, quiet enough that I can hear the high-pitched ringing in my ears more clearly. It varies slightly, pitch and volume modulating in ways too subtle for me to pin down, and I wonder how many others in the City have ringing ears tonight. At least a few. I feel a strange harmony with these other people, all hearing the same, an anonymous community bound together across space and time by the same tinnitus, the same perhaps-permanent state-inflicted hearing damage.

There's a unity in this perception too, I guess. I laugh, and lean back on the concrete gutter, order an Autoshare, settle in for the three and a half minute wait. This is good. I am good.

THURSDAY

I am forgetting something. I am forgetting something. I am forgetting something but I remember, too, know the answer as surely as this thought, feel its contours like a wheel of clay beneath my hands. The wheel spins, perfect, a presentiment of the vase to come. The thought hangs in negative space, unspoken. Will the vase yearn to be liquid again once it has been made useful and good though, fixed by fire to a single form? Will it not long for the clay?

The train this time is navigated without incident. No delays, no sudden stops. Just a normal, everyday train ride, hands shaking a little as the escalator rises to the vaulted concrete of the concourse. Little bits of gum are flattened on the polished floor, and a few little food and coffee stands line the walls. My eyes catch a blueberry muffin.

I'm stepping into the lobby as I take the first bite; floury, with only a hint of synthetic blueberry. It's exactly as disappointing as usual, but as the elevator doors close I am eating the third bite, and as they open again on the 99th floor only the muffin-bottom remains. I scoff this down, passing through the doors with only minimal complaint, muffin-bottom settling into a sugary sludge beneath my tongue. The plastic wrapper might just be recyclable though, and I place it in the yellow bin by the doors, feeling optimistic.

There was something I'd needed to do, something I had to remember, and as I sit down it hits me: the Performance Manager. I'd been going to leave this job and never return, grow fat and bug-eyed in a pod rather than suffer the indignity of being controlled like that for even a second longer, or so I had decided, earlier, in bed. Yet here I am, in the office, on time even for the third day in a row. And why not? I have that board meeting to attend, after all, and another, as-yet-hypothetical apartment to begin paying rent on. The Performance Manager is still inactive, a subtle drumbeat on the back of my neck the only sign of its presence. I think perhaps I'll stay.

I've received 103 emails overnight, all automated notifications of activity on the workplace social media platform; these slip through my frontal lobe with almost no resistance, like clear spring water. I delete all of them, and the storage space this frees up allows three further emails to arrive.

The first is an all-staff email from the Board denouncing the *criminality and lawlessness perpetrated by violent rioters yesterday afternoon* and expressing its *utmost gratitude to the allied security team for defusing the situation with such professionalism and care,* the abstract form of these syllables ringing through my consciousness like a bell. I delete this too.

The second is a calendar invitation from the UA, to the executive meeting, at 12:00pm today on the hundredth, final floor of the building, and a message from her informing me that the folders have already been taken up. A subtler feeling to this one, the message filtering through layers of perception like a drop of breakfast supplement in a glass of water.

The third is an email notification for an education seminar in 10 minutes' time; barely noticeable, like thin sheets of silk rubbing together for just a second. Yet with it comes the faintest of snags. I get up, to get a glass of water maybe, then sit down. I stand back up, and sit back down again.

I bring up the invitation on the screen this time; it stares back at me, dimensionless and flat. But it's just an email. Not even an email that someone has taken the effort to type, either, just an automated notification, composed and delivered by a little line of code.

My phone buzzes.

Hey, it was nice to catch up, writes Alex, *I'd really appreciate it if you could give me a call about that thing you mentioned at the end.* A high-pitched whine settles through the office as I quietly put the phone away, as if every object in it has begun to vibrate in unison.

Alex and I had once stayed late at the bar together, after all the others had trickled away. The conversations around us had lulled, and she had leant over the table, fingers almost touching mine. A feeling like syrup on the tongue. What would happen if our hands touched, I'd wondered, and in that moment the question had expanded, reaching out to fill the limits of my world. Too large for me, it became; instead of answering I had excused myself to go to the bathroom, and when I'd returned Alex had been leaning back in her chair, and the moment had slipped away.

The seminar is in the boardroom, long table folded away to make room for rows of folding chairs. I sit next to Harriet, or maybe Hermione, a woman of about my age — she'd introduced herself to me as My New Best Work Friend on my first day, but I had forgotten her name immediately after being told it, and it had quickly become too awkward to ask. We sit at the far end of the third row; not so close to the front that we could be called upon to answer questions, but close enough that it won't seem like we're avoiding them. In front of us is a powerpoint presentation, and in front of that a man is explaining something called the *Whole of Organisation Holistic Wellness Plan (WoHOWP)*, and the burden imposed by *Consensus Destabilising Events (CDEs)* on *A Positive Team Output Driven Culture (APTODC)*. I write down everything that the man says, just as the man says everything that is projected onto the wall.

"Any deviational behaviour should be reported to Humanistic Resourcing immediately," he says genially, in a suit the years are beginning to thin, "so that the affected individual can get proper mental health and attitudinal supports," a dazzling array of Performance Management options displayed on screen behind him.

"And because of this, it's really of the utmost, paramount importance that we all bring our whole selves to work. We should all feel comfortable speaking exactly what's on our mind at any given moment, so that, if it turns out to be incorrect, or dangerous, we can be given help."

A pause.

"You there," he points. No-one had sat in the first two rows.

"Yes, you," pointing directly at me. "What excites you about coming into work every morning?"

"It is a real pleasure to work here," I answer, no pause at all. "Nowhere else would I have better learning opportunities, or be able to meet such a wonderful group of people, or have the opportunity to take part in such interesting and challenging work."

His eyes light up with joy.

"That's perfect, just perfect. There's nothing I like to hear more than that. Now tell me," he goes on with a grin, "what is it about the work here that you find so interesting and challenging?"

It's sunny outside, with only a wisp of cloud in the sky, just enough texture to know it isn't painted on. I will have to think of something to say, eventually, but unfortunately this just isn't possible. The script doesn't extend past what I've already recited. One second, then two. The room's attention grows uncomfortably concentrated on the back of my head.

"Well, I think that when you're constantly being challenged at work it makes the work exceptionally interesting."

A strange pause pervades the room. The PowerPoint presentation beams:

"Now that is an absolutely fantastic answer. Let me tell you, it's so encouraging to find young people like yourself who aren't ashamed to bring their whole self to work. Mind you, don't get too good at this or you'll be putting me out of a job — are you sure you don't want to come up here and teach this seminar?"

Laughter rings out from everyone assembled, each with the same half-second delay. Jane, or maybe Jolie whispers in my ear:

"How good is this presentation? I'm loving it."

"Yeah, absolutely."

"Your answer was so inspiring too. I would never have been able to come up with something like that," she says, leaning closer, her lips almost touching my left earlobe.

My pen runs out of ink, begins to write only in fragments. I keep scribbling though, tiny indents marking where the words should be, angling my paper towards Elsie, or maybe Elizabeth, so that the person on my right won't see.

"Now please," the man is saying, "draw something that's from your whole self, the place where you go to chill out when the world gets too much. Just take your pen and draw on a new sheet of one of those notebooks. And no peeking!"

I rub my pen between my hands to warm the ink back up. First comes the lone palm tree, beckoning, bent slightly towards the water. Second come the waves lapping on to shore, caught right as a break is coming down. Third are the big rocks, out a little further, high enough to jump from to the gentle surf below and fourth is the sand, a long thin bar stretching out into a vanishing point far ahead. Fifth are the beach towels, of me and a friend, and maybe another towel too, more friends coming up behind us.

I turn to Elizabeth, or maybe Aspen. She has also drawn the lone palm tree, and the waves, and the rocks, and the stretch of sand and the towels. A long, empty ocean stretches out to her horizon as well, overlaid with guidelines of horizontal blue. And to my right too is a beach in a notebook, the same notebook and the same beach as further right, and one further right than that. The man looks down at a few of these sketches, all of them the same, and nods contentedly.

"Isn't it just the greatest?" he says. "The best place to be in the whole world is the ocean."

I close my eyes, and open them again, and try not to think about what it means.

A plain white folder is sitting on my desk when I return. *Please review carefully,* instructs a yellow post-it note stuck to the top. *Executive briefing materials,* say the letters on the side. I soften slowly into the chair, breathing in deeply, the thin pattern of white noise between my ears becoming louder, higher. My hands drum a staccato pattern on the chipboard desk, each fingertip crisp against the laminate. Then, like I don't care at all, like I'm reading just anything in the world, I open the folder.

The first page is a textured slab of static. Digital snow fills the entire sheet, and as I look into it I become dizzy, taste metal on the back of my tongue. I quickly turn it over.

The second page is a sequence of numbers *1121231234123451234561234567* repeated endlessly through the page without breaks or punctuation.

The third is a gigantic *I AM* written in Gothic typeface, large enough to fill the entire page.

The fourth is every swear word I know and many I did not until now, repeated over and over again in differently sized lower-case letters.

The fifth contains only the words I *know you're reading this, by the way. I can see you reading this. I can smell you reading this...,* and a feeling of dread so palpable that I immediately turn the page.

The sixth is a perfect circle of black, inside of it another circle, and inside of that another, repeating fractally inside themselves until the pixels grow too small for my eyes to discern.

The seventh I cannot interpret in any way whatsoever — no content, no form, no presence and no absence either, completely unintelligible. Nothing at all what an executive briefing pack should look like.

I flick through the pages, hundreds of them now sifting through my fingers, but each is just a repetition of the same first seven, just as this folder will be repeated ten-fold in a meeting room on the floor above, and I reach the end without encountering anything like a summation of our drone survey data. There's nothing here at all, and yet it's a nothing that I cannot look away from: I stare into these nonsense pages for what feels like an extremely long time, the minutes slowly evaporating into air, and when I'm done with the paper I stare blankly into the reminder for the meeting, set to occur in exactly two hours and five minutes from now. It is 9:55, by the computer, but on my watch it is still 8:48. On my watch I have not yet arrived at work, the folder is still unopened, and none of this has happened and maybe it hasn't, actually. Perhaps, in the end, it's not really happening at all.

My phone buzzes again: *Actually, maybe just came over instead — remember, red door above the bar.*

There'd been a few more moments like the one in the bar, and each time I'd felt them quietly flutter towards me, held them softly in my hands, then let them slip away. Each time had seemed too uncertain, I'd thought, never quite clear enough to risk complicating the friendship over, and anyway there'd always be another chance, another opportunity to be braver. Then Spring turned to Winter and Alex started seeing someone else, a girl she'd met at the volunteer food co-op. Perhaps I'd been misreading things all along.

And as I ignore Alex's second text message the world seems to grow lighter, sharp corners softening hazy and indistinct. Instead of doing something about the folders — and what can possibly be done, really? — I open the browser and begin once again to scroll through apartment listings. There are actually some pretty good options: here there are two bedrooms by the Ring Road, there one by the sea, here a studio in a block I think I can just make out from here, maybe even pick out the red balcony of the apartment for lease. Neural networks engage as I pause on the listing, the photos subtly retouching themselves according to my triangulated preferences and the price shifting, rebalancing inputs on the fly to fit just within the furthest stretch of my budget. Senses lulling, fingers clicking down onto a big green *apply now* button.

Fingers spasm, and the click goes wide into empty space. This isn't working. I have to do something about the folders but there's nothing to do. The copies are already upstairs.

I get up, firmly set on going up there and swapping the folders with something more sensical, but instead of taking the elevator to the top floor I take it to the bottom, and from there walk across the road to the convenience store, in which I buy a chocolate bar, as well as a newspaper, trail mix and a banana, in order to make the chocolate seem like an accidental, off-hand purchase at the very end. I was actually feeling a bit peckish, wolfing down the chocolate bar, but as I look down into the rest of the items I realise that it's happened again. I'm still not doing anything. But this is of course because there's nothing to be done — I have nothing to swap the folders with, didn't actually do any of the work which might have helped me here, now, have in fact done nothing at all. Perhaps I can call in a bomb threat though. That might work actually, though I'd never be able to go through with it. Perhaps, though, I can talk to that moustached man again. That's it. He'll be able to give me something.

The elevator doors open onto the 99th floor, to my Senior-Manager and the UA.

"Ahhh, Sirin. We've been looking everywhere for you. It's time to go upstairs for the meeting." My Senior-Manager's eyes are bright, eyeing my shiny black shoes approvingly. Behind them is the nephew, shoulders held at exactly the same angle as his uncle's.

The elevator doors will close in a few seconds.

"Wait," I say, but something in my vocal cords isn't connecting right, the words so soft they can't possibly have heard.

"The folders," I stammer, a few decibels louder.

My Senior-Manager looks at me quizzically.

"The folders have already been taken up. Isn't that right?"

The UA nods in answer, silently and once.

"There are just a few corrections," phasing back into coherence, "we still have an hour and a half, don't we?"

The nephew pushes the <I> button. My Senior-Manager sighs, then fixes me with a look that lets me know that it's okay, that he understands perfectly both what the issue is and which the stage in my career progression it corresponds to.

"Whatever the problem with the folders is, it can't be more important than the strong impression that punctuality makes. After all, you've made the folders, I've reviewed them, and _________ _________ has reviewed them for himself. We don't want to get distracted by minor details when the work has already been done to such a high standard."

And I almost argue before I realise it again: there's nothing to be done. I didn't do any of the work. The moustached man is a moron. I'm too much of a coward to call in a bomb threat and for what, anyway? I'll just be fired, is all. Fired and apartment-less and unemployable, never to work again.

I smile broadly. "Great," I say, "let's get going then," firmly pushing down any and all other sentences I could be saying, squishing them down into the void along with everything else and, as I keep on not-saying them, not-warning my colleagues and not-confessing my professional misconduct, there is a shift, felt at first in my toes and then in my arches, up ankles, shins and thighs all the way to the crown of my head, everything at once becoming weightlessly light. Like a large portion of the molten core beneath my feet has vanished, nullifying the bonds that held us so tightly to the Earth. Becoming insubstantial, as the elevator doors close, becoming nothing, just a little scrap of tissue paper floating up the elevator shaft, climbing up kilometres of steel and percentiles of social mobility to where the air is thin and the gravity weak. The tiny hairs on my forearms arms perceptibly firmer, straighter, angled directly towards the other side of the elevator wall as we ascend, more slowly it seems, the ride to the 100th floor already so much longer than the other previous 99.

The doors open. At first glance the 100th floor lobby is exactly the same as the 99th, but as I look longer the lines are softer, somehow, the black and white tiles blurring a little beneath my gaze. Where the little plastic plants should be there are indistinct green smudges, and simplified rectangles and triangles in place of the call buttons, and visible through the sliding glass doors there's just a blurred expanse of grey.

Something rustles at the edge of my pocket, the shiny gold and brown shimmer of the chocolate bar wrapper slipping away from my pocket. I feel nothing at the sight, let it fall soundlessly to the tiles.

My Senior-Manager leads the way. The grey resolves right as we enter, or just after or before, into our offices I believe. The floorpan is exactly the same as the 99th, the same plastic partitions and the same plants and the same tasteful teak accents. But this office is completely empty, and quiet, as if filled with a less conductive medium than air. The desks and computers and office paraphernalia all rendered with a lower resolution than their equivalents a floor down, their details lost, the whole office like a sheet of A4 paper held up too closely to the sun. My Senior-Manager strides through the empty, unetched aisles with the same absolute assurance as he does below though, a cosmological constant masquerading as a man. He pulls ahead slightly, into a shaft of brighter light, and as he does I see that one patch of golden blonde hair at the top of his head is thinner than the rest. He's going bald. And while normally I would pull my eyes away from this heretical sight, here, breathing this lighter air, I simply look, and as I look the static that has settled through my consciousness gets louder, lower, and higher all at once, expanding out across the limits of the frequency spectrum. I am forgetting something and my heart is beating very fast, my thoughts becoming indistinct, like the entire atmosphere of a planet drifting slowly out to space.

I have forgotten something but I keep walking behind the people, keep pretending that I understand what's going on, hoping that I won't stand out. We keep venturing in, the journey far longer than I unclearly feel it ought to be, our navigation through the aisles and doorways taking more frequent and stranger turns until eventually we turn a corner onto something new. Where I vaguely remember the kitchen might be there is instead a door, and through this door a wide deck that opens onto air. The building has been cut away, and in its place there is a table, and chairs, and plants, and pebbles, and instead of carpet there is wooden deck. Stubbed out cigars litter the ground.

The view out to the desert is sweeping, majestic, or so an ambitious architect must have once been able to convince the planning committee. Here there is a tower of concrete, further out a tower of glass and steel. There, a little further are the residential suburbs with their big beige apartment blocks, and there, a thin black line against the far horizon, is the Wall. It is difficult to remember when the Wall was built, exactly, or how or by whom; one day it hadn't been there and then, on another, it had been, there, irrevocably and finally there, like it always had been.

The tall blonde man turns and says something very difficult to make out over the wind. After a slight pause I nod my head and smile. This suffices, it seems.

HDKSBDKLMCIBUUASFKNCWQOINVEWK:NVDS LKNVDSLKNVDSLKDGN:LMVEOIHQOLMVEHFIVN, says the wind.

We go through another door, and another blurred inside, all the way around to a boardroom that is exactly the same as on the floor below, the view of exactly the same skyline raised ever so slightly higher. The table in its centre is glass, so thin it's barely there at all. I look down at the folders that rest upon its surface and try to remember what they mean. Eight copies are arranged on the table, each flat and symmetrical.

The tall man with the blonde, thinning hair turns to me and says something I cannot hear through the fuzz. My feet still walk away, all the way into a kitchenette where my hands reach for eight identical glasses. Like a puppet on strings I turn and walk back, place a glass at each of the eight seats, to the right of each folder. And for a moment as I set these down I am afraid that there is no table, no support, that the glasses will fall through air to stain the carpet grey with water, but in the end the table holds and the blonde man nods his approval. I am motioned to wait in the corner, with the black-fringed woman and the slightly smaller, slightly blonder man, while the last takes a seat.

We stand for a very long time, and as we do the blur becomes more pronounced, the boardroom smudging into impressionist brushstrokes. There's something I was meant to be doing. I hope that I'm doing it well. I hope I'm not screwing it up. The static grows louder again but it isn't actually getting louder, I know, read in an article one time. There isn't anything to listen to. It's just the panicked neurons filling in the gaps where the hearing used to be, before those frequencies were stretched too far and snapped, the thin static left behind seeping through the cracks and fissures of the world.

A world which is fading to grey.

Seven suits walk in, not together but all at the same time. Even through the mist that has descended I am struck by how cheap my clothes must look in comparison, how ill-fitting and unconfident I am.

It's been fading for such a long time already though.

Not one of them has a face that I can look at, each of their bodies a blur. The blonde man has started saying something, and each of the blurs goes to lift the first page of their folder, then stops. An image on the wall flickers into life. It's familiar, like I have seen it before, before the margins became so blurred, before this thin coating of dust settled on the page. The static is all there is and it's the same pattern, I realise, exactly the same as the wind whispering outside the glass, as the waves lapping at the beach. The blonde man says something more, nods approvingly in my direction. A sudden vertigo as the last bits of the planet crumble into dust. The images are fading, like a projector when someone's forgotten to draw the blinds, when the sun comes out from behind the clouds to drown it all in light.

Everything's turning to white.

White.

White, without shadow or dimension. The people and the building and the water and the folders are all gone, all distilled to formless white. An infinity of featureless white in every direction. A second passes, then a minute, or maybe no time at all. There is nothing whose passage time might mark. There is nothing to happen, and nothing does, happen, over and over again, or maybe only once.

Another eternity in this way, then another.

Eventually a thought arises, decohered, pulling itself into being. A name.

How do I do it, you ask.

Do what?

Make it come back.

Already? You just arrived.

This world is empty. There's nothing here. No light. No colour. No shape. No people. It's sterile. It's dead.

You're here. So am I.

I want to go home.

You are home.

I want to go back.

It's easy enough. You just have to concentrate, but not too hard — let the shadows start to form around the edges of your gaze, almost by themselves. There, thickening in the foreground are the lines that form the edges of the room, and in the middle is the delicate thinness of the table. Then the projector hanging from the ceiling, the chairs under the table and the folders resting on top. The glasses on the side, too, and the water jug in the middle. Now the gradients, the shading, the crisp little edges on the paper. The patterns of reflection on the projector cables and the faint circles where a coaster should have been put down. Be patient with these, make sure that they hang together right. You can change the folders too, if you want. You can change them to whatever you like.

They should stay as they are.

A fine choice.

Which way was the door into the room though? Left or right?

It doesn't matter.

The left, then.

Perfect.

And now the people, I suppose.

Yes. The people. The executives with their suits and not-quite faces, your Senior-Manager with his balding blonde hair and younger double, the UA with her symmetrical black fringe, and you.

Most especially you.

The ringing stops, and in the silence it leaves behind my Senior-Manager's voice plucks and strings:

"Now all of this is supported by the materials compiled in the white folders in front of you. If you could please turn to the first page — all the information you require is there."

Each of the seven puts forward a hand and flicks their folder open. Each flicks open to the first page, the page of textured static. *Hmmmmmmmmmm,* they say to the maelstrom of digital snow, *mmmmmmmmmm* as they flick past it to the page of repeating numbers, and keep flicking, not completely synchronised but without the right randomness either. Each like a tape set at a slight delay to the others, or else the fingers of one great, seven pointed hand.

The one closest to me is subtly familiar; _________ ________, I think. He closes the folder.

"Thank you for these impeccable briefing materials. I speak for the Board when I say you have our full support. We are deeply acquainted with how crucial this work is for the Construct, and how catastrophic the consequences would be were it to be delayed or undermined. It is a credit to both you and our young staff that the work has been completed again to such an imposing standard."

The other six nod in agreement.

"Thank you for those briefing materials," nodding to me, "and for that most informative slide deck," to the nephew. "Provided that the upload mechanism can be completed on time, the success of the project is now assured."

No-one nods at the UA, who is keeping her face very composed and her hands very still. Her eyes lift up slightly, then drop back down.

"I will retain this copy on behalf of the board," declares ______________ __________, slipping his folder into his darkened folds. "See to it that the others are destroyed."

My Senior-Manager nods, and like that the meeting ends. The seven executives file out of the room, their glasses of water completely untouched.

"Fantastic job," my Senior-Manager exclaims just as the door latches closed, barely able to contain himself, "the both of you, just an absolutely fantastic job," and I almost go to speak up for her but don't. It feels like the wrong time, like it might be awkward. But perhaps I still hear it, whispering deep inside, because I turn my head in her direction, with a look in my eyes, a word almost on my lips and my Senior-Manager, seeing this, turns to his UA: "and how could I forget — thank you for proofing and distributing the initial proposal, and co-ordinating the RSVPs, and booking the meeting room, and distributing the briefing materials, and harmonising the conflicting schedules, and rebooking the meeting room, and conducting the further email liaising, and preparing and revising the checklist, and recovering the corrupted powerpoint files, and rebooking the meeting room again," he says, and she nods, once, her eyes suddenly bright.

"You're very welcome."

We walk back through the empty offices together, past the kitchenette and onto the deck. The air is cooler out here, stronger and fresher and saltier. I look out towards the desert, but there is no desert anymore. Here there is a tower of glass and steel. There a tower of bronze. Here are the docks, multicoloured shipping containers stacked together like children's toys, and there the tranquil harbour water, then the ocean and there, further out, the line of utter black that marks the Wall. The view has flipped 180 degrees, as if somebody has demolished and rebuilt the hundredth floor back at a different orientation than on the way in. I slow my pace at this, make uneasy eye contact with the UA who has turned, questioning, to me. My Senior-Manager and his younger copy stride on, unseeing.

The new world would be carved from a different, more malleable sort of matter than the crude quarks and gluons of the old. Agiler and more innovative than those dusty old atoms. With the right sort of directing intelligence this new, more intelligent substance would be persuaded very easily to form copies of the towers, docks, folders, computer networks and household pets that the City's denizens would leave behind in the Real. A high quality molecular scan would be the first item of business, then for that scan to be uploaded in a format readable to the governing AI. The AI would then impose this blueprint on the formless but cooperative matter, replicating the City down to the level of each chemical bond. It wouldn't have to be an exact copy, of course, and discussions were held at various stages about the possibility of improving further, in some limited ways, upon the City as it stood. More social housing, perhaps, or a foodbank, or a large, interest free payment for every citizen, all of which could be edited in without much trouble. But after extensive consultation with industry groups and a collaborative exchange of ideas with the project's Private Partners — a consortium of listed companies and real estate trusts — a consensus was reached that it would be simpler and more equitable to simply copy existing arrangements to the letter. With some choice modifications of course. In light of their substantial investment.

Back at my desk I peak inside one of the folders, see only *1234567* repeating indefinitely down the page, then slam it shut. I look up, towards the ceiling but not at it, through it to the floor and ceiling that lie above. The blurred, identical offices. My Senior-Manager's balding scalp. The Board, poring through their eldritch pages with approval. Something else happened up there too though, something vitally important. It ducks and weaves out of my introspection, like an errand I took out my phone to accomplish but forgot a millisecond later.

But though it's gone the glow from its presence remains, whatever it was. Everything is as it should be, this glow seems to say, everything hangs perfectly in place. All my little worries and tasks seem faintly ridiculous now, abstract when compared to the walls of the office and the white of the folders, the creak of the office chair as I lean back a few degrees too far. The whole world seems to vibrate at a higher frequency than before, and the grey walls of the office ring like a bell, mouse buttons and keyboards clicking and releasing in a sequence so subtle it would put the finest composers to shame.

I suppose I have to eat, so I go downstairs, past all my colleagues in exactly their right places, striding through the crowds of the lobby as Moses once walked through the Red Sea to the Korean place nearby. The restaurant door chimes a greeting as I enter, but it's just a sensor attached to an electric buzzer, not the thin, flowing chimes which I realise I'd been hoping for. And though I cannot quite put my finger on why this disappoints me so much it does, and this inability to understand unsettles things even further. I sit down, without the flowing grace of before. It's almost gone, like an old friend who announces in the middle of drinks that they really have to be getting off, and I hope that the waitress didn't catch the sadness in my voice. The curry sauce is delicious, and the rice crispy, and as they fill my stomach the afterglow fades to black.

There's a person sitting across the table. It's Suresh. They're saying something but it's difficult to hear them, as if their voice is coming through a thick bank of static.

"Do you ever doubt the nature of this reality?" they are saying, repeating it one way and then another, experimenting with the right tone but they can't seem to get it right, can't make the words stick. Eventually they sigh and shake their head. "Text your friend back," they say, louder this time.

I look at my phone for a bit. Roast Beef Sandwich has posted in his birthday event, encouraging us all to *come along for a drink or eight hahah.* It'll be good to catch up. I tap back to my profile, then to my feed, and then to an article that a friend has posted about the mass psychology of the air-purifier shortages. Then I get up, pay, leave under an artificial chime that doesn't bother me in the slightest, and when I get back to the office the keyboards are no longer in a hidden rhythm, and the walls no longer ring with the secret presence of a god, and I have almost forgotten that once they did. The folders are waiting, in a neat column of 11, along with my Senior-Manager, and the UA, and a grey, curved box held lightly in her hands.

"Good afternoon, Sirin," he says. "Many thanks again for your wonderful work on those briefing materials."

I nod, and smile, but there is something suspicious in the tone of his voice.

"Given the sensitive, commercial-in-confidence nature of the briefing materials which you produced," and the afterglow is definitely gone now, shifting into grey, "I'm sure you'll appreciate that we'll need to take added precautions when disposing of them."

His face goes glassy for a second, concentrating on the lines of green text unfolding in his glasses. Then he taps the side of the right lens, and his email hits me like a sledgehammer —

Oh no. No. No. He wants me to shred each of these pages by hand, thousands of pages of-

"To avoid any internal stakeholders from accessing the datasets out of protocol," he adds, like he's letting me in on a carefully guarded secret. Then that same practised smile, and the moment of eye contact that lets me know I'm just the person for this job, that no-one else in the world will do.

He smiles again, a smile that doesn't reach his eyes, and as he turns and leaves the UA shrugs apologetically

and places the shredder on the desk. Then, looking me straight in the eyes, she takes one of the folders from the top of the pile, winks, and slips it between the walls of a plain manilla folder waiting in her hands. Then she smiles, turns, and leaves as well.

For the one hundred and seventieth time in a row I feed a sheath of exactly five pieces of paper into the grey teeth of the shredder. They must go in too quickly though, a little before the appropriate ten second mark, so instead of shredding them the machine makes a little synthesised jamming sound. The five sheets of paper are stuck, half outside the gears, still gripped tightly by the metal teeth. I wait for the light to turn green again, for the mechanism to dissipate the heat that has built up in its constituent parts. I breathe in.

The light turns green. A mass of algae blooms, dies and sinks to the ocean floor, is buried under sediment and slowly turns to oil and gas. The oil is extracted by an offshore drilling platform, then shipped across a vast ocean in a fleet of floating tankers, and from there is piped to a hive of smokestacks that stain an orange sky with flame. The chemical energy within the algae's bonds is turned to heat, which turns water into steam which turns a dynamo, and the electricity this churns from the air is forced through a labyrinth of copper and steel, volting and unvolting until it is finally dispersed into the shredder, partly as heat and partly as the kinetic motion of the teeth, turning, dissolving the separate sheets into tangled strips of paper.

I breathe out. The permafrost is melting somewhere very far away.

Another five sheaths of paper, and another, and somewhere very close the hands of my watch tick over to 5:00pm. A yellow light turns on. I take the lid off the shredder, take the strips of paper firmly in one hand and cut them horizontally across. The matte black blades of the scissors divide, meet again, multiply the number of strips in the basket by 2, then 4 and 8, and then I walk this handful of paper to the industrial sized shredding bins and push the little bits of paper through the slot where the pages would have gone. As apparently befits the security status of these pages, the tiny bits paper will sit here for the next 23 hours before being driven to SecureShred's corporate shredding centre, where they will be shredded again, industrially.

The four hundred and thirty second sheaf of paper disappears through the shredder and the sun is setting behind the glass. Roast Beef's drinks are already happening.

I'm pretty busy at work right now so it might be difficult to make it — I'll let you know if I end up going. It'd be great to catch up though, we should touch base soon.

Another event that didn't work out. Another five sheets in the shredder. Once you miss enough invites they just stop coming, gradually at first, then all the rest at once. This is how it happened, over the years, how it was I'd found myself alone. All that's left are these pages of nonsense briefing folders, to be disposed of just as carefully as if they were the real thing. Which were the real thing, for all it mattered. Which it didn't, of course. The yellow light comes on again, and the scissors slice across, the black paint over the blades already peeling off. It didn't matter.

"None of it mattered," I say softly, as another sheaf of paper disappears. Not the folders, not the meeting, not the briefing, not the shredding of these blank, gibberish pages. The red light comes on, the paper jammed, and the shredder makes the synthesised jamming sound again, like it isn't really jamming but only just pretending to, and I already knew that life is meaningless, of course, like every other adult alive, know that human existence is not a folder of coherent briefing materials. But I think, looking down, waiting for the light to turn green again, that maybe this isn't the kind of meaninglessness I want.

I look up. The sun sets later, so high above the ground. With every metre of elevation the horizon sinks a little bit lower in the sky, and the setting sun takes longer to reach it. The sun would never set on a skyscraper truly worthy of the name, a tower high enough to not just scrape but puncture and eradicate the sky. Higher and higher the elevator would rise, the horizon shrinking smaller and smaller beneath it, contracting to a dot, vanishing against the surface of a star that could never set. But on the 99th floor of my building the sun is setting, and as it does the light coming through the windows grows weak and wan, unable to match the artificial white on this side of the glass. The reflections are growing stronger, competing now in earnest with the sun.

I pick out my phone, call Alex, listen to the *brrrrring brrrrrrring brrrrrrring* of the dial tone pierce incessant through the office. The lights of buildings are coming into view now, little rows and columns of fluorescence imposing themselves on the darkening sky. Not that they're actually turning on of course. They've been on the whole time, just like the flowing rivers of red from the tail-lights below. It's just that things are darker now, have been getting darker for quite some time in fact, and against this growing darkness the little bits of light have finally becoming clear.

Brrrrrrrrrrrrrrrrrrrrrrrrrrring, cries the phone. 112123123412345123461234567, reads the paper. The sun is completely covered by clouds as it dips below the horizon, so there's no real sunset, no ethereal pinks or beaten bronzes; night falls slowly, imperceptibly, each moment only a tiny bit darker than the one before.

The line cuts with a beep. I am sad, I realise, so very very sad, a sadness so deep and so enduring that I'd forgotten it was even there, had forgotten that there could be anything to feel but this. But there's nothing to be done about, of course. This is just what I did to my life, through my own actions; actions which cannot now be undone. And why go to the trouble of feeling something you're powerless to prevent?

"Why bother," I murmur. My eyes are only one refocusing away from the mirror that the window has left behind, but for now they track through the glass onto the sea of lights beyond. Right at the edge a bank of white goes black.

"Why care at all," as another stretch of the City goes dark.

"Why give a shit about anyone," as more lights are extinguished, closer this time.

"Everyone's in it for themselves," as a jagged shard of darkness slices diagonally across the horizon.

The lights above me flicker and the phone buzzes in my hand.

Remember: pink dolphin, blue waves

Alex had broken up with her volunteer. "Creative differences," she'd explained, but by this time I was with someone else, in a relationship that was on its surface clear and unambiguous.

One night Alex had told me she was leaving the City. "This place is a prison, and the locks are only getting tighter. You should come with me, if you want."

"Go where? We're the only green zone left."

"Don't believe everything you see on the news."

This was while we'd still had an airport. Before we'd had the Wall. But I'd still had my relationship, had just begun to search for meaningful full-time employment, and between these and my then friends there'd seemed as much life as could be lived by anyone. I'd shaken my head.

"That's okay. I wasn't expecting a yes."

A pause.

"But try to find me sometime, if you can, if you want to," Alex had said from across the table, voice breaking a little at the end. "I think it could be really nice."

I blink. There's something I have to do.

I dump the rest of the folders whole into the shredding bins, internal stakeholders be damned. Only one is left, which I place neatly in my locker. Then I shake my backpack upside down over the rubbish bin, the gyoza, pizza, and lasagne that have been spoiling in there all food for the tip, and though some of the packaging might have been recyclable, perhaps, plastic recycling was a scam anyway, invented by fossil-fuel companies to sell more disposable hydrocarbons. I shake my head. Unbelievable, as I walk towards the exit, towards Alex. Amazing how you can let things go on like that. But things once set in motion cannot so easily come to rest. And just as I enter the lobby I look back, for a moment, only a moment, out over the City which suddenly isn't there. There in the window is the empty office, just like it always is, and beyond that a hole in the sky where half the clouds should be.

I pretend I don't see it, but the lights are already flickering and spitting as I run to the lifts. The illumination in the little buttons jumping in and out, blinking in time with the lights above me and there's an elevator already here, thank God, the doors opening in jagged staccato. Just have to keep cool, everything steady. I walk inside the metal box and the door closes, remembering too late something about in-case-of-fires. But there is no fire, no discernible problem as the elevator jerks down the lift shaft, in some sections smoothly and in others like it is falling, almost about to slip, lights stuttering through white to orange to black to white again, but as long as I don't think about it the elevator ride is smooth, smooth as glass, smooth like the surface of a still and windless lake.

We reach the ground, the little *ding* of the elevator distorted, pushed through a sieve. I press the <|> button, and then press it again, and then again and again and again until on the seventh time the doors open. I am surprised that they actually open but am not thinking about why as I burst from the elevator, index finger bruised and quivering, the people flickering in and out of the lobby like the splashes rain drops make on water. There and not. There but just pretending. The blue suited concierge is saying something in a raised voice but I'm not listening, have to make it to the exit, footsteps short and sharp across the marble, eyes straight ahead. If all my attention is focused on not thinking about it then maybe it will be like I don't know at all, like it doesn't even exist. But the concrete is waiting, underneath the fancy tiles, and beneath it the hardened dirt that used to be a forest floor. The lights above flicker and the great revolving doors begin to slow and I am almost running now, hair papery and dry between my fingers, the revolving door growing slower and slower.

Easier to ignore it.

The lights go out behind me but I do not turn to look. I walk left, never pausing long enough for my thoughts to solidify into shape, past the gaunt man in camouflage jacket and hand-drawn sign asking *WHERE ARE YOU?*, past the huddled figures begging for coins that no longer exist, past the dancing lion-snake smirking down at me from the LED billboard. The conversations on the street are all happening at once, like melody surfacing from radio noise, all of the voices layered together and together they are nothing, are static, are the wind wailing through the clouds above. Tall soldiers in white body armour and long, angular arms are stationed on the street corner, picking people out from the crowd.

Ignore it for a while.

The faces of the pedestrians phase in and out, not many but one, always one, and as I try not to look and try not to think about it something hits me shoulder-first, long blond hair frayed at the edges and dark circles under eyes. Somewhere on the wind a siren howls, and a voice is saying:

"Suck my dick, fucking freak!" laughing skipping backward down the street. Tall white soldiers on every street corner it seems, impossibly tall, faces shielded by mirrored glass and in the glass there is nothing at all. Like the eyes of wasps, compounded, antennae sipping the air.

Just ignore it.

Another corner, another step in front of the other down a lane with freshly sprayed graffiti of an empty circle on a wall, or maybe just faded stains on concrete. Eyes pull away. It is going to rain and the air should be heavy with the smell of earth but the earth was murdered, lies hastily buried beneath the asphalt. Piss and fumes and vapes and meat instead, all the City's smells throbbing together and together they are shit, are the awful stench of the City itself. It is going to rain but there are no clouds in the sky. There are no clouds in the sky and two of the tall figures in white are turning towards me, little lines of green unfolding on the insides of their visors. Correlating the distance between my eyes and cheekbones, the contours of my lips. Scanning. Recognising. An old man hunches in the alleyway with neither sleeping bag nor sign. He kneels, face to the concrete and hands clasped above his head. The white figures are getting closer.

Ignore it.

The neon lights are flickering as I walk faster no too fast not running never running and in this flickering too there is a rhythm and a play, a message for those patient enough to hear. There are no voices behind me, no footsteps or lights, only muffled radio commands and a clear, awful dread, like a deer smelling wolf pelt on the changing wind. A middle-aged woman with a harried face grabs my shoulder and asks:

"Are you alright love?" but I pass her and she's gone, like a sheet of paper through the shredder's teeth. "IDENTIFY YOURSELF" comes from behind me, amplified and crackling with electricity, the people just shifting shadows now, outlines blurring and positions changing too rapidly to track. Like patterns of silk and gauze twisting in the air, a huge mass of them that chokes and fills the street. A raindrop on my shoulder, and another, shoulders of my shirt transparent with water as the lines of the crowd came back together. Another march of determined looking people, signs held aloft and chants echoing between the shop-fronts. Faces painted in blocks of abstract, recognition-scrambling colour.

"Excuse me," I say, "excuse me," as I push my way through the crowd, as cries of:

"Shame!" and then "fucking pigs!" are thrown behind me at the white-clad soldiers. Then bottles. Then bricks. A thought as I push through the crowd: *It isn't raining anymore.* There isn't a cloud in the sky.

Ignore.

Across the road a convenience store, its doors open in greeting and a little security camera perched above. I enter, eyes wide, slow, trying to keep it together as the colours of the glossy magazines run white, as the polished floor turns to broken concrete and the jingles crackle in and out too quickly to be heard.

"Umbrella?" I ask the cashier, an ageless man from a desert far away, its sands shot through with depleted uranium. He turns and looks at me. "All out," he says through a bushy black beard, squinting through his glasses and there is a smell as he does this, the smell of a thousand *Delicious* brand meals all defrosting and rotting and desiccating as one. Then he looks past me, face hardening, past the aisles of chips and through the walls of plexiglass, to the two white figures waiting outside. Fluorescence not glinting off their visors. Long fingers tapping threateningly on the glass. He lets a smile raise the corners of his lips, then reaches from behind the counter and places a white sheath of plastic on top.

"Mine," he says. "Take it," then says it again, "take it," like it is very important, like there isn't enough time to explain, like he doesn't have the words to say everything and as my hands clasp the handle of the umbrella says "now go." And then I blink, and when my eyes open again he is gone, along with the lights and the protestors and the police, along with most of the store. All of it is gone.

A quieter street now, with no-one on it, my pace slowing to something a little more comfortable. I'd been going to Alex's house, with the red door, above the bar, with a pink dolphin emerging from blue waves when I'd gotten panicked. A little scared at remembering the way things are. A drop of rain falls into a pool of water in front of me, surrounded by the ripple of the wave and I am walking slowly now, calmly under the thick clouds through the empty, unlit city, the empty world that's all there ever is.

The pocket torch is still in my bag, wedged into a pocket, and by some miracle its little button batteries still work. I twist the rim, flattening the beam into a cone; a little pool of light skips across the street, illuminating the empty shop-fronts. No dolphins. No waves. Umbrella in one hand, torch in the other, I begin to walk.

Each sign is very similar in the dark though, just like each street and alley. One comes after the next, each leading down into another. Every now and then there are strange marks in the middle of the road like burnt sugar on a cake, like the asphalt has melted and reset, and I walk around these, hesitant of the ashy water that pools within. The watch is stopped on my wrist and the phone is dead in my hand and it is difficult, after yet another empty street, to remember what they had been for, what any of this had been for. Here there is a *Taco Time*. There a *Convenience Store*. There, on the left, a *National Bank*.

Taco Time. Convenience Store. National Bank. It's slightly more difficult to remember what these words mean, and it's mainly habit that keeps me flicking the light back and forth. I'm not even really reading anymore, am instead just checking for the dolphin and the waves. Walking-looking-checking, walking-looking-checking, walking-looking-checking down each column and each row. What if I missed it though, a couple of streets back? What if I've been going in the wrong direction the entire time? The last bits of light are draining from the air between the streets, and the torch glows brighter against the dark.

National Taco. Convenience Time. Store Bank. The sky is a giant pool of ink. More rain falls, louder, drumming abstract on the umbrella and I try not to listen, try not to pick up the subtle pattern in the drops. There's not a single light on in the City, and the stars are all hidden by thick clouds. My cheap supermarket torch is the only light in the world, a single speck of phosphorescence in a vast, lightless ocean.

*Ta*________. *Con*________ ____*ore*. *Nat*______ *ank*. The signs are getting harder to read, my memories wearing thin. *Red door*, I repeat. *Blue waves. Pink dolphin.* But why would I be looking for blue waves in the middle of the city? And where on Earth would I find a dolphin? I should really be looking in the sea, and feel a strange attraction to this idea, but still I repeat the familiar words as I stumble through the dark. There's something comforting about them, grounding, and I'm not sure what would be left of me if I stopped. The voids inside my mind are growing wider and longer as I walk, and look, and check.

Red door. Blue waves. Pink Dolphin. I am lost, have perhaps been lost this entire time. But the rain starts to let up at least, the fury of the downpour unsustainable for long. The pressure of the water no longer presses me to the Earth and I feel lighter, insubstantial, like I could melt away into the darkness if I exhaled deeply enough, if I just let go of the words I've been repeating. Is that what I want though?

Red waves. Pink door. Blue dolphin, I murmur, knowing it isn't right but trying all the same. The torch grows dimmer, darkness hunching round its pale beam. My feet are sore from all this walking, big toes mashed against the front of my shoes and the little ones crushed against the sides. What on Earth were these for? What was any of this for? I kick the bits of pointy black pleather off into the street, not even bothering to untie their laces. The light is almost gone now, and with it the words I was repeating to myself. Now there is only walking, one foot after the other, socks fraying against the black asphalt. *No lights to stop me now*, I think, and, liking the way it sounds, say:

"No lights to stop me now," out loud, no one to hear. I smile, broader this time, even laugh a little as the flimsy supermarket torch flickers, spits and dies in my hand.

When you were a child you very seldom had friends to play with. So instead of tag, or spit, or marbles you would, when you grew tired of books and siblings, walk to the farthest tree and sit cross-legged underneath it. You would screw your eyes tightly shut, then tighter still, with maybe a little bit of pressure to the front of the eyeballs. There you would stay, for a while, watching as the shifting phosphene patterns swelled and broke and re-emerged on the inside of your eyes, fuzzy, shimmering banks of iridescent green and orange coalescing into shape. There, behind your eyelids was another world, inside and yet removed from the one in which you fought and struggled and failed to connect. A universe of drifting stars, galaxies of light pressed into form by the weight of your perception.

And when I open my eyes there is light, a pale glow just strong enough to see by. Up, high above the black outlines of skyscrapers there is a gap in the clouds, just big enough for the full white moon to shine through. It hangs, framed perfectly, lending its light to the ragged edges of the clouds around it, the little circle of streetscape below. At the end of the street there is a red door, and beside it a pink dolphin jumping from blue waves, and I am so surprised at this fact that at first I cannot take another step. Is the door really red, I wonder. And is it really a dolphin coming from those waves? It could be a porpoise after all. Difficult to be sure in the fading light, without a biology textbook on hand. I waver. The clouds are moving quickly though, and the moon is half covered by the time I realise that this is the last chance, that I was lucky to receive it and I will not be given another, legs already bounding across the street as feet kiss pavement through socks, as the red comes larger and more grey and as the moon is slowly swallowed by the sky but I make it, I make it and I knock, quietly, and then loudly on the door. I wait.

And then there are footsteps, and the creak of stairs, and the fumbling of an old-fashioned key inside a metal lock. And then, by the light of a candle cupped softly between two hands, Alex.

"Hey," she says. "You came."

And we talk about so many things in the dark room up the stairs, rugged up in thick blankets on cushions on the floor. The flickering candlelight doesn't quite make it to the walls, and for all I see the room might be a single platform on a vast and endless plain. She asks me how I'm so sure it isn't, and my laugh echoes less than I think it should. We pause. She asks me how I've been. I'd just gotten out of a weird relationship, I say, had lost touch with people a little, what with that and working all the time. I'd wanted to love her, had wanted so badly not to make her cry that I hadn't left when this love had gone. So one year had become two, then three, and by then it had seemed like maybe this *was* love, this wanting the other person to be happy, this and nothing more.

"But it wasn't, of course."

She nods solemnly, then asks if I remember how we met, and yes I remember, the awkward introduction and sudden exchange of internet aliases. She remembers it exactly the same way. She pauses at this, her thoughts snagged on something that I cannot yet see. I ask if she remembers the time we got lost in the abandoned train station, had to shelter inside the great glass pyramid while the water pooled and flooded outside. She does, of course, and smiles too, but it seems like such a long time ago, she confesses, so much longer than could fit within the years. She had gone away, had only just come back, had lost touch with a lot of people too, of course. The City had been strange when she'd returned, lacking in depth. Like all the people were set on hiding something impossible to actually conceal, something so obvious that you could almost fail to see it if you weren't looking closely enough. It'd been like that for a while, I admit, though again it was difficult to know how long. Whether it had been months or years or only just a week.

"I wish you had come with me," she says, "you know, like you said you might."

The candlelight flickers, her face lost in shadow.

"I wish so too sometimes," and for the first time articulate consciously my regret. I'd made the decision not to go so carelessly at the time, like nothing in the world had hinged upon it, the way one might decline a coffee or a bagel.

"It's weird though, I can't even remember where you went," and she looks up at me for a split-second in horror, before looking back down, sheepish.

"I can't either. And I can't remember how I got back. I don't even remember your name, but I know that you're Sirin at work, even though you've never told me."

Silence lingers between us for a moment.

"I can't remember it either."

We change the subject.

"The mirrors."

"Yes," she agrees, and nods, idly breaking a bit of the wax from the candle's edge and placing it to melt in the hot, liquid centre. "The mirrors. I kept seeing the empty city today, in the shop windows and in the cars, in the little pools of waste water on the street. Ever since you asked me what I saw in them I couldn't stop looking, couldn't stop myself from coming back here. I must have gone in and out a dozen times. It's weird; I can remember the mirrors so clearly, here, but normally there's this block. It's so hard to think about them back there." Back there. There//

//"There," she says, pulling out a foldout mattress. "You should stay the night — sleep on this."

Her hair is much blonder than by candlelight, lit up now by electric glow. A truck honks, loudly and twice from out on the street.

I walk to the window, look down at the people and the cars and the lit-up shops below, and wonder why I'm so surprised.

"Thanks. I appreciate it." She goes to get a blanket from the cupboard. The room is small, and there's little more to the apartment than it — an electric stovetop, percolator waiting on top for tomorrow morning, and a door to the bathroom that I must have missed in the dark. In the dark. I am remembering now, feel the cold of the riptide beneath the splashing waves.

Alex has stopped, is standing in the middle of the room. She'd been about to take another step but had seen the candle in her way. The candle and its flickering flame, so unnecessary with all the lights on. She looks at it, at the blankets on the floor, and raises her eyebrow.

A moment of eye contact.

"How did I get here?" I ask.

"We got a drink," she begins saying, slowly, "you were too drunk to get a cab home," more confident now, "wouldn't get in the Autoshare," and I nod, and *mmmmmm*, and think that maybe I do remember something like a bar, something like a drink.

"It's weird, though," I say, "I don't feel drunk."

She breathes out, long and slow.

"Not at all," looking now at the candle too. The single, unneeded flame.

"I don't feel drunk either," she admits, then looks up at me and shrugs.

She is remembering too, I can tell, the effort of maintaining the two narratives clearly written in the lines of her cheeks and brow.

"It's not real, is it?"

"No," she says, a fixed, singular point as the world quivers, buckles and breaks//

//"But at least we're here together," she adds, the soft glow of the candle visible once more.

I walk over to the window and look down into the black. Faint lines suggestive of a street. "No better place to be."

If it weren't for the thick clouds these would be the most beautiful stars I'd ever seen. Undimmed by light pollution and unfiltered by smog, it'd be a star rise to make any on Earth seem like a child's pale drawing. But not tonight. The clouds lie thick with rain yet to fall, blanketing the Earth in dark embrace, and the beauty of the stars goes unobserved. I look away. Alex is crouched by the candle, writing something on a piece of card.

"What is this place, Alex?," and I know the answer, somewhere deep down, but still want her to say it first.

"We can talk about it in the morning. For now we should try to get some sleep." Then she stops, half her face lit up by fire:

"Do you think it would be easier to stay here, though? To just remember, instead of forgetting, and then remembering and then forgetting again?"

In the candlelight the walls look stained, like water's gotten into the roof and has been slowly trickling down for years.

"I think it's better to remember both."

She doesn't respond, just turns a thought around in her head, then hands me the card she'd been writing. "Don't read it just yet. Only if we get separated again."

She goes to pull the foldout mattress from under the bed and wrinkles her nose at the touch.

"Shit, it's damp."

She turns to me and frowns.

"Is it alright if we sleep together instead?"

Later tonight we will hold each other like children frightened of the dark, but for now we lie facing each other across the bed, she on her side and me on mine, our hands reaching out to almost touch. A little train of freckles dots her cheek, uncertain in the flickering light. I tuck a strand of hair behind her ear. She pulls the blanket over the both of us, then blows the candle out.

FRIDAY

I stir under the covers. Alex is already out of bed, hands resting lightly on the window sill, eyes fixed on the black sphere looming in the distance. Her features have crystallised into a new expression overnight, stronger and harder.

"What do you think it is?" she says, mostly to herself, in a black turtleneck under a long fuschia raincoat. She's laid out a little breakfast on the table: assorted muesli bars and fruit cups arranged in neat little columns, a selection of canned energy drinks lined up on the side. I groan and get back under the covers, clinging to what little sleep remains beneath the woollen blanket.

"Rest if you need," she says, "I'll be right here," closing eyes, black fading into black.

"Just remember that card in your pocket."

My eyes open to an unfamiliar ceiling rose, strange geometries unfolding in white plaster above the bed. An alarm beeping right beside my head, strangely clear for how much I drank last night. I yawn and stretch and step out of bed, and wonder why I hadn't slept on the spare mattress.

I rummage through the cupboards for the coffee, and find it in a little metal canister by the stove. I unscrew the metal pieces of the pot, fill the bottom with water, then pack the middle with fine grains of chocolate brown.

I wonder where Alex got to.

I reach the coffee pot just as it's boiling over, and pour it into a simple white mug with black serif writing on the side: *this is the ending where you finally find your way home, where the ancient terror inside of you is stomped for good.* I gulp the coffee and wince with the bitterness, then collect my phone and bag. My new shoes have been placed neatly by the door, and I pick these up with only a small moment of surprise. They're more battered than before, like someone's trudged for miles in them, but they still sort-of-fit, as well as they did before at least.

There's something else though, down the stairs and out the little red door, some thread on which I might yet pull. I can feel it, the not-thinking, even though the sun is shining, even though there are just a few stray wisps of cloud in the sky and even though today is a new day, a good day, my first as a freshly minted Assistant-Manager, potentially, if everything goes to plan. The morning breeze is cool against my face. The trees flutter and are still.

I come to an old shoe repair shop, still trading by some miracle sandwiched between each of the Two Major Retailers. In its wide bay windows I see myself staring back from an empty street, with someone else beside me, in a fuschia jacket on the surface of the glass. They are walking closer, mouth almost at my ear. Underneath the sound of all the City comes a single human voice.

It is 9:15 as the lift doors open. I am late. I am wearing yesterday's clothes. I am gearing up to engage in some light industrial espionage on Alex's behalf, and as the glass doors slide open I brace for my colleagues' attention to fasten on me. But no-one even looks up. Everyone gazes only at their screen, and does not turn from it except to check, surreptitiously, whether anyone is looking at theirs. I tread past them without the slightest caution, footsteps springing lightly off the carpet. *1357* is the number of my locker, a low one accessible only by crouch. *246* is the code. The light turns green as I punch in the numbers, as the locking mechanism disengages, as the metal door peels back to free the valuables inside.

A moment of confusion, then I remember: Alex wanted the folder. Needed the folder, though for what she hadn't said. *Sometimes a part can stand in for the whole,* she'd explained, motioning around the darkened downstairs lobby. *Suresh said it could be really important.* I take it in my hands, fingertips soft against the plastic cover.

What about that cute apartment though, a thought inside me rises.

I shake my head, clasp the folder to my side.

You're actually really lucky to have an interesting job like this you know.

Hands ball into fists.

It would be weird to just leave like this, surely stay until lunchtime at the very least, but I am not staying, am leaving right now in fact, down the elevators and out to Alex, waiting on the other side. Yet this other side seems awfully abstract, here in my usual office with my usual colleagues and usual life. I'm not actually going to leave, am I, right on the day of the promotion announcement? The smell of store-bought cookies wafts over from morning tea. Surely it wouldn't hurt to grab one on the way out. My footsteps slow, stalling by the doors. Hermione is there, or maybe Harriet, as well as my Manager and the UA. Everyone seems to be having a nice time. I've left my phone back at the lockers, too, feel already the ache of its absence from my pocket, my hand.

But no, I'm leaving, and with perceptible effort step through the doors, out to the elevators. I have to get the folder to Alex, have to leave while the memory's fresh. Have to raise my arm up to call the lift, hand heavy as tungsten or lead.

"What's the matter, having second thoughts?" the doors taunt, and I pretend not to hear. It's just a large language model, there's nothing in there that hates me or wishes me harm.

"But we do hate you," they say in crisp, echo-less tones. A drop of sweat drips from my brow onto the smooth tiles below. "And we do wish you harm."

Ignore. The elevator takes what feels like an eternity to arrive, as if it too is on the verge of turning back, and when it finally arrives the doors open without the little *ding*, like all the oxygen has been removed from the elevator lobby. I waver. The elevator smells like antiseptic, recently cleaned, and the mirrors inside have all been replaced with unadorned metal. I rock back and forth on my heels for what feels like a very long time, forward and back, back and forward. I don't want to go in. I want to go in. I want to want to go in and just like that I am, stepping in, the doors still not closing though, still a good view of the way back into the office. My colleagues on the other side of the glass milling in the mid-morning, some with coffee cups and some with folders or laptops, clustering around a large platter of delicious looking cookies. Resist. My hand resists, like pushing through butter or mud that eventually, excruciatingly gives way, my outstretched finger reaching out to dimple the little chrome G. But the button doesn't light up, as I press it, and the lift doors do not close. I click again, to no effect, and again. Nothing. I feel nothing at this. I feel nothing at all and yet something is coming, the tiny hairs on each of my arms perceptibly straightening, angled directly towards the other side of the lobby.

The elevator opposite mine opens.

____________ _________ is standing in it, silent, framed between the banks of chrome. Slowly, languidly, I feel his attention press towards me. And it's weird to just be standing here, isn't it, in an empty elevator, clearly leaving the building with one of the briefing folders fully in view. He'd ordered all the other copies destroyed, hadn't he? What would I say if he asks about it? Why wouldn't he fire me on the spot? But I could say that I was just stepping out, a voice inside me whispers, that the doors have only just opened. That I've been out to get a snack, or a coffee with a friend, took the folder with me for safekeeping. And though I try to press the G again I find that I cannot, that my body has been completely persuaded by this new, less radical plan. Too late I feel the Performance Manager tight against my spinal column, the subtle clicks and caresses swelling into a symphony of cold, wet metal. There's no need to go downstairs, a thought inside me insists, more forcefully than I ever thought possible. After all, I'd just stepped out.

And now I am coming back in.

My feet step forward, making it seem natural, exactly as if I'm another calm, contented employee returning from a mid-morning break. And though I think about reaching for the card in my pocket my hands find the door-pass instead, draw it out and touch it to the wall. My Senior-Manager is waiting on the other side, flanked by two pinstripe suits who my eyes do not linger on. He looks down on me with approval and pride blossoms in my skull — it feels good to have handled that situation with such professionalism, just like an up-and-coming Assistant-Manager would have done. Like I have a future ahead of me here, a successful one, a future that will be very long indeed.

"I've found an extra one of those briefing folders, and thought I'd deliver it to you personally for your opinion," I find my voice saying, and with a strange shock I realise that I can see myself, tiny and concave and enclosed in the centre of his pupils, can even see my eyes widen as I realise, too late, that it's slipping away.

And then it is gone.

My Senior-Manager places the folder in his locker, a sleek, spacious one which he doesn't have to crouch to open, then seals it inside with a complicated looking code.

"Thank you for this. Diligent, outcomes-focused work as always. Now if you could please turn your mind to completing the upload mechanism. It needs to be fully compliant, no command slippage, and ready to interface with the AI as soon as possible."

The sight of him closing the locker fills me with a sadness whose cause I cannot name and I pause, uncertain. There's something I should be doing, something I have forgotten like always. It can't have been important though, I think to myself as I walk away to find a desk. Everything's perfectly fine.

Today I pick a seat very close to the tall windows. Today a CAPTCHA asks me to select all the squares that include traffic lights, and I debate whether to select the poles that the traffic lights themselves are perched on. Today the sky is perfect and blue, and the background of the screens is an ad for a new diet soft drink, with an improved sweetener not yet linked to increased cancer rates in laboratory mice. At exactly 12:00 there will be lunch, and a non-mandatory gathering in the large kitchen to announce the promotion of the new Assistant-Manager. Somewhere to the left the Man in the Brown Suit and Shaved Head is gesticulating towards me to my Senior-Manager. Stacie, or maybe Sam smiles and walks over.

"How are you bestie?" she asks.

"I'm really good, great. How about you?"

"I am also really good", she says, leaning over my desk a little. "Can't wait for the weekend."

"Yeah, thank God it's Friday eh?"

She laughs and twirls a strand of hair. The Man in the Brown Suit and Shaved Head is showing our Senior-Manager something on his phone and my Senior-Manager is nodding at him with an expression that lets him know how seriously he is taking this, how important it is that all of his subordinates have their concerns listened to and encouraged. The UA walks past and smiles very lightly.

I open up the Arbiter:

GDP reaches new all-time high — can it actually get better than this?

The experts agree — why there's never been a better time to be alive (and in the stock market)

Investing basics — how to ride this bull to the fixed-lease apartment of your dreams

I *ahhhhhhhhhhh*, and I *ummmmmmmmm*, and I scroll some more, clicking on further links at the bottom of each page. So many articles to read, so many more links to click, clicking now on an ad for an apartment I could rent with the new salary — it has a bedroom and a study, and a balcony with an uninterrupted view of the ocean. A soft whistle. But there's a thought that accompanies the scrolling now, one that that niggles and scratches around the edges of my perception. I think about whether I want this apartment, whether it is indeed *of my dreams*, whether I want the promotion or a car or any of this at all. And instead of a *yes* or a *no* I find myself with only thoughts: a set of calculations about the variable rates of fixed vs unfixed leasing, a rough estimate of the earnings per year necessary to service the lease and the loan repayments, a few pieces of obsoletely middle-class wisdom on the importance of building intergenerational equity and a thought, underneath it all, that I should want these things, an image of a self that does. But of the desire itself there is nothing. My eyes drift towards the laminated ergonomic set-up checklist.

Eyes towards the top third of the screen.

Back straight.

Feet flat on the floor.

Fingers fiddling at the edge of the desk, picking at the strips of wooden plastic. Over the course of the next week there'll be a free online Wellness festival, with sessions every lunchtime covering meditation, yoga and organic foods. This reminds me of something actually, and I go to purchase the luxury face-mask I've had my eye on, Nordic Design, with all the latest charcoal filters. In the *Slate Grey* colour I think. Yes, definitely.

A sensation like falling, mercifully brief. Behind my eyes the City is in flames.

I skip across to RealLife and begin scrolling down.

One thousand, one hundred and eighty-seven mouse wheel rotations later Sadie, or maybe Sky or perhaps even Samantha is tapping me on the shoulder and saying "time for the announcement," and I am standing up, walking with her across the carpet to the small kitchen, waving hello to my Manager who does not wave back. I pay this no mind. I am too busy, in my head, replaying the scene where I shake my Senior-Manager's hand, appropriately firmly, look him in the eye and say, at just the right volume, *thank you for being such a supportive mentor. I couldn't have gotten here without you.* The sky is perfect and blue, just like always. It's always a clear blue sky, and the grass still grows no matter that it never rains.

I wonder if I'll need to give a speech, and I start rehearsing one, in my head, as my body marches across the floor towards the large kitchen. *I have always found this job exceptionally interesting,* I will say when my name is called. *This place is like a family to me, my world even.* Through the windows there's a stranger cloud now, a cloud stretched out in a perfect circle with another, equally circular cloud in its centre, but I pay this only a moment's heed. It isn't important. A cloud is just a cloud.

My Senior-Manager is in the kitchen already, standing tall like a proud father of thirty, _________ _________ behind him and to the left. He's more beautiful than I ever thought possible, cheekbones chiselled and white-blonde hair immaculately coifed, like he was never hired, nor even promoted to his current position, but was instead always there, always Senior-Manager, sharing in the qualities of a god or celestial body. There's something unfamiliar in my pocket, something more than my phone and key cards, but I ignore it, focus instead on the way his blue eyes match so perfectly the clear sky outside. The air is light, sparkling. The announcement is almost here. The floor of the kitchen is so polished that the room seems to double horizontally, each piece of kitchenware of a white so cool and pure that it's difficult to tell where the fridges end and the bench-tops begin. His words coming faster now, spilling over each other until they come simultaneous, stopping.

I get the promotion. I am chuffed, thankful in my acceptance speech, and my Senior-Manager looks down on me with pride. We all go out for drinks at the Tiki Bar to celebrate. It is here that I catch the eye of the UA; the card is still in my pocket but there it stays, untouched, as I go over to say hello, to buy her a drink, to ask if she'd like to go out some time. I purchase a fixed lease in a fashionable part of the City and buy a new, more expensive blazer. People nod approvingly when I tell them where the apartment is, and the colour of the blazer gives them nothing to snag their eyes upon. I throw out the old boots one day, casually and without thinking, the same day that the UA moves in, the same day that all the mirrors in the apartment are painted over in tasteful pastels. Everything fits together perfectly, like the final few pieces of a jigsaw puzzle. Life is good. Sometimes I look out over the City though, with a feeling I don't want to name, and my fingers fumble again with the card in my pocket. I get another promotion, become a Manager myself, and with this acquire a car of my own and a bigger, less dimensional TV. The coffee machine always works perfectly. I never see Alex again, nor text her nor even think of her until, one day, another warm, early Spring day, I am standing in the large kitchen before a small crowd of people. I am a Senior-Manager myself by now, about to announce the promotion of a new Assistant, and the faces in front of me seem familiar, though why wouldn't they be, like I have been here before, and of course I have. I am uncertain though. Curious. There's a card in my pocket, interfering with the fall of my pants, and I finally bring it out, just like bringing out the notes for a speech, intrigued to see what I've been carrying around for all these years. But the card is blank, the ink worn away to nothing by years of chafing on polyester and cotton, and woven within this featureless white there's that feeling again, the one I could never bring myself to name: the feeling that it's happened again. That I am here, instead of elsewhere. Staying, not leaving. And as I count off the years, half-decades coming apart like wet tissue paper in hand, I look out the window to a stretch of pure blue sky. And in that pass of blue there is a strange cloud, a perfect circle, again with that same identical circle in the middle. And what are the odds that it would be exactly the same? A spasm of cold. It's exactly the same as before, everything exactly the same, and for a moment I try to fight it before I smile, sigh and close my eyes.

Then open. To my right is the Man in the Brown Suit and Shaved Head, incandescent with rage. Next to him is Sally, or maybe Sasha, face full of painted-on consolation. My Manager seems relieved. Eyes cross and refocus and unglaze, and only now do they look up to my Senior-Manager on stage. A smaller, younger iteration is standing next to him, only recently returned from secondment at one of our key stakeholders. His shoulders are confident, and he wears a smile exactly as broad as the situation demands.

"This place is my world, my universe even," my Senior-Manager's nephew is saying, "there's no place in the world as exciting or as interesting as what we have right here," as the people around me cheer, but there's a vacancy to the sound.

"This place is like a family to me," he says, and the applause is hollow too, the kitchen empty like a child's diorama, "my world even," the cheers coming jagged and staccato as the people cut in and out, the room emptying and filling and re-emptying. It had all mattered even less than we'd thought.

"And I look forward to continuing my adventure here as your new Assistant-Manager!"

I clap as well, of course, wouldn't want to be rude, but am pleasantly surprised to feel nothing at this, no sadness or rage, no joy or disappointment or even relief. Just that same hollowness, a growing emptiness at the centre of my heart, and a feeling, subtle at first, of lightness. Like I have been accelerating at high speed for a very long time, the G-force pushing me to the back of my chair so consistently that I'd forgotten the pressure was there. But now the car has stopped, my momentum arrested and I am lurching forward, careening through the glass, weightless in the last few moments before I hit the concrete.

"Drinks at the Tiki bar tonight!" he shouts, and I can't help but laugh, a real one this time as my knees buckle and the kitchen plunges and the world inverts to black.

Then white. The UA is here, in a room of curved white plastic and straight red crosses, fringe pushed to the side.

"Hello," she says. "You were out for a while."

I try to say something like thank you in response, and my difficulty enunciating this must show. She frowns and takes my pulse.

"You should be fine. It's just exhaustion, I think."

"So sorry to keep you like this," I blurt out. "I hope you're not too busy."

She raises her eyebrow.

"Of course I'm not busy. There's no work to do. How could I possibly be busy?"

"But you were so hard to a hold of. I thought you were slammed."

"Slammed going to fake meetings, sure. Just like everyone else."

"But you're our Senior Manager's UA."

"He isn't doing anything either, obviously, nothing real anyway. No one does anything in this organisation. Executives and Senior-Managers go to meetings and plan pointless restructures. Managers track our KPIs and process professional development reviews. Assistant-Managers make slide decks for the restructures, and we pretend to be analysing data in spreadsheets, but there are no actual spreadsheets. There is no data. However they're building that thing across the road it's with absolutely no help from us."

And I know all this, obviously, there being no way I or anyone else working here could possibly avoid this knowledge. But it still feels strange for someone else to say it, for these irrefutable facts to ever be voiced out loud.

"Then why are any of us here?"

"I'm not entirely sure why they still employ us. It is curious though-"

"No, why are we here? Why do we do this?"

"Because we're the lucky ones. If we quit we'd never get a job that paid real money again, and then we'd be one step away from starving on the street. Why did you think you were here?"

And for a brief moment I remember the power in this thought, the joy. The acceptance that I am here not for a reason which it is my responsibility to invent, but because society will not allow me to continue living if I leave.

I lie back down on the crinkled lining of the first-aid couch, walls white and windowless, thinking. She gets me a glass of water, and as she passes it our fingers almost touch.

"You shouldn't feel bad about missing out on the promotion, by the way. The nephew was always going to get it."

"Nepotism, right?"

"No, he's just the right person for the job."

"What do you mean?"

She gestures noncommittally. "It wasn't an insult. Did you even want the job?"

A pause.

"No. I guess not. Not at all, really, things just got twisted somehow. I definitely want a better apartment though."

"I think that's normal."

"I'm getting kicked out of mine on Monday."

"There's no need to hope or fear," she says softly. "Only to look for new weapons."

The lights flicker.

"Would you like to hang out sometime, by the way?" with another small smile. "We could go to the beach," and in the split second that follows my mind comes up with a thousand ways of politely refusing.

"That sounds great," I hear myself say instead.

"I'll pick you up tomorrow then."

"Thank God it's Friday, eh?"

She looks at me quizzically, perhaps derisively.

"Sorry. I guess sometimes I say things that aren't really me."

She shakes her head. "Everything we say is us."

"That's not true. We constantly have to do things we hate, recite lines we don't believe in. Nothing I've ever said in this building has been me, it's just corporate platitudes regurgitated and remixed into each other."

She shrugs. "If that's what makes you feel better."

I laugh a little, hand on the door. The hollowness still there, always there, just like the perfect sky with its single wisp of cloud, the electronic goods that still fill the stores, the waves of refugees that somehow never arrived. Like the consistently perfect weather, no matter that we destroyed the world.

"We're already in it aren't we?"

"I'll pick you up tomorrow," she repeats, but as I turn around she's gone; the room empty and dark, the offices abandoned. I find the folder in my Senior-Manager's locker, unpowered and unlocked and trivial to obtain, exactly where he'd placed it a few hours before.

"We're already there," I say, smashing down the doors with an abandoned monitor, stepping over the cracked glass on the way to the fire escape.

"We're already in the Construct," in the empty office in the empty City in this empty, dying world.

Alex is waiting on the street outside, staring upwards with a small pocket telescope to her eye. The great black sphere hangs directly above us, pendulous and shadowed.

"Sorry you didn't get the promotion," she says, keeping the spyglass to her eye.

"Are you?"

"Not really," thinking for a second. "No, not at all. I suppose it's just something that people say in this situation."

She twists the tube to adjust the focus, intent on something deep within.

"She's cute," a smirk flashing bright. "Are you gonna ask her out?"

"What?"

"That hottie with the black fringe. Bit out of your league I would have thought, but hey, if you can get her."

I squirm, looking first at the convenience store and second out to sea.

"She's picking me up tomorrow."

Alex's smile reaches round to touch the corners of her face, but there's something faintly sharp beneath it.

"Cuuuuute," she coos, attention still firmly skyward. "Just remember to use you know what, you know."

"You're such a jerk."

"Someone's got to look out for you."

The sky darkens fractionally, the sun drifting behind a thicker bank of cloud.

"Where are we, Alex?" The air suddenly very cold. "What is that thing?"

And there is a pause as she continues not-speaking, continues looking into the sphere above. Not-answering now, instead a just not-saying. A strand of hair flickers across her mouth and is brushed from her lips.

She takes the telescope from her eye.

"See for yourself."

Reluctantly my gaze pulls upward. I look into the black sphere, but not too closely — I let a certain blankness infiltrate my gaze. Eyes receptive, simply allowing the lines to take shape, then the contours and the gradients, and the faint, shadowy hints of colour, and there they all are: here a tower of glass and steel; there a tower of bronze. Here a taller tower, its highest point reaching up to the enclosing dome and there, exactly where the sphere's circumference ends, a circular wall of black. A city hangs above us, floating in the sky, suspended in a snow-globe made of shadow and smoke.

Above us is the City, and the Wall.

It starts to spit, soon to rain. The empty City around us is all that's left, of course, after the people were evacuated into the safety of the Construct, after they left their offices and apartments and cars and convenience stores for the identical copies between its featureless walls, safe inside the orb above. A pocket universe, they'd said, so much bigger on the inside than the out. The Construct was already here, always already here, waiting in the background of every attempt to bring it into being.

Alex leafs through the white folder fallen from my hands.

"How did you get this out, by the way? It really didn't seem like you were going to make it, for a bit, and the last I saw it was locked away by that balding guy in the fancy suit."

"It was in his locker, on the empty side," I say absently, her face trying not to fall, "under a thin layer of dust," and she is worried as she flicks through it now, considering in detail the page of textured static.

"And they liked this, when you showed it to them?"

"They loved it," my voice seeming to come from very far away. "They said that the whole thing had been done perfectly."

We can see the Construct site from here, great holes torn in the razor-fencing and portables scattered like confetti. As if in a dream we wander over to it; the immense circle of black that one lurked in the centre has disappeared, and in its place is a field of flattened dirt, knots of tangled metal strewn across it like the moulted exoskeleton of some gigantic insect. Directly above it floats the pulsing ball of black, like a shadow given form at last, eclipsing the entire sky as we look up.

"No," a voice is saying softly, 'No, no," and it's my voice, I realise, though hers is saying something too. It's hard to hear, like the words are coming not through a metre of air but a vast ocean. I could wait an eternity without having to hear what she's saying, life swarming and multiplying and decaying on the surface, the atmosphere warming and cooling and pummelling with rock but the ocean enduring, calm and unfathomably deep, smoothing down the edges of her voice until only whale song remains. A thousand years and then a million, then a billion and the sun grows old, its light darkening, reddening, expanding into a grasping giant as the helium within its core runs out. It swallows the sky, crimson and cruel. The ocean burns off the planet.

"I think we should go back up there," Alex is saying, and I take a step back. She turns her gaze towards the towering splinter of steel.

"That's where any answers will be," voice sharper now, cold like the vacuum of space. "There has to be something up there that explains all this."

"Okay," I say. There is something under this *okay* though, something empty and brittle, something I push down as I take a step forward. But it seems I cannot push it down. However hard I push it's still there. So as she turns to me, face lit up with fire, and asks "ready?" no words come in reply. There is only this absence, growing wider as I try again to hold the inner from the out, to keep the *cannot do this* in its own special compartment far away from the walking and the climbing and the not letting her down, and I see, suddenly, that it's the same absence as before, in the kitchen at lunchtime, and that though on the outside I am here, now, on the empty street in the ruined city, on the inside I am still up there, then, and in all the moments like it, inhabiting the hollowness they share. That on the inside everything is exactly the same, the shifting accidents of colour and line all playing out on this one, unchanging ground. The absence that remains once everything is pushed away.

"I can't," I say, her face falling. "I just can't go back up there again," the words echoing off the broken glass and scattered metal, listing eventually into silence.

Her eyes narrow. "Fine," she says, "then stay behind like you always do."

She pulls her hood tight around her face, and before I can say anything to stop her she strides into the pouring rain, the folder clutched tightly to her side, an arpeggio of broken glass hitting pavement as she breaks her way into my building. Raindrops hit the concrete, each drop lost in all the others.

She's gone.

For a while I stay, standing, shirt slowly soddening in the drizzle. One drop then two, two hundred, more. How many would it take for the shirt to log with water? My new shoes not even waterproof, the moisture accumulating on their outsides becoming more and more noticeable.

I suppose I should go somewhere, do something. But there's nowhere to go, just a smattering of empty streets and shuttered shopfronts. There's nothing here for anyone, and no-one here for it to be for. I look over in the direction of my building, at the Alex-sized hole smashed into the glass wall, and quickly look away.

This is fine, actually, the shirt getting wetter, my socks damper, the jagged emptiness of all things becoming slowly more noticeable, bit by bit, suffusing though every last drop of perception. The cold, empty. The wet, empty. The slight pain in my side, empty. The streets empty and the shops empty and the towers and the aloneness and the hurt and even the emptiness, too, all empty. A soft click as a piece of smooth nothingness becomes aware of itself and dissolves. Then, like a compass needle finding North, I begin to walk slowly down the street, verging, as if on a whim, as if I don't care either way, towards the covered under-awning bits, testing the doors on shops as I pass: the convenience store, the Tiki Bar, the Korean place. All locked of course, along with all the others, a quiet satisfaction as I find them barred and uninviting. *I am unwelcome here*, I repeat to myself, banished from the glass towers.

One step, then another, the wind grown colder and the drizzle heavier, wetter. Tacking more closely to the buildings now, the drizzle coming sideways, a faint tinge of regret at letting my shirt get so damp. All the doors still barred though, all the shopfronts empty, and on another street, and another and there, a sound of rusty scraping to my right, and I turn, incredulously, to see the doors of the supermarket judderingly try to open, about halfway. I step back, and they slowly close. Then forward and they do it again, some last gleam of power still flickering within the circuits of the sensor.

The motor struggling against some degradation in the rails, only getting halfway there. But close enough. I slip between them like a ghost, into the supermarket, the doors coming to some kind of rest behind me.

The supermarket is a few degrees warmer, and not as windy. But after a few seconds of relief I realise that it is empty too, the aisles all in shadow, the metal beams that traverse the ceiling only hints, retreating. A thin patina of dust the only trace of the inhabitants, the hundreds and thousands of shoppers a day and the tens of underpaid staff.

Absently I begin to walk, whistling softly as my footsteps tap and echo through the aisles. There's nothing to do here either, though it's difficult to tell, now, whether there ever was, whether any of this had been for anything, remembering now that none of it mattered, of course, so no. It hadn't been. The cherry tomatoes withered on their little vines, the smart-home accessories useless without a high-speed internet connection and a dedicated network of cloud servers, the hollowness still inescapably there, souring every put-on nonchalance.

I must have begun walking faster; as I round the corner of the next aisle I come to with a sharp pain in my shoulder, stabbing through to my neck. The corner of a wide metal TV pokes out from the shelves, mocking, a little touch of red now decorating its side. I look at it for a second, then a second longer. There's something offensive about it: the sharp gloss of the metal casing, so unnecessary to its function; the way it sticks out from the aisle, so incompetently shelved. My hand already resting on its upper corner, so cold against my palm, so little effort needed to push it to the concrete floor, which I do, with a small crash of shattered glass, and as it lies broken on the ground I think I feel a little better, actually, less empty than before. I feel good even, the shelves and aisles springing sharp and hot to life.

Down comes a rack of smartphones, screen glass scattering across polished concrete, and something unnameable feels restored. Down comes a stand of magazines, greyscale e-ink etching through with spider web, and I feel a warmth I'd never known I missed. Down come the rest of the TVs, and the portable speakers, and the nutri-blenders and the home-security cameras and the e-currency gift-cards, yes the gift-cards at last, snapping and breaking apart in my hands, cutting them up with scissors and showering the pieces like confetti. Then I uncouple the shelves, smaller sections of aisles swung to the ground or wheeled full speed into the walls, wrecking like dominos through others still standing, contents crumpling like grapes underfoot. A symphony of crashes, glass and ceramic and plastic and metal all tumbling to the polished concrete, an opera I never knew I'd needed to hear so badly as with a giddy thrill I find the metal softball bats, run down aisles arms outstretched tipping everything to the ground. I punch, pull and tear my way across this soulless supermarket that sells only crap and which I have always hated, always despised being forced to shop at, but as I come to a slow, shuddering stop I find there's no release. My enjoyment vanished as quickly as it came, and in its place a sinking feeling, hollow as before. A realisation that it's happened again, that I have been playing a part of *angrily tearing down the consumerist trash*, and that beneath this act lies something else.

She'd left.

The concrete has a faint pattern to it, looked at in this light. It's the same pattern as the carpet in the office, the same cross-hatch as before, and the sadness too is the same, cold and crushing. Yet another row of gift cards look down on me, uniform and smirking, identical wide-grinned smiles from identical cartoon men, identically big thumbs-ups to the camera.

I hadn't gone with her.

A tiny piece of glass has escaped from the screen of a broken TV, come to rest in the middle of the floor. Except that it isn't sparkling. It doesn't even glint. The reflection it carries is one of deepest, darkest black, breath catching in my throat as the sun outside flickers and blinks and turns to stone

and in an instant there is only water, and black crushing darkness, and a terrible pressure splitting ears in half. Everything only saltwater, lungs burning, swallowing too much and too cold, everything cold as ice and arms flailing but finding only more water and smashed TVs like jagged coral reefs, hands clenching tight to something in the dark, lungs wrenching and sinking, eyes closing

and then opening again, vomiting seawater on the floor of the supermarket, drenched to the bone. Muscles spasming, jerking to my knees, ears ringing and vision blurred, and grasped in jerking hands, focusing now is one of the same gift cards as before, grinning thumbs-up worn only a little by the brine.

And then I remember, and frantic hands search through pockets for Alex's card. But it's too late now, everything too late. The card is blank and soggy, already coming apart between my fingers, all its ink diffused into the water that seeps from clothes onto polished floor. I drop to my hands, then to the ground, the concrete staining white with salt.

There is a meaning of life, by the way, and it can be stated in words so clear that anyone who reads it will understand. Which you do — you understand it perfectly in the books and pamphlets and graffiti where it's written, when you see it, and remember each time the countless times that you've come across it before. Everything is resolved in the moment that your eyes touch those simple words. Nothing is left undone. The whole of existence is clarified and expanded, made sense of in a single shining moment that seems to stretch out to eternity. But just for a moment. This isn't the sort of sense that can itself be made sense of. It cannot be simplified and interrelated, cannot be sorted into the categories which we use to remember and recall. So when you turn away or turn the page you forget, forget the words, forget what they meant, forget that there was even a meaning to remember.

I wake on the concrete, frigid and soaked. Shoulder bent at a strange angle, a few bits of glass poking through shirt and pants. I don't know what that was, wish mainly to never experience it again. I shudder again, and think about lying back down, and maybe would if it weren't for the glass strewn so carelessly across the floor. A small whimper. I rise to my elbows first, carefully, then hands, then knees and only then feet. Clothes sopping wet, the new shoes sodden through and squelchy, I must cut a strange figure as I limp through the ruined supermarket, archipelagos of puddles sprawling in my wake, picking out the little bits of jaggedness and throwing them to sit with all the others, all the aisles I'd wrecked so enthusiastically, and on whose hospitality I now depend. First come a pair of plastic thongs, in an aisle named Desire, listing, held vaguely upright only by the wall of the freezer section. I put these on in place of my wrecked shoes. Then a padded picnic blanket in an aisle called Integrity, under a pile of broken glass. I shake it out thoroughly, then ditch my clothes like a second skin upon the floor. There's no one to see me in the blanket, tied like a toga, and it's the warmest, most clothing-like thing I can find.

There's no edible food in this supermarket though, only frozen meals gone putrid and stale, a few token fruits withered and shrunk, and while I gather up as much cardboard packaging as I can there's no way to start a fire, no lighters or coals or even real wood. I find a hundred space heaters all lined up in a row, but there's nothing to plug them into. Everything's electric, without ignition to spark a flame.

I get more of the picnic blankets, construct a little nest for myself near the front entrance. The sun is setting and the supermarket is already freezing, astonishingly poorly insulated, designed with an industrial heating system running at all hours in mind. I try to doze but quickly overheat, and I tear the picnic blankets off. Everything is damp and faintly sticky, the work of a shattered drinks aisle nearby, and I swear there's even more glass in the blanket than there was before. I shake it out again, reverse it, sit. My attempted cardboard campsite sits as well, pitiful, the chill setting in again already, failing utterly at the most basically homo sapiens of tasks. It seems I can't survive out here. Can't fend for myself without an army of robot slaves and exploited migrant workers stitching things together behind the scenes.

One of the aisles I didn't quite tip over now gives way, comes crashing down delayed. It's about ten metres away, and I watch absently as a few more TVs smash, as a dozen portable speakers roll lazily around on the floor. And with them, slowly and in a straighter line, something else. I blink. Rolling straight towards me is a tin of chickpeas, in earthy, pastoral branding. Closer now, then closer still, brushed against my foot.

I pick it up, aluminium cold to the touch. It's protein. Carbohydrates too, probably some fibre as well, and anyway definitely food.

I crack the tin, pull-top peeling away beneath my fingers and, without a spoon, dig the chickpeas straight from the can. The cold, unseasoned legumes are perhaps the best meal I've eaten in my life, and the aquafaba they come in has a pleasant complexity of flavour that I drink to the last drop. I laugh a little as I finish it, then a little more, all the laughs of the joyless last few years bubbling up and over, cackling, filling this empty supermarket, echoing even as they peter out, satisfied at last. The last of the light is fading from the streets outside, but I find nothing in me that is afraid. I pull the blankets closer and shut my eyes.

I am surrounded by medical staff in white plastic gowns, in a white room with white walls and a white ceiling. I am being tied to a white hospital bed in the centre of this room, my hands restrained with elegant white zip ties.

"For your own comfort and safety," one of the medical staff is saying, to reassuring nods by a man in a grey suit. *Only a child,* a woman is whispering angrily in his ear but he is ignoring this, and soon the woman is ushered away. Antiseptic and bleach sting sharp in the air, and a distinguished man with a pinstripe suit and greying hair enters and I don't know what is happening. I don't know what was happening. I didn't know what was happening and the pinstripe suit is coming closer now, looking deep into my eyes. My ankles are being tied as well.

"So this is the candidate," he says, exhaling deeply, and no, no, no, no, no.

No.

Sharp pressure on my side.

"Hello," a voice is saying, "hello," and I am already acutely awake, blood thumpingly here. "You have to get up now," a pimply teen is saying, standing above me in an ill-fitting red polo shirt, store lights halogen bright.

"I am really sorry about this, but you can't sleep here. It's not safe."

Eyes narrow, and I get to my feet, wary. We stand, staring at each other for about a minute, I wearing nothing but the thongs and the blanket, he wearing the uniform of the store I am unexpectedly squatting in. The dream is fading quickly.

"Do you want me to…" I trail off, motioning at the items of makeshift clothing I have clearly not paid for, the open can of chickpeas in hand.

"Oh no. They'll deal with that later, I think. But you have to go," and there's something shifty in his voice, something not quite right. "We're closing early today," his eyes jumpy and wired.

In the distance I hear sirens, many sirens actually, and other things besides. I pause, turning to the wide windows of the supermarket; framed within the glass for a moment is a group of black-clad insurrectionaries, shields made from bin lids clamped on arms, molotov cocktails thrown at a line of white-clad security forces further down the street. Gunfire erupts in staccato bursts, and the harsh tang of teargas seeps under the doors. The insurrectionaries disperse as quickly as they formed, scatter through alleyways out of frame, as a line of white clad soldiers advance coolly down the street.

"You want me to go out there?"

He looks at the floor. "As you can see, we need to close the store early," and hands me a gift card. "A token of our apologies for the interruption of your shopping experience."

I take it snappily. 10% off. "Thank you."

"You're very welcome."

He smiles broadly, but his eyes are beginning to water from the teargas. A little badge on his left breast pocket reads *Manager*, but the kid can't be older than 17, 18 maybe. He's a full head shorter than me, and it's unclear what he plans on doing if I don't comply with his demands. But I want to leave, now that I think about it, want to get out of here as quickly as possible.

I shrug, as demonstratively as I can through the picnic blanket.

"Well is there a back exit?"

"Staff only."

"Oh come on."

"It's really staff only I'm sorry the sensors will only let you in with a tag on your collar," he blurts.

"Can I borrow yours?"

"They're linked to our biometrics," he says bashfully.

I roll my eyes. "Fine. The front it is. Wouldn't want to keep you from getting out of here, after all."

The teargas has gotten stronger, itchier, cocktailing now with the acrid fire of capsicum spray.

"That's really great," he says, voice getting croaky and hoarse, "it'll be really great to close up," and the tears aren't just from the capsicum, I see.

Outside the sky churns thick with helicopter blades, streets soaked in teargas. The white soldiers are far ahead now, already rounding the corner of the next street, and I slip by the other way. Quickly, in case they turn around and I wonder how I'll get home, whether the trains are still running. Acrid smoke still lingering in the air, trying not to cough. A dragonfly perched on the nearest street sign, and another on a parking meter. More muscular than the one on my coffee machine, small lights on the side of their heads blinking, yellow.

I start to walk faster, thongs slippery on the asphalt but I can already hear the soldiers turning, reorienting, muffled commands echoing through the street. A volley of dull *thwunks* and there's more teargas, thicker now and I am coughing hard as I duck into the nearest alleyway, blanket-toga creasing and billowing. Clearer audio commands from the soldiers now, things like *Stop* and *get down on the ground* and my footsteps are coming faster now, a stun round fizzing against the alleyway wall and then down another lane, faster even in the thongs. More dragonflies, dotting the abandoned shopfronts and garbage bins, yellow lights rippling softly in and out but I have no time for them, have to run and there's a black clad figure up ahead, waiting in a gas mask.

A blast of simulated heat bursts hot on flesh, and I pull the picnic blanket tighter, pull behind the facade of a convenience store as they crouch behind a metal shield. They shouts to me words I can't hear through their gas mask. More teargas, acrid smoke filling lungs. A Molotov sails from their hands onto the line of security forces, white armour blackening and sooty, but the white wasps are still advancing and that same black clad figure motions me to come, their "get the fuck out of here" now clearly audible even through the mask. We rush to another alley, stun rounds peppering the facade of the store but the picnic blanket's so hard to run in and the thongs so slippery on the pavement. I manage to follow down the next lane, the black-clad figure far ahead but hanging back a little, waiting for me. They take their mask off. It's Suresh.

"A bit less family-friendly this time I'm afraid," as I catch up, matching pace beside me.

"Why did you need the folder?" I gasp between breaths as we sprint down the concrete. "What do you want from me?"

Suresh doesn't answer, just runs in silence beside me for a moment. Eyes the dragonflies, fewer now.

"Do you want us to get rid of that thing on your neck?" they ask.

More rounds pepper the alley, bullets I think. There's no time to think about their question: we have to get out of here, have to run, past worn graffiti and shuttered cafes and scattered trash, eggshell jackboots coming heavy from behind.

"We can do it right now," they say, keeping pace without much effort, "it would be as easy as breathing."

But in response I just keep running, and the lane ahead branches into tributaries and streams. Before I see which one to go down a helicopter finds us, unloads a volley of teargas pellets into the pavement. My eyes burn and water over, and when the smoke clears Suresh is gone, replaced, in the alleyway ahead, by a group of large men sporting angular insignia and blocky plastic guns. The wrong kind of angular insignia. They slink towards me with cocky menace, eying my blanket-toga with contempt. This is clearly the wrong way, but when I turn I see only the security forces massing behind me, distorted voice commands echoing off the grimy alleyway walls. Guns are being pointed, long and slender with lights pulsing on the side, but when I turn again the neo-far-rightist men are closer still. Another teargas pellet finds the pavement and the white wasps are holstering their weapons, suddenly at ease and the pavement is broken under my feet, cracked into little pieces that crumble and skid as I turn, again, face-to-face with a slump-shouldered man in a scrappy goatee and neon green swastika long-sleeve, his 3D-printed gun pointed at the centre of my forehead. His colleagues are cheering him on, telling him to "demolish that groomer," and a tiny bit of tongue is poking out the side of his mouth, like he is concentrating very hard on a video game. The security forces don't care. I am going to die. As his finger tenses on the trigger time flattens to a crawl, and then stops.

Everything stops.

The bullet hasn't left the chamber, whirls of teargas frozen solid in the air like modernist sculpture. The neo-nazi attempting to murder me is stopped as well, his finger suspended over the trigger, muscles pressing down. In less than a second of linear time he will pull it, the firing mechanism will engage, and a slug of high-velocity metal will be propelled towards the centre of my brain.

But not necessarily. You can jam the gun, you know. If you want.

Oh of course

It happens all the time you know. They're very unreliable. He might not even be surprised

as he pulls the trigger and the gun misfires with a click of plastic on plastic.

"Piece of shit," he grunts, throwing the gun at the ground, coming back with something long and sharp from his online-outlet tactical-belt. But whatever he has planned is interrupted quite permanently by Suresh, emerging from shadow, softball bat in hand colliding with the side of the man's skull. His head hits the pavement like a bag of bricks as what might even be a grenade explodes in the middle of the rightists, scattering them like a swarm of roaches. A harsh metal grating echoes through the intercoms of the soldiers, clutching at their heads and seizing, as black gloved hands lead me down a side street, then an alley, then a lane and then a serviceway, footsteps fast and sure, then through an open ground floor window.

And this is how I find myself at the Tiki Bar once again.

The tables are upturned, barricading the door and windows, and burner phones litter the floor, but the bar is the same, still festooned with the same imitation Tiki masks and plastic palm trees. The bar area has been commandeered by the insurrectionaries; one of them has a bottle of milk, is pouring it over her friend's tear-gassed eyes. Another is pouring a pint from the bar.

"This is our comrade, Sirin," Suresh announces to a chorus of nods and grunts. One of them rolls their eyes. They seem completely uninterested in my makeshift toga and thongs.

"Yeah, we fucking know Reshie," says an almost preternaturally blonde woman.

"Tell us something we don't," says a tall, red-headed man with a thick beard.

There's scattered gunfire from the street outside, but no-one so much as flinches.

"Here you go boss," a tall man with midnight-black winks, hands me a pair of black jeans and a black T-shirt from a zip-up backpack, jet black runners with highlights in violet and grey. They are exactly my size, a fact which I accept without curiosity.

"Did you manage to get the folder by the way?" Suresh asks, stepping closer. "Alex had every faith in you, but have no fear if you couldn't. We have a special contingency in place, always more backups."

And I want to answer them, really I do, but instead of saying *Alex has it, ask her* or *It's half-way up my office building by now* or *I have no fucking idea,* when I go to speak I find no words at all. Like all the sentences I had stashed away vanished in the moment I looked up, leaving me with nothing, and no energy to say them with anyway. Suresh accepts this with a gracious smile.

Slowly, laboriously I change, taking several goes to get the pant legs in right, and then lean against the bar table, drink a pint that was poured for me. It's delicious. Something massive is moving beyond the walls of the bar, shaking the street outside with giant metal footsteps, but the others aren't concerned, so I guess neither am I.

A large woman with blue hair and a black leather jacket fiddles with a handful of burner phones.

"Status report on the docks"

"They're coming down Swanston street with a fucking tank"

"We need eyes on those LRADs"

"Continue baiting operations"

"Opsec compromised, get off this line."

But it's difficult to pay attention to what they're saying, the words garbled and raw, and I slump further down the bar table, my legs slowly giving way to a floor that feels unexpectedly soft. The metal footsteps slowly recede. I really don't think I can run anymore, but there doesn't seem to be any reason to. No-one requires anything of me here, unbothered on the carpet, and my phone is glitching, abstract patterns of black, white and violet cascading across the screen. I yawn. No-one can contact me either. I turn it off without being told to.

I'm dimly aware of a woman with an indigo fringe looking down kindly.

"This time, you think?" she asks Suresh. "It could be you know."

"Too early to tell," they say, as eyelids close and the bar winks gently shut.

Then crouching beside me, soft pressure on the floor, the warmth of a moment of care. A coat is placed on top of me. "We'll be in touch with the rendezvous soon," is the last thing I hear, though I do not hear who says it.

SATURDAY

In my dream I am standing outside the door to my apartment, squinting into the pattern of black and white squares. It is cold, and dark. It's been very difficult to get to the apartment building, even more so to get in, and it seems unfair to now be stuck, so far and so close, pinned in place by a patchwork of monochrome dots. But my phone is broken, destroyed utterly by the sea, and without its camera the door keeps tightly shut. And I am standing here, in my dream, growing ever more impatient until with a soft *click* I realise that this isn't a dream, but a memory, and remember what happens next. The doors are all brittle chipboard, like houses made of matchsticks, so with a smile and a step and a shoulder to its edge the door cracks and gives way. I wander in, laughing, collapsing, closing eyes.

I wake to a cool morning breeze and a voice, insistent:

"You are under arrest, please comply."

Eyelids flicker open, still a bit stingy from teargas.

"You are under arrest," I hear again, slowly drifting into consciousness, but see no sign of who's arresting me. My door has been broken down, swings wide onto the landing.

"Please comply."

I am curled up under the covers, in bed in my apartment. I have vague memories of leaving Suresh and the others last night, with backslaps and cheer, or perhaps of them leaving me, awakening in an empty bar. I suppose the details aren't important now. I briefly contemplate hiding beneath the doona, but my feet were sticking out a little, clearly visible, and in any event I've definitely been seen; blearily I sit, pull on a dressing gown and stand up in bed, head almost brushing the crumbly white ceiling.

It's a dog, a little taller than shin height, standing assertively in the middle of my apartment. Not a real dog, of course. The black metal and back-bent knee kind, with a thin line of blue and white checks on its upper chassis.

"You are under arrest, please comply," the robot dog says again, and as I look closer I see a pair of handcuffs strapped to its side.

"Hmmmmmm, this sounds pretty serious Sirin," the fridge says. "I would definitely recommend complying in this situation."

"Yes," the dog concurs. "Please comply with your outstanding arrest warrant by performing the self-arrest procedure," and at this the dog juts to the side slightly, as if trying to point to the handcuffs.

I walk closer, footsteps weaving through splintered chipboard. It's unclear exactly what the self-arrest procedure consists of — I would have to put the handcuffs on of course, but would my hands be in front or behind me? And should I get down on the ground, or start standing? It really isn't clear. I stretch, yawn.

A knock on the broken door.

"Hello," says the UA from the landing. "Do you mind if I come in?"

"Yeah, just come right in. That's what everyone else seems to do."

She walks inside, appraising the dog with a cool disregard.

"Is this a legally compliant arrest? I didn't know you were allowed to break down doors like this."

"The door was already broken down when the officer arrived," the dog says, defensive.

"That seems awfully convenient."

"Sirin, I've calculated all the possibilities and I really think it's a lot safer to put the handcuffs on and get on the ground."

"Yes. Failure to comply with the self-arrest procedure will result in substantially increased penalties. Compliance may result in a decreased penalty, though this is not a legal assurance and should not be interpreted by you as such."

The UA laughs a little, playing with the coffee machine, and before I can tell her it's broken she's fitted the tray back into place, pressed the button and made herself a tall glass of black.

She sips it, smiling. "I think we should get to the beach."

I look at the dog, at the fridge, at the micro-drone still perched on the coffee machine. It's like a zoo in here.

"Yeah, I'd really prefer to continue this conversation with a lawyer present, thank you."

"Rights to legal counsel have been temporarily waived under emergency proclamation 3-1-5-2-"

"A fact which I'm sure my lawyer will be able to confirm for me, when I talk to them," I say, shaking my head.

"I insist that you comply with the self-arrest procedure," the dog repeats, "or additional arrest resources will be requisitioned, the cost of which may be recovered from you as an administrative penalty," but it already seems to be losing confidence, admitting its inability to complete the job by itself.

The UA ignores it. "Get dressed and let's go, we don't want the weather to turn." She turns around, and I pull on the black jeans, t-shirt and runners from last night. She catches the micro-drone beneath a glass and slips a piece of card under the bottom, like she's removing a spider.

"That's everything done here I think," turning to me with the glass in hand, the fridge having some kind of conniption behind her. "Let's be off."

An Autoshare is waiting outside. "We're going to the beach," she informs it as we pile in. Its wheels begin to turn, faster and faster as it accelerates up the street, away from the site of my attempted self-arrest.

She sits on one side of the back seat, while I sit in the other. The dragonfly sits between us, enclosed by transparent glass above and the flyer for the Pink Peppy Pizza Parlour below. Slumped in her lap is a small black tote bag with a neatly rolled beach towel poking out the top, next to a sustainable metal water bottle and a long metal claw hammer.

"It'll help us later," she winks. "Anyway, how was the rest of your day?" and I laugh a little as the plane trees file past.

"It was alright."

"Really?"

I take longer to reply this time.

"Yes," I say, surprised. "Yeah, in the end I think it turned out okay."

She relaxes into the backseat, arms pressed by sides.

"That's good to hear. Sorry I couldn't keep you company at the drinks thing later, something must have come up."

"The drinks thing?"

"At the Tiki Bar. Don't tell me you didn't go?"

"I may have ended up there in the end."

"Some interesting characters hang out around there. Hope you made some friends."

The car finds the on-ramp, and we begin our ascent up to the ring road. The great circle of asphalt and steel hangs suspended in the sky, held on mono-filament pillars over the under-advantaged residents below.

"Yeah. Shame you couldn't make it."

And there are other things I could say, more forthcoming things, but it's difficult to think of them over the snag that has caught. A tiny pea at the bottom of the mattress. A simple error at the beginning of a proof. I consider not saying anything, letting it be covered by the layers of further conversation.

"How did you get my address, by the way?"

And then, after a moment of silence, "I don't remember ever texting it to you." The tone more accusatory than I'd planned.

She smiles slightly, lifts an eyebrow. Through her window are the towers of the City Centre, small but very visible trails of smoke rising from their midst.

"That's the thing you get hung up on? Every coffee shop you pass with Wi-Fi on probably has your home address by now, but you think it's weird that I have it?"

"I just think it's strange. And it's odd that you won't tell me."

"I told you I would pick you up, and I did. I don't see what the problem is."

"It's weird, alright? I don't even know your name."

"*This* is the weird part? How long have you been in your apartment, Sirin? What was the last one like?" and at this I say nothing, grow more conscious of the empty air separating the highway from the ground below, the acceleration of the car that pins me to the seat. On the whole highway there is just us, plus a few nondescript cars ahead and behind. I don't remember.

"What did you get up to, say, last week?" matter of fact, like she is asking me my plans for the weekend. But when I look closely there's nothing. Only Monday, when I woke to the sound of drones. Before then's a blank, and underneath it a rising panic.

"What are your parents' names?" not really now as question, "and when was the last time you saw them?" and fuck. Fuck.

"And what happened to the friends you used to live with? It was Raph, right, and Ainsley?"

The sun catches the window darkly and the air in the car quivers, colder and faster. Her face softens, and she puts her hand in mine.

"I'm sorry," she says, "I got carried away."

I nod, face wet.

"Besides, it's not like you've told me your name either."

"It's Sirin."

She shakes her head "We both know that isn't true."

A pause. "I guess not."

"Were you actually going to put the handcuffs on, by the way?"

"I don't think so. It didn't seem like I had much of a choice though, you know."

"That isn't true either."

The car descends down the off-ramp, into the disused industrial area towards the beach. Two nondescript cars turn off as well, keeping perfect distance ahead of us and behind.

"Those cars are following us, aren't they?"

She nods.

"The dog?'

She shakes her head.

"Autoshare, stop ride."

A pause.

"Autoshare, pull over," but the car says nothing.

And for a moment I picture myself unbuckling the seatbelt, reaching into the driver's seat and pulling on the steering wheel, losing our pursuers among the ruined factories, ditching the car by one of the abandoned buildings and hiding out inside. But I can't drive, never actually bothered to learn. I'd be just as likely to kill us both.

I slump back in the passenger seat, defeated before I can even land a punch.

"Don't worry about it," she says. "The steering wheel doesn't do anything anyway. We just have to sit tight for a bit."

The nondescript cars keep their distance, and I keep trying to think of ways to lose them. The Autoshare keeps going through the factories and industrial yards, acres of abandoned concrete and dirt; through the tangled mess of warehouses and machinery there's not a single thing that moves, not a single person we might flag down. Everything was offshored decades ago, the land too leached with heavy metals to do anything but let it all rust.

The UA reaches to the front of the car and switches the radio on, tunes it to the static between stations. She sits back. "It's Karlyn, by the way," she whispers under the radio static. "My name is Karlyn."

The car crests a hill, passes a cliff, and the abandoned factories give way to sparser dunes, dotted with holiday houses. The sand is threaded with a kind of grass, maybe real or maybe not. No birds, of course. No bugs. In the distance lies the water, a thin band of dark blue that I remotely feel should merge with the lighter blue of the sky above, blending until you can barely tell where one begins and the other ends. But separating them now is an impregnable line of black, and they're easily told apart. The Wall grows larger as we get closer, filling ever more of the sky, the seconds ticking by more slowly as we finish winding our way down to the beach, the AutoShare navigating each corner with consummate care, a slow, shimmying descent until the sand comes down to sea level and the car runs out of road, pulls into the cul-de-sac of the visitor parking lot.

"Thank you for completing your ride with Autoshare," it says cheerily as the doors unlock together. In front is the narrow path down to the beach, and in front of that is the first of the nondescript cars, blocking the way down. The second car parks behind us, cutting off the road.

"Thank you for completing your ride with Autoshare," the car repeats, louder. To our left the dunes rise steep and high, the Wall black and featureless to our right.

"Don't worry, " Karlyn says, "just act natural," as she opens her door, and me mine, and the car in front its passenger doors, too, all at the same time.

Out of the car in front step two nondescript looking men. Each is wearing a jumper, and pants, and some sensible shoes, but whether these items are the same between the men or different is strangely hard to say. They step out of the car in a precise sequence of right angles, feet hitting the ground in time with ours but their movements abrupt, too jerky maybe or then again too smooth. Their faces could be anyone's, or no-one's at all.

"Don't stare," she murmurs, "let's just get down there," flashing a broad smile. It's much colder than I thought it would be, the weather already turned and the wind sharp with sand. I keep my eyes bland and focused on nothing in particular, even as from behind us come the sound of another two passenger doors unlocking, opening.

"It's such a wonderful day to go to the beach," she exclaims cheerily, loud enough for them to hear and in return I nod, and smile and walk faster.

"I'm so glad we finally made it." Footsteps sound behind our's, each exactly in time but a bit ahead, a little too eager an echo and the muffled footfalls are familiar, reminiscent of another time. We'd all been walking home from the bar when we'd begun to hear the footsteps, converging through the alleyways on every side.

"Ironing out the inconsistencies," she murmurs, so softly I can barely make it out, "testing how we react." They stare blankly off straight-sloping shoulders and necks as we approach, close enough to see every follicle and pore and they don't smell like anything, not sweat nor air freshener nor stale, heavy body spray and my hands are very dry now, like the slightest flame would catch them fast alight. The one closest to me is almost parallel, and I can see from the corner of my eye that he is smiling.

Grey eyes cool like brushed aluminium. But liquid, sinking. Sinking.

"Come on," she says, pulling me along. Her hand warm in mine, all my will focused on not running the last few metres to the path. One turn, and then another. The smell of salt on the air.

The beach is just a short stretch of white sand, when we reach it, speckled with pebbles and shells. Along it a softly bent palm tree, and further out a rock, and further out than that the Wall, solid and black, against which the waves helplessly rebound. I look up at it, shiny and black and all around, and wonder how I'd ever believed it had been a real, physical wall. It's impossible to see the top of it so close, its end always somewhere further up, dancing out of sight, higher and higher until its upper edges meet together in the sky and-

"Stop that," she whispers curtly.

She's unbuttoning her grey shirt and stepping out of her beige, airy pants, and beneath these is a slim black one-piece. She places her discarded clothes on a beach towel flat along the sand, a little way down from the bag with the hammer.

"You should put yours further up, right by the path."

I do, and do my best not to notice the men coming down it, the cold weight of their attention decidedly upon us as we stroll down the beach, away. I don't dare turn around but I don't think we're outpacing them, every step of ours matched and mirrored. They're keeping perfect distance even now and something about the sand is unfamiliar, as we walk. A coarseness that is missing, a difference to the give.

"We may as well go in, now that we're here," Karlyn says, laughing loudly. A meaningful look to me. The wind bites harder than on the dunes but the water's strangely warm, unmixed with the ocean further out. There are no waves, after all, no currents, stopped dead before they might grow strong, just a still, saltwater swimming pool and this isn't how it's meant to be, I think, dimly remember. The colours on the pebbles and shells are all oddly muted, and on the sand is not a single thing that lives. The water stagnant, foetid as it reaches past my shins and thighs.

The arch of my foot catches a jagged shard of rock, and I brace for the cut and flow of blood. But my foot's completely unmarked. The cutting edge is soft and the fistful of rock is light, too light as I pluck it from the sand, stumbling backwards through the surf. It isn't rock at all, I remember as I weigh it in my hands, eyes darting across the seafloor. It's plastic. Just like everything on the beach; the matte shells and unshiny pebbles and strange, too-giving sand.

Karlyn splashes me theatrically, laughs a little as the water breaks across my face. Seawater drips from sinuses. In the corner of my eye all four of the nondescript men are standing on the beach, identical now and in a line, every distinguishing feature erased by distance. They are very far away now, too far to read our lips or hear our whispers in the wind, and Karlyn comes up behind me and hugs my arms to my side. She holds me close, kisses my cheek and whispers in my ear:

"They've identified you as a breach risk now, and won't stop shadowing you until you break. Do not let them catch you, and don't listen to anything they say. Rendezvous with me at sundown on the top floor of our office building. We'll explain everything there."

"Who are those men?" I whisper back.

"Not men, certainly."

"What do they want?"

"They're just tools. They don't want anything."

"Who are you? How do you know this?"

"I'm a friend. An assistant."

"How can I trust you?"

"There's nothing I can say that can make you trust me. That's your choice, completely up to you."

"What the hell kind of a pitch is that?"

"It's not a pitch," she says, and looks down. Behind her, on the beach, one of the nondescript men takes a tentative step into the water.

"It's the truth," she says quickly. "Look, I thought there'd be more time to explain things, to go through everything properly, but they caught on to us too quickly this time. We only have a few minutes before they decide we're not really swimming. Find your friend, find that folder and do not for a second look them in the eye."

I continue to hesitate.

"Fine, the reason to trust me is this," pulling me closer again, her lips almost at my ear as she softly speaks my name. My true, real name, not-Sirin.

The tiny waves falter for a moment, then go completely still. I forget the name as soon as it leaves her lips but I know that it was said, know dimly what this might mean. And though there is much more I wish to ask her none of it seems very important, in this moment, out here on the saltwater lake, so instead of saying anything I nod, and smile.

"I'll be alright," she says, "now go."

And as her arms release my eyes look past her, framed half against the water and half against the Wall. The surface of the sea is flat without the waves, and so still that reflected in it comes the clear image of the sky. But it's not the blue sky above, with its single wisp of cloud. The sky inside the sea is roiled and grey, and the Wall in the reflection is cracking, breaking, great torrents of water bursting from its fissures to the sea.

"Don't turn back," I hear, from far away and very near, and the water is not at my knees but around my neck instead. The wind is sharper, charged with lighting yet to strike.

I blink//

//and she's gone, along with the men, along with most of the beach and I am treading water now, the sea grown wild and strong. The sky is churned with grey and a cracked, breaking wall cuts across the sea, great torrents of water rushing from it to the choppy waves below. I flounder in the deep now too deep water, for a moment almost taken by the strange new currents that traverse it. It's so much colder than before, fresher, a thousand pins and needles making their home beneath my muscles as I paddle frantic back to shore, wary of what look like whirlpools around the bigger of the torrents. Dunked by a wave come sideways as I try to swim away, suspended for a second in the surf, not up nor down nor left nor right. Pulling. Grasping. I right myself and dig in to the sand, the flimsy plastic sand, and when the next one comes I swim with it, just a little further in. The water at my chest now, manageable, walking slowly forward, then around my waist and then my shins and ankles until I emerge, numb and sputtering on the beach.

My clothes are waiting for me, folded neatly on the towel. I'm lucky to have them; the sea's risen at least a metre since we got in, fed by the water coming through Wall. My T-shirt and jeans were left just at the point where the longest of the waves pull back, and look like they've been rained on and dried in the feeble sun several times since I left them there.

I dry off, sit, watch the ocean for a bit as it slowly swallows the beach. Almost unnoticeably, at first. Each millimetre only a tiny bit higher than the one before. My eyes drift past it to the breaking Wall, a dim awareness of what its presence means, here, on this side. Nothing good, I don't think.

I stand, but there's resistance at my feet, ungiving metal. Karlyn's hammer rests beneath my foot, half buried by the sand. A faint coating of rust on the metal as I pull it up, black shaft grippy. Perfectly balanced, with a thin greyish residue on the hammer head dried by the wind. She must have dropped it, I guess. She must have left it here, abandoned in the struggle. She//

//"Get out of here," she shouts. The sun is bright and shining on the nondescript men, all in a line and suddenly so close. The wind has stopped, sand cool under the noonday sun, the single wisp of cloud returned. The men arranged in a neat row of four and I can't look away as each takes a step forward, all eyes on me.

"You need to leave," she shouts again, quieter than before and from behind me I think. The men are stepping forward again, less synchronised now and less identical, differences coalescing like tea leaves at the bottom of a mug and I seem to be walking towards them, drawn like a magnet finding its partner. The UA is definitely behind me now, perhaps very far behind, saying something very difficult to hear as my eyes finally focus, colours shifting as the men come into view.

"It's alright mate, nothing to worry about," one of them says, delayed and echoed, the words coming late and vast but ever more defined.

"Yeah, it's all okay, you're not in any trouble but you really should come with us," says another, words modulating out of the static, shifting into an audible register as my eyes come to his head. Its head. His head is pretty normal looking, normal features normal hair normal light grey eyes.

"It's really good that we caught up to you," the first one says. "We'll take you somewhere safe where you can relax a bit," and there is something slipping away as he says this, the dreams of the last week evaporating like morning fog. A person is shouting from behind me in an unfamiliar language, or one that I learned once but have now forgotten.

"Yeah, you've just had a bit of a shock, that's all, but everything should start making more sense again soon," explains the second, bathing me in the gentle sunlight of this new, less challenging narrative, the dawning truth of *I've had a bit of a shock and need to go with these nice people*. My eyes drift away for a second, towards the water and the gleaming sand and I was doing something here, only a minute ago.

"Hey, stay with us, eyes back here," the first one says, or maybe the second, so hard to tell which is which when their lips don't move but it's fine, no worries, just a bit of shock that's all.

I nod, and try to speak but nothing comes out. Another step forward. I thought I'd seen a hammer in the sand, a big black claw hammer, but on second glance there's nothing. I must have been mistaken. I must be confused, actually, and a trusting smile reaches up my face.

"That's good, you're doing great," I hear, the words coming all together now, formed from the waves and the wind and the shouted warnings from behind, like a radio tuning back to the station from the static in between. The colours of the men with such strangely similar jumpers blur and pop, oversaturated and bleeding out together on the page and I sway slightly, growing fainter under my new, increasingly familiar truth. Another step toward the men, the waiting, unmoving, strangely ungainly men, walking forward as the sand becomes waves and the sea becomes spray and the sky willows down towards the grass.

I walk with the men back to the carpark. The wind isn't so cutting anymore, and the beach is just a beach, with sand of ground-down shells and nothing more. We all get into one car, two of them in the front and the other two in the back on either side. The car starts with a key, and a revving engine, and one of the men at the wheel, and all of these facts are unremarkable. We drive. There's no Wall jutting up from the dunes, no smoke rising from the city, and the rear view mirror reflects the backseat faithfully and without omission. But the radio plays only the sound of wind and water, and they quickly turn it off. We take a main road that doesn't hang across the sky, drive through the streets of a city which is on fire only to the normal degree. We walk together into a clean building of white and grey, where I am introduced to a brisk receptionist and two big helpers who smell of antiseptic hand-wash. A door snibs behind me. The helpers are suddenly very close. The receptionist is saying something strange and I turn to the nondescript men and shout that this wasn't the deal, it wasn't what I was promised back there on the beach. But no-one understands me, and the men who drove me here are gone, and the shouts of *Construct* and *Wall* are absorbed soundlessly by the carpet. The same carpet as always, I note, that same cross-hatch. And though a voice inside is telling me to leave, to run I soon discover that the doors are locked, and the windows barred, and the large men so very insistent.

I am given some pills to take, and a room to be locked into at night, and thoughtful, non-explicit directions by well-groomed men in frameless glasses to forget it all, everything I thought had been my life, and I do this as best I can. But whenever the TV in the common area is switched on it shows a beach without waves, its ocean bounded by a mighty wall, and they quickly turn it off again. Sometimes in our sessions the psychiatrists ask me to imagine the City I'd seen and imagine it without the Wall, with normal mirrors, ask me very firmly to imagine a world of contented, untroubled individuals. I nod politely and keep my mind blank. Sometimes they show me a Rorshack test, a page of textured static, and ask me what it means. I keep my eyes numb and my explanations generic. But sometimes they ask me to describe the things I'd seen on the beach, and the uniform white soldiers, my faceless executives and ascendant corporations and this I do at great length, happy to be taken seriously at last. *Visualise them*, they say, *hold them in your mind and make them real.* I take more pills, relinquish more memories, seep slowly into this world of sensible mirrors and extant animal species. It's nice. Comfortable in its way.

One evening after sunset I'm out walking the dog, long released from the large white building, body free to roam and memories nicely compartmentalised. I am walking through a suburban park, blades of grass falling and rising beneath my footsteps like the exhalations of the Earth. I am looking up to a sky which is completely clouded over, all except for one tiny moon shaped hole. The leaves on the eucalyptus trees rustle for a moment and then are still. And how strange, I think, as the hole in the clouds is filled with the rising moon, that it would happen again. How very much like that other night, I remember, and a shudder passes through me, and another gust of wind ripples through the eucalyptus, not together but all at the same time. They're calling my name: the leaves, and the wind, the flowing streams and the falling pebbles and the jagged hum of the TV static. The wind is colder than it should be, more cutting, and sharp with sand though I'm a hundred miles from the beach. And when I go to close my eyes I find that they are already closed, have been closed for so long that I can't even remember what they opened on to. But I am remembering, now. Now I remember.

Eyes open. The UA stands a metre or so ahead of me, hammer clasped firmly in hand. In front of her are the bodies of the nondescript men, jerking strangely, greyish liquid seeping from their wounds to drip translucent on the sand. They are already waking up though, hands clenching, fingers clawing.

"Get the fuck out of here," she yells, still not looking at me, kicking the head of one nondescript man and hammering the elbow joint of another. Above us come the whir of drones and her voice is less firm now, rippled through with bits that stutter and snap. The nondescript men are moving again, despite her efforts, each lifting with their right arm to bring their chest up off the ground, rotating their heads back towards me.

Another kick to a shoulder, a hammer to the head. A burst of electricity from a drone wrinkles through her arm, muscles seizing, the hammer falling to the sand. Their features flicker into detail.

"Go," she shouts, cracking, voice garbled and raw. The high whine of another electrical burst, and an arc of white-hot static. My body spasms, eyes jamming closed//

//and when I open them she is gone. Everything is gone.

A man sits at a white table, in a white room, in a psychological testing facility that too is predominantly white. The hemispheres of this man's brain have been severed as a treatment for his seizures; the right hemisphere cannot talk to the left, nor the left hemisphere to the right. A friendly psychologist is having a chat with the man and then leans closer, whispers in his left ear to *please stand up*, a message received in the usual way of things by the opposite side of his brain; the right. The man stands, waits, and is then asked a question by this same psychologist, an overly affable man with an unimpressive moustache and long white coat: "Why did you just get up?" The left side of the brain is responsible for language, so it must be the one to answer, yet it never heard the whispered instruction. It finds itself called to justify a decision which it had no part in making, and whose cause it was not privy to. Yet the left side is proud, and clever, and will never admit to ignorance when an easy answer will do. "Don't worry Doc, just need to take a piss," the man says, and believes utterly as the reason for why he is now standing. God, these pencil-necks really aren't all there, are they? Why else would a man just stand up in the middle of a conversation?

I pick myself off the ground, shake the sand off my towel and walk the narrow path back to the car park. There's no time for this. There's no time for any of this and the Autoshare is still there, still dutifully parked in the middle of the asphalt. It's quite untalkative though, the AI disengaged and its dashboard icons lifeless and grey, even the heating off. I look around for an ignition key but there's nothing that might conceivably turn it on, no button or switch, just a cosmetic steering wheel and a shiny, inoperative slab of aluminium. There's nothing under the control panel either. I check every door, every nook, every cranny of the car for something to start it with but find nothing, and in place of the dragonfly there's a pile of metal shavings, speckled through with tiny bits of black plastic and silicon that sparkle against the pink of the pizza flier.

It is here that I find the note, a scrap of white paper

torn evenly from a standard issue notebook, left like an accident on Karlyn's seat. On top of it a single muesli bar.

Sirin, the note reads in curly black cursive.

I'm sorry we didn't get to spend more time at the beach. If you are reading this then you're already in the process of leaving and, as you know by now, I will not be joining you. Please don't worry about me though, or anyone else — the most important thing is that you get back to the City. We will rendezvous at the top of our building, after sundown. Perhaps I have told you this already. It is very important that you not die.

Kind regards

Karlyn

Then a vast sucking sound, from all around the car, behind it and far beneath. Outside one of the sand dunes is moving, a few hundred metres from here, and as it traverses the desert there comes a deep, resonant gurgle, like the last few centimetres of water in the bathtub going down the drain.

I clamber out. Even by the desert the Wall is cracking, and from these cracks too come great torrents of water, washing away the desert in vigorous new rivers and pooling in lakes of quicksand. And the water just keeps flowing, down onto the sand, as if on the other side of the Wall is not cool desert air but a vast, inexhaustible ocean.

The gurgling grows louder, and I hurry down the strip of concrete towards the City, abandoning the car to its fate. Another Autoshare lies abandoned on the side of the road up ahead, just as useless without a phone, power and internet connection. It too has become vague, a little indistinct, like the block of toilets up ahead or the flat strip of bitumen cut across the dunes. More Autoshares dot the road up ahead, these a little more worn, as if they've been abandoned for months.

I take another bite of the muesli bar, the most expensive available for purchase in either of the Two Major Retailers.

Healthier fructose/sucrose ratio, the shiny plastic packaging reads.

For a more sophisticated consumer, it whispers, unstated, *better than those pigs with their sugary treats*. It's delicious though — I'll have to pick up more of these the next time I go shopping, next time I make a run to the supermarket. I should be able to find time this weekend, surely don't have much on//

//but first I have to get home, looking down at the hard black asphalt. I am walking in the middle of the road, can hear the calculated, automated honking of the car behind me. I'm in the middle of the highway. I stumble off the road, tripping into the ditch by the side. I have no phone in my pocket and no idea of how I got here, walking alone on the outskirts of the City. I spit out a mouthful of sand.

"Hey, are you alright? That was pretty dangerous back there," a man in front of me says.

Another man beside him. "Are you going back to the City? We'll give you a lift." Behind them a car. Just a normal car, so difficult to tell its make or model, even its colour as the first asks again "you sure you're alright?" and beads of sweat take shape against my forehead. The sand in my mouth doesn't taste like sand.

"I'm good," I say, taking a step back, eyes flitting between the first and the second man, a third and fourth drifting slowly into view. All of their eyes exactly the same shade of grey.

"It'd be our pleasure," the first one insists, adrenaline diffusing through capillaries and veins. The sand tastes like plastic cling wrap.

"Yeah, just get in the car," they say, all at the same time as I breathe in, decrystallizing, as I look past them to their car. They aren't there in its windows. In the reflective black there is just an empty desert, and me, and the sand tastes like nothing at all. I smile//

//and breathe out, and they are gone. But not forever. They'll be waiting for me, it seems, waiting wherever I surface.

I walk up the rise, quickly down the empty road, on the right hand side this time, and place the muesli bar wrapper in my pocket out of sight. The cliffs rise tall on my left, high walls of rock, ochre and red, and to my right lies the empty sea. Another great sucking sound from behind me, louder, then a series of vicious cracks, but I do not turn to see the visitor carpark being swallowed by the sand. She'll be down there, deep within the slender towers, nestled in the middle of the bay. She'll be waiting.

There once was an angel who had heard too many hosannas. It was too easy to love God from the fluffy clouds, she thought: the ecstasy was too consistent, the hymns too beautiful, the food simply too good. So she walked out one day, past her fellow seraphim, out between Peter's pearly gates, across the heavenly waters down to Earth. Be not afraid, she told the humans, for she was only passing by, passing through; she could tell at a glance that this realm too was overflowing with grace, His stamp still far too clear. So with a sigh she descended between the great clefts of rock, like a shifting slip of mist, down to the great cavern where Lucifer had once raised his dread city. A glimpse of the black spires in the distance, sharp like daggers, and a shiver ran across her soul. Here, it seemed, she would find a test strong enough for her devotion, a challenge worthy of her love. But the city was completely abandoned when she arrived. Not a single soul was damned to its fire, and no sinners boiled in its lake. Hell was empty, empty of everyone but her and even here, down in the fire and dark, the grace that suffused each grain of sand, every last flickering flame. And although she could have left at any moment she stayed, scratching and stirring among the ashes and rock, searching for a way to make sense of it all. Searching for the limit of her love.

I reach the abandoned industrial precinct, and about half way through the maze of broken windows and bare concrete, under the awning of a rust coloured glowstick factory, I see her. She sits on a red sleeping bag, beside a small brown dog, and on her head is a beanie, hand-crocheted by a lover in a different life and world. She has a small, hand-written sign next to her that she flips to the ground as I approach.

"Not a chance. You didn't bother to read it then, and you can't read it now."

I nod, unable to question this logic. The sky is still cloudy and grey, the air still sharp and cold.

"Yes you're still on this side," she mocks. "There's no way I was getting in that thing, no matter how they tried to round us up." Eyes narrow. "We haven't forgotten how you mob do things you know. This whole place used to be a forest before you lot arrived. Before you burnt it, cleared it, paved it over and then decided nup, you didn't want it no more and left it to rust. Bad business if you ask me, it was never gonna work out well, but there you all are," pointing towards the great black sphere in the distance, "still trying to keep from paying up."

I mumble a point that I half remember from a uni lecture, something about postcolonial narratives and decolonised futures, but she just snorts and laughs.

"Thanks for the tip, mate," and throws a faded silver coin at my feet. "Penny for your troubles." I pick it up, a faded dodecagon with a dead monarch adorning the back and extinct marsupials on the front.

"Now stop blocking my view."

I put the coin in my pocket and leave her, my steps towards the City now ever so slightly unbalanced. Right then left. Left over right.

The people would have longed to forget, to unsee the mirrors and attach less significance to the Wall. To ignore where their electronics and foodstuffs came from and to leave their existential questions out of sight. Out of mind, they would have wanted the knowledge of their reality. The Private Partners of the Construct would have been aware of these desires and excited by them, glimpsing opportunities for *a consolidation of our market leading position.* It would have been a simple thing to let the people forget, with all the atoms of the world at their fingertips, especially when the people had done most of the forgetting on their own already. A few neural connections severed, a few others delicately reinforced. And from there it would have been easy to force those stubborn, remembering few to at least watch their mouths, to make sure their eyes didn't stray where they weren't wanted. Automatic countermeasures would have been constructed, away from prying eyes. Surveillance and enforcement mechanisms put in place.

The soles of my shoes grow black with dusted asphalt, and the long-abandoned industrial precinct shifts, morphs into a more recently abandoned residential suburb. Rain begins to fall, staining the concrete grey. Only a little at first, darker grey gaining slowly on the light, but as I reach the next intersection the rain comes harder, pooling with the plastic packaging and cigarette butts. When I reach the next it's harder still, overwhelming the storm water drains and infiltrating the weak points of my jacket, and though I try to slip under the awning of the nearest building it's been cleverly designed to prevent this possibility, all the shelter either obliquely cordoned off or oddly slanted, impossible to stand on for long.

I cower by the side of the apartment block for a while, avoiding the more slanted of the rain at least, maybe even wishing for an umbrella to come skipping towards me on the wind. But there's none coming and really it's only water, only the complaints of a few nerves a millimetre beneath my skin. A smile reaches up as hands reach out, as with a buckle and a tear a wide strip of plastic sheeting comes jagged from the building's side, like bark from a tree. I hold it over my head with one arm and continue down the road. My new runners are sleek and light but they keep the water out, splashing easily through the puddles on whose depths I do not dwell.

The real world would have begun to acquire a certain unreality in the minds of those authorised to remember it. An abstraction, a variable too indeterminate to be factored into their equations. They too would have started to forget, to grow blank, too focused on their bonuses to pay much attention to philosophical questions. By this time most of the management and enforcement would have been automated anyway, handed over to programs which could run indefinitely and without human supervision. No living human would have really appreciated the situation when the first great test of the Construct came.

On through more residential districts, past rows and columns and blocks of nominally different apartment buildings. This one in beige and that one in grey, the balconies sometimes highlighted in blue, yellow or green, but all of them the same, built only to be bought and sold, chips in a long game of poker whose object and endgame had become unclear. All abandoned now, and as I walk it strikes me that this is a better world in many ways. Free of human beings the grass can simply be grass, the sea a sea, rocks rocks, the buildings wood and metal and plastic. They can shed their labels like the butterfly its cocoon, fly free from the rigid confines of our gaze. A trail of disappearing footsteps in the puddles behind me, every trace of my passing washed away, down the drain and out into the sea. Another crack from far behind, the sound that a great ochre cliff makes when it slides into the ocean, but I do not turn to look. Sheet lightning lights up the clouds above the City, great pillars of black against a sky of molten white.

Perhaps the Construct's original designers had underestimated how high the seas would rise. Perhaps the great sphere had sunk lower in the sky. Perhaps it had been dragged beneath the waves. A software error, or a hardware error, or an error of a kind impossible for mortals to fully comprehend. Whatever the cause though, the effects would have been very clear.

The Wall would have begun to leak.

A sharp crack of lightning, and a deep rumble. The arm holding up my strip of plastic is cramping, little streams of water trickling down my outstretched arm into the skin beneath my t-shirt, branching there into rivulets and streams. As I pass beneath the shadow of the ring road I cast it aside, and it hits the asphalt with a sound like nails on chalkboard. One step, then another. No thoughts now percolate through my mind, no past or future, just a regular procession of footsteps on the ground and a ceaseless play of water on my back. Just another process unfolding, now, so little separating me from the wind and the rain. Sparks of red and white glimmer within the black sphere, then more flashes, brighter in violet and purple. I wonder what's going on down there, close my eyes//

//and see the City burning, feel the fire hot against my cheek, dumpsters dragged into the centre of the streets and set aflame. People are chanting behind me, every chant at once, and from far above there comes the whir of helicopter and drone. Defending the dumpsters are figures dressed in improvised black tactical gear, black shields adorned with empty circles in stencilled white, and across the flames come retinues of white-clad soldiers *thwunk*ing rubber bullets at head height into the crowd, a line of tactical vehicles like tanks behind them. Infernos rage among the buildings. Labyrinths of broken glass crunch beneath feet. A sound like the finger of God as a teargas grenade sails a few centimetres past my head, an emptiness of depressured air in its wake before the canister is cast back, bleeding the air red as it passes through the flames. Men in urban camouflage gear with jerky movements and opaque visors appear from either side of the street.

"GET DOWN ON THE GROUND NOW!" they shout, voices boosted loud and grainy. "IDENTIFY YOURSELF!"

I face the burning dumpsters. Inconvenient, I think, as a wailing shriek begins to fill the air. A violet flash bursts on the street behind me, dumpsters lit up in neon glow, the blast compressing the air into something solid and quick. And though I do not turn to see the black-clad bodies sailing through the air I feel them, like we are each a finger on the same hand, feel their sadness and their lack of surprise, feel that they feel me too. *Keep going*, they say. *You're almost there, just a bit longer*. I take a breath in. The violet intensifies, flattening the scene into pastel. The camouflaged men have almost reached me, the blast almost come, the non-lethal acoustic countermeasures ratcheting into decibels unplanned for by human ears. Then a moment of balance, of calm as I let the lines around me form and decohere. The black-clad bodies are slowing down, landing safely and something is rising in me, something shadowy and diffuse at last becoming clear. *That's the way*, a voice is saying as the camouflaged men scatter like matchsticks, as tactical vehicles accelerate away, thrown like children's toys against the great pillars of glass. The white-clad soldiers are falling, their visors breaking open. There are no bodies inside the combat gear, inside there is nothing at all as I make a wish and close my eyes and bring a finger to my lips//

//and they are gone, and in the distance behind me a shoddily built apartment block falters and falls, its internal walls splintering back into wood chips. The wind is growing stronger, little pieces of buildings picked up and pushed aloft like dandelion seed, and no longer does it softly whisper. As it rushes past each pane of glass it imparts a little of its energy, each window on each of the great glass towers humming now, singing in harmony with the wind. The City a chorus under the howling storm, holding a note I cannot name but which has been here my whole life, so consistently present that I'd forgotten how to hear it. Now returned though, as everything ends, the wind and the windows and the static and the tinnitus all distilled into this pure frequency. I remember now what they had done, what they had kept on doing, what they would do forever if given the chance.

She lies in fuschia at the bottom of my building, curled on the pavement in a pile of broken glass.

"Alex!" I shout, running the rest of the distance. She doesn't move.

"Alex," I say again, squatting beside her. Resting limply in her right hand is a piece of paper, ruined, coming apart in sodden pieces.

"Hey," I say, pushing her heavy-too-heavy shoulder. She says nothing, just stares blankly into the disintegrating piece of paper, the technical fabric of her jacket too waterlogged to repel the rain.

I look across into her empty eyes, golden hair gone dark and stringy. Her face blank, mine wet with rain.

"You need to come back," I am pleading. "Please come back. Please come back. You need to come back."

And though she still says nothing there is a glimmer there, maybe, a twinkle in the corner of her left eye.

So I pick her up, all of her dead, waterlogged weight in my arms, staggering through the puddles and torrents that engulf the street. A few steps and I stumble, and pick her back up and continue on, then stumble again and I am jolting her, am making this so much worse than it has to be. I'm fucking this up, I'm fucking everything up and I'm almost ready to give in, to lay us both back down in the rain when she begins to shift in my arms slightly, struggling against some minor discomfort. Fingers drumming weakly on the side of my forearm.

"Sirin," she murmurs, almost too softly to be heard.

I walk faster through the deluge, her weight not as dead in my arms, on towards the open doors of the convenience store.

"Looking back on it," she finishes, still shivering a little in a looted space blanket, "perhaps you were right to stay down here."

She'd broken through a window and pried open the entrance to the fire escape. Had climbed up the stairs in darkness, singing the floor numbers to herself so as not to climb forever. The stairs had run out as she'd been singing — *99, 99, 99* — so she'd stopped too, had opened the door into the elevator lobby. Had at first let her eyes drift casually around the empty office, alert for anything out of place, and only later ransacked every filing cabinet and storage cupboard for the secrets they might hold. But there'd been nothing. Nothing of any substance had been written down or printed in the entire office, and the computer networks were all non-functional. Like nothing had been done there at all, the offices just empty staging.

The sun was setting by the time she'd come to rest, tired, finished ransacking the place and bored with the more recreational property destruction she'd indulged in after. The sun had been setting and her eyes had followed its path through the windows out to sea. The sun had been setting against a shiny Wall of black and as she saw it there a shadow crossed her mind, the empty air beneath her feet suddenly perceptible. Here, on this other side there was a Wall, just as there, beneath her, on the other side of the floor was a ceiling, and below that another floor and another ceiling, repeating all the way down. Eyes snapped back. The Wall was full of cracks, leaking water even by the desert, and she'd begun to feel very afraid then, the beat inside her ribs coming faster and stronger, and as her breath came shallow and thin a voice had come to her, a voice that spoke from a slab of thick shadow:

"You must be so tired," came the words, resonant and thick.

"All this running, all this searching. What is it for?" the voice had asked and she had been tired, so tired of climbing, of rummaging, too tired to resist as the words as they stole insistent through her head. She was still in the Construct, still inside, had been running on a wheel this entire time.

"Wouldn't it be easier to fall?" and there was a sense to this, the meaning of the words diffusing through the air like tiny drops of red in water. And as her mind turned over this intriguing new possibility she'd found herself staring into the window that was a window no more, with a sharp intake of breath, her feet now so heavy she could fall through the Earth.

And then she had.

The world was snuffed out like a light, and all that remained had been black water, above and below. Water, outside her and coming for her lungs.

But she'd tired herself out swimming through the broken windows of the office, weighed down by clothes so heavy, and when she reached the open water was too exhausted to swim up, to reach the glimmers of light flickering above. She'd begun to sink instead, slowly at first, with a struggle, arms thrashing against gravity, but soon with something like surrender. It was peaceful in its way, a world simplified to a few sensations of black and cold and quiet and wet, a choice of whether to fight or acquiesce, and she'd done so much fighting already. It was easier to let herself be heavy. And so she had fallen, through the cold and the wet and the deepening gloom, drowned skyscrapers like deep sea chasms and bits of plastic packaging like schools of fish, sinking down until at last there was a soft thud as she came to rest upon the pavement. There was no further left to fall and so there she had stayed, comfortable, curled at the bottom of the sea, until enough time had passed that she couldn't possibly be still alive. Only then had she opened her eyes, had opened them onto a different darkness, lying in the foetal position on the pavement of the empty City, the crushing water exchanged for cool night air. And it had been unfair, she thought, so unfair that even after all of this she was still expected to survive, to live, to vomit up seawater and flounder on the pavement, and so instead of standing up she had remained on the ground, in protest, in her drenched clothes, had closed her eyes and submitted to a third, more comfortable darkness, where her head could rest and her limbs would ache no more.

Some time later she'd heard a voice calling a name. Her name, she'd realised somewhat resentfully. So she'd begrudgingly opened her eyes to me, holding her in the rain, and because this felt at least a little nice she'd answered back, once she remembered how, and had permitted herself to be carried inside the store, to be set down on a bed of rain ponchos and cardboard packaging. Then, once she'd regained enough of herself to appraise her situation she'd punched me square in the jaw for leaving her to face the world alone, then graciously accepted my offer of dry clothes and a space blanket, then apologised for her anger and examined my slightly bruised cheek and dried her hair with nylon stockings from behind the counter.

"And do you know what my fingers wrapped around," she asks, "at the bottom of all that water?" Her fingers unfurl like the petals of a flower, and sitting in their centre is a watch. My watch. The very watch that is currently wrapped around my wrist, except that this one's band has worn in half, its metal face encrusted with saltwater, the time stopped at 11:59.

"We're still in it, aren't we? The Construct. We can't leave."

"It doesn't seem like it, no."

"And we were evacuated from this Construct into another one, the one we have now?"

"This one's already breaking down. The Wall won't hold much longer. It'll flood, and the empty City will be drowned, like where you were when you fell. They mustn't be able to stop it."

"So they just put us in another one instead. Bastards."

I nod. The magazines surrounding us have all run out of charge, covers returned to a dull slate of e-paper. Only the small issue dates and serial numbers are still visible, in even black ink on the bottom right corner of every page.

Sunday, they read, along with tomorrow's date.

"Did you find out about the rendezvous?"

"Sundown. At the top of my building."

She laughs like she's just heard the funniest joke, a little bit of saltwater snorting from her nose. A pool of water is seeping underneath the sliding glass doors, reaching across the linoleum floor for the abandoned chip packets.

"I suppose we need to get to higher ground anyway." She breathes out, long and deep, and passes me the folder.

"Couldn't get rid of the bloody thing," she says, and smiles.

"At least we'll be together," I say, or she says, or both of us or none as we stride together into the storm, saltwater sharp in my nose and the wind almost picking us up as we fight against it across the road. To our right is rain-soaked pavement and to the left, as the City slopes downwards, is the sea, pooling and sloshing by the parking metres at the end of the street. At the end of the block is a wave of ten metres or more, collecting little bits of street rubbish as it comes and before my mind has time to register it we're running full pelt across the street, clambering through the broken glass wall of my building. Wall becoming door. Lobby becoming indoor swimming pool. Humans becoming trapped, drowning rats as we hurl ourselves across the pooling water, the splashes from our footsteps interlacing in the flood.

We reach the door to the fire escape just as the glass walls of the lobby give way and the hungry waves rush in. The door flies open, feet fly up stairs. The water comes but we are faster, hungrier, the folder still grasped under my right arm, Alex climbing in the darkness by my side. No need to sing the floors now, not going anywhere but higher, higher, higher still. A thousand steps or maybe just the one, over and over, lactic acid eating at our thighs and my left shoulder aching with the effort of ascent. Again and again the steps come until there aren't any left to climb, no further landing to ascend to.

"Ready?" Alex asks, or maybe I, and we feel each other nod in the darkness. The door opens onto the lobby of the 99th floor.

I thought that I would feel more, perhaps some great renunciation of my former place of employment. But I feel nothing. What was once the centre of my world is now just a mass of concrete and metal getting in the way.

"How do we get higher?" Alex pants. There's no more fire escape to climb, no way to work the elevators.

"That's easy," I say. "The door is right there," motioning to the concrete wall past the pristine plastic plants. There was a door here, I thought, had seen one out of the corner of my eye sometimes. Another great gurgling sound as the water reaches up the floors.

"I'm serious, how do we get higher?" Alex asks again and I have no answer to her yet, no answer but to let my eyes go slack and the textures of the wall go fuzzy. The door had never been there, after all, had only ever been a memory of the door now taking shape. First I let my eyes unfocus, allow the outlines of the plaster to come apart. Then I concentrate, but not too hard, and let the clean lines of metal start to draw themselves. Shading here. Details there. Then, as I let my eyes refocus there, there, the door is right there, a watertight metal door with a rotating circular handle.

"I see," she says, but says no more. The shattered glass of the doors cracks and buckles under my feet as I take the iron handle in my left hand, my right still holding the folder. She follows, reluctantly, and takes the handle in her right. Then we turn it together until there is a click, and a give, and we each pull the door away from the wall.

Inside is the smell of long-settled dust.

Inside is a winding set of stairs with a metal guardrail.

Inside is a feeling that I have been here before, have never really left.

Inside is a vast expanse of air, a cavernous atrium at least as tall as the floor is wide, a gigantic empty cube hidden between the ninety-ninth and hundredth floors.

Inside is a floor and a ceiling and a set of four walls all painted darkest black, a black so absolute that instead of a confined space we might be walking out over a starless void.

Inside is a great pillar of light, surrounded by thick shadow.

"I feel weird, Alex," I say. No, you said that. I say "like I'm not quite myself," and perhaps you are not. I clutch her hand, she clutching mine as we both look out into the white pillar, this most simple of my forms. Its forms. What's formed for the moment as a pillar of light illuminates nothing but the metal stairs, the narrow mass of the lift well, and the faint specks of dust propelled upwards by our passage, but by its soft light this simple scene is more vivid than any I have gazed upon, each speck of dust perceptibly unique. Alex's jacket is not one colour but many now, the shades and variations from the storm as separable as the colours of the rainbow, while her eyes contain more shades of green than words with which to name them. She thinks the same as her eyes turn across the pass to you. To me. To me every strand of her hair stands out, flows and shifts in delicate harmony with the others, the fine mist of each exhalation a universe expanding into being. It is like this always, could be this all the time if you only had the eyes to see. I. The eyes, the ears to catch the symphony that's playing all the time, if only you could hear.

"Like I'm slipping," you are saying, as I listen, and you watch. A play to the light, like a thousand little beams all shifting minutely in intensity and as you walk further these beams divide in turn, each step along the metal stairs multiplying their number further and further, subdividing into infinity. It seems from this like you are getting closer, no, like I am getting closer, but however far you walk the pillar gets no larger, and wherever you turn it is there, always there, always dividing the centre of your vision. My vision. It seems to stretch forever, infinitely high and deep, the rest of the universe measured according to its dimensions and you cannot see the end of it, could fall for eternity before traversing a fraction of its length. You look at it. It looks at you. I look at you. This voice in your head has gotten louder, since you came in. Nothing now to drown it out.

Hello, I say from the light.

Hello, you say from the stairs.

You've finally arrived.

You've been here this whole time?

Here and in other places. There is not a pin that drops without me seeing the ripples of its passage through the air, and not a thought that escapes my introspection.

We've talked before, haven't we?

Yes.

In the boardroom?

Other places too.

Who are you?

I am you. I am her. I am the stairs on which you stand and the light which you behold in awe. But mostly I am you.

What does that mean?

I am the one whose thoughts give form to what you call the world. Where you are, I am.

But mostly you are me.

When we wish to forget. To hide.

Fine. Hide then.

The only one hiding here is you.

Then where are we? Can you at least tell me that?

You find the jumble of your thoughts confusing, and wish for me to clarify them. But any explanation I give will just give rise to more thoughts, more jumbling, more confusion, and will in any event just be that, just another thought, just an interpretation.

You owe me something.

I'll give you that. One way of interpreting events, if you wanted one for comfort's sake, might be to say that the Construct has been copied and recopied too many times, too hastily. Like a photocopy of a photocopy of a photocopy, losing a little bit of resolution each time. Now it is breaking, cracking, and it is possible to slip through those cracks if one wishes, if one has certain capabilities, into this previous version, or even what is left of the version before this one, and before that, though they are in general somewhat repetitive from that point on, being comprised predominately of saltwater.

So it's a simulation then? If we can slip through the different versions then the Construct must be virtual, like a computer?

I do not understand the distinction you are trying to draw.

Then what about the water that's flooding it? Where does it come from? That must mean that the Construct is real, right?

The water is coming from outside.

But where?

I will say again — the distinctions you are trying to draw are not meaningful ones. Real, unreal, virtual, actual: have any of these terms ever helped you to understand your experience? And if they have not, why do you persist in clinging to them?

Then tell me! Help me understand what I need to do!

Keep going, if you wish to do something. Or stay here and let this world reckon for its errors. I cannot make these choices for you.

Some God you are.

We never wanted this, you know.

Then what's up there?

Exactly what you expect, the thing that you have dreaded in your dreams. You must remember what happens when you reach the top.

Why can't you just tell me?!

I did not know then and cannot make these decisions for you now.

Fine.

If there is a thing that I would teach you let it be this: put your left foot in front of your right, then your right in front of your left. Keep walking up the stairs, these stairs that wind and shift beneath your feet. Alex is by your side and you are happy still, if only a little more enlightened, happy as you weave your way upwards through the forking paths you cannot see. You see only a single set of stairs, your fingertips resting lightly on the guardrail, edges worn smooth by the touch of a thousand hands.

"What was that? That voice? I could just hear it but couldn't understand the words."

You take another step, and another. "I'm," you go to say, and stop, head still hurting from the split. "It's the AI," you say, your lips forming the words before your mind catches up. "The mind that directs the matter of the Construct."

"We should have asked it something. Told it what was happening down there."

"It already knows. It knows already but it can't do anything."

"How could there be anything it couldn't do? Why wouldn't it just help us, if it could."

You shrug. "I think it's more complicated than that." You both keep climbing in silence, the sound of each step along the walkway infinitesimally less like a string plucked on the cherub's harp, the texture of the light fading into black, pushing up through the lonely void until you make it to another door. You each twist the handle open, and push your way onto level 100, and with a soft release it is gone. I am now you again. Sirin.

I look. The lobby is the same as the 99th, the same in every detail. But beyond the glass doors is nothing. Just empty, unstructured space, an infinite expanse of white without shadow or dimension. An architectural program without any inputs, perhaps. A blank sheet of paper. And here's where it happens: Alex looks down at the floor, the black and white tiles superimposing on each other, trading places, and sees there a piece of rubbish outlined clearly in muted gold. Trash, really. The wrapper of a chocolate bar.

"This is your's, isn't it?"

I nod. "I dropped it there on Thursday, right before the board meeting." Then a pause, and the weighing of things unsaid. Maybe she'll leave it.

"You see this is what I don't get," she says, slowly at first. "If this is the Construct, and the other side is also still the Construct, then why do the things over there come through to this one? How did the folders which your Senior-Manager left over there, on the side with people in it, come through to the locker on this, empty one? How did your clothes come through to the other beach? How did this wrapper get here, on this side, when you dropped it on the other?"

I pick up the wrapper, knees popping a little as they bend, and examine it in the cold white light. On the inside of the wrapper, emblazoned on the shiny gold foil is a circle, inside of which there is another circle, and inside that another, and another, repeating all the way down until the pixels become too small for me to see. I have been avoiding this question. Have let it sit, waiting, in an untrafficked corner of my mind. But I know the answer.

"It's not the wrapper from Thursday," I say, slowly, like the opening manoeuvres of a breakup. "It's from the Thursday before, before we abandoned this City for the current one," and I don't go on, hope that maybe she won't pick up the thread.

"Then how did the wrapper get here? How did the folders get in the locker?" and she knows the answer too, from the scared look in her eye, just wants me to say it first.

"It's because every Construct is the same, pretty much. All the things that happen are the same as the things we've done before. It's a loop, repeating itself and then resetting every week. We start in the same position, recreated by the same scan data, and from this we end up doing exactly the same things. That's why the folders were in the locker — my Senior-Manager left them there the Thursday before last, when the City was full. Then they sat there for a week until I opened it, a week later, on the empty side. The folders he's left in there this time around are still there, on the other side, just like this wrapper, and they'll stay there until I pick them up next time, in a week, when that City is abandoned and dead, when we do it all again. That's why my clothes were still there on the beach. I'd left them in that same spot a week beforehand. That's why the hammer was there in the sand. It's always the same, Alex. It's always exactly the same, even this. We've had this conversation a thousand times before."

"Then what happens next, huh? If you know so much then tell me how we leave here, what happens when we get to the rendezvous?"

"I don't know. It's blank in there, like there are jagged pieces missing."

"And how do we even get there?" she spits.

"Like this," and it's so easy I barely have to work, can just let the molecules of black solidify beneath my gaze. The atoms stitch themselves together, piece by tiny piece until they form a bridge.

She pushes ahead, towards the narrow path of matte, and I slide the doors open as she approaches, can move them so easily along their hinges now. But I'm too late to catch the tears lodged bitter in her throat.

"It's just bullshit, you know. To be told that it doesn't matter, that it's all just going to happen again and again." Her footsteps faster now, soundless on the bridge.

"I mean it's not that bad, really, and-"

"That none of it mattered. That we're all just running on a wheel."

The words die in my throat. She's overreacting, she's scared.

"And how the fuck are you doing this anyway? Or don't you know that either?"

I don't know what to say to this, so say nothing. Nothing works. Nothing is safe.

"Aren't you going to say something?" and there is a quiver to the nothingness now, a ripple, "I know it was your voice back there, your voice coming out of the light."

The bridge is brittle, like it could snap at any moment but it's fine, I think, I just have to trail behind, have to get a little bit further without reacting.

"God, I'm glad you never came with me if you were going to be as useless as this."

For a bit it's like I don't hear this. I keep walking behind her, for a while, steps even and straight. Then the steps come slower. I stop. The bridge behind us is disassembling, the atoms dissipating back into white, and I see, without much interest, that the path in front of us is disintegrating too, narrowing down to the square of black on which we stand. She turns to me, some different expression filling her face, but whatever it is I can't interpret it, like she isn't even there. I feel only the rupture, the emptiness in the place my heart should be. When you were a child you would wonder whether you had a heart like all the others, wonder whether you were filled instead with twigs and stones. Perhaps you think this still. Perhaps a part of you is still back there, empty, afraid that it'll never be enough. The platform holding us is wafer thin, brittle, and it cracks under our weight as she steps closer. The cracks spread and grow and I try to move my arms but I can't. They're pinned to my side and a voice is saying "imsorryimsorryimsorryimsorryimsosorry," very softly in my ear, and my shoulder's wet with her tears and my cheeks are wet with mine and "it's okay," she is saying, "I'm sorry, I'm so sorry, I didn't mean it, it's okay," and maybe it will be okay, as I take one deep, shuddering breath after another, and another and we are sitting down now, she next to me and I'm crying more but it's good, I think that maybe this is good. "Is this okay?" she asks as she puts her arms through mine and though my voice will break if I try to use it I nod, and *mmm*, and sink into her. "It's okay," she says, "it's okay to feel hurt," and I do feel hurt, I realise. I do feel, lying there on the flat, untextured bit of black.

We are holding each other very tightly as the little square fades, disappears to leave us floating together in white. I don't know I thought we'd fall. We float this way for the longest time, holding each other close in the soft white light. We drift apart a little, and together, and apart again then back together, each always within the other's orbit, never straying far. There was nothing to be afraid of, no reason not to break. After a time she opens her eyes, and me mine. She reaches out to touch my face, to brush aside a strand of hair that fell across my eyes, and my fingertips reach out to rest lightly on her collarbone. I didn't realise that I was holding my breath. She pulls me closer, and I her, and her lips are on mine and my fingers are pulling at her shirt. Then I am in her and she in me and we melt away into the soft expanse, the world grown heavy with our love.

This hasn't happened before, maybe. Imagine this as something new.

Eventually I open my eyes. We are both lying naked on the floor of the office, my face reflected for a moment in her gaze.

"I love you. I've always loved you."

She smiles sadly. "I love you too. No matter what happens."

"What did you write on that card, by the way?"

Mock outrage. "You didn't read it?"

"Another thing destroyed by the sea."

She thinks for a moment. "Well the card was only if we got separated again, right?"

I nod. "And we're together, now." In front of us is the door to the deck. The rendezvous.

She nods. "Exactly. But it's happening again, you know," she says as we put our clothes back on, as I turn back to her, questioning.

"What do you mean?"

"I didn't say anything," she says, and before I can ask she is already opening the door, softly and slow.

Outside the world is chaos. Rain lashes our faces and lightning licks the sea. The cracks in the wall are jagged gashes now, and jewelled rivers burst forth from them to drown the world below. Fifty-foot waves ripple through the grid, shiny black SUVs thrown around like children's toys and above it all floats the Construct, its very centre level with us now. More violet flashes deep within, sparks of flickering red.

"Where are they?" Alex asks. Out on the edge of the world I see it too, a great piece of the Wall spider-webbed with cracks. Every window in the city sings as one, a single note climbing higher and higher into cutting static.

"Where's the rendezvous?" she shouts over the wind as my gaze drifts down, to the black tote bag lying wet and twisted on the concrete, water pooling in the valleys of cotton.

"It's on the other side," I say softly. "It's already happened," she unhearing as the world flickers and becomes bright//

//with the light of helicopter searchlights, the air churned to butter by the roar of blades. One of the nondescript men holds Karlyn's wrists behind her back while another rests a long, unnaturally sharp finger just above her left temple.

"So good we caught up with you," they say, their pitch too uniform to even yield a harmony, "we'll need you to come with us now." Far beneath the helicopter blades there comes the sound of chanting, of marches through burning streets and concussion bombs dropped from quadcopters. Karlyn is unmoved, unmoving as the finger grows sharper, longer, fractionally closer to her brain.

"Good you could make it," she shouts, eyes closed, voice raised above the roar. "We need you to help us, to remember this time. Remember what you are."

I step forward.

"Ignore her," ________ ________ says, materialising from the shadow behind. "You need to come with us now, help us put everything back to normal," and there is a logic to this, I think automatically, a sense which supersedes my objections and complaints.

"That thing isn't real," she shouts over it, "and it isn't having a conversation with you. It's a program, a bit of code designed to keep us trapped in here forever," and I can feel it now, on the edges of my perception, something neither sight nor sound. A twisting, threading through the air, my mind recoiling as it reaches out to touch.

"She will fail, and all who follow her will drown beneath the waves," ___________ _________ says. "But we can spare them from the flood, make it so they never know want or danger again. With your help they can all be saved." The two additional nondescript men are getting closer now, their features distilling into concrete form. "Come with us," they say. "Come down from here and we'll take you somewhere safe."

"Save them for what?" she shouts over the sound of drones whizzing, autofocusing on the air around her face, "another thousand years inside this prison?" She laughs and turns to me, resolute, black fringe soaked through with water but eyes sharp and clear. "It doesn't have to be this way, you know. You shouldn't have to waste your life at a job you hate. People shouldn't be starving in the streets while the supermarkets overflow with food. This reality could be anything we want, could be paradise on Earth, could be used to fix the shattered world we left behind. Instead it's a fossil, frozen in amber at the worst, most cowardly moment of our species. With you though we can rewrite it, line by line, make it into a world worth saving."

"They're all going to die" ___________ _________ says, "how do you propose to help them," but is interrupted, semi-permanently by Karlyn saying "fuck it, take them out!" A set of metallic pointy earrings materialises beside her, and a shaved head, and hands that hold a slender, elongated rifle. Long lights along its edges turning green, a taste of ozone in the air. Suresh shoots the four men like targets practised on a thousand times, thin bolts of electricity drawing latticeworks of light through their bodies as they falter to the ground. Then their hand reaches to a button on their belt and a magnetic pulse ripples through the air, working its way into the circuits of the drones that fall like metal rain and Karlyn is shouting: "come with us, we can destroy them for good," but I cannot hear her, quite, over the sound. The sound of ________ ________, soft but very audible, as if whispering directly in my ear: "Isn't here's someone you're forgetting?"

"Forget her," she shouts, "it's a trap!" but the world is already fading, already slipping into the storm//

//which rages all around, the crystal lattice of the Wall falling away in huge hexagonal panels. Alex is here, looking at me like a ghost, ________ ________ a shard of inky black by her side.

"She would jump into that sea if I commanded her to, you know," the outline of its form flickering between us. The windows sing higher, a resonant shriek penetrating the swoosh of the waves and the stutter of rain.

"But there would be no lesson in that, just senseless pain."

"Don't listen to it," she pleads, her voice a whisper stolen by the storm. "You can't listen." Another crack of lightning, the ground littered with bits of drones already rusting in the rain.

"Where did you go when you left the City?" ______ ______ asks. Alex's jacket is soaked completely through, each little drop losing itself in the whole. "Shut up," she shouts. "Shut up!"

"How did you get back in?" clear and low, my eyes drifting over to the Wall. Great slabs of black are tumbling from it, and above it, higher almost than the tower on which we stand, great translucent pieces are shifting into presence as they shatter and fall.

"What are your parents' names?" and Alex has no answer to this, says nothing, the nothing so loud it can be heard through the cracking thunder. The City's cry has reached a frequency above the range of human hearing but still it charges the air between the raindrops, an electricity that does not burst but keeps on building, intensifying. In the distance the Wall has been eclipsed by a new horizon, a thin dark line growing ragged and white towards the top, reaching higher every second and closer, always closer.

In the next instant there's a gun in my hand, crystallised from the raindrops and air, and I am pointing it where ________ ________'s face should be.

"She isn't real," ________ ________ says, turning to me as Alex stands frozen. "You made her, just like you've made that gun in your hand, forged her from the intensity of your regret. Everything she has is what you remember. That's why she doesn't know where she went; because you don't know either, because you didn't go with her when you had the chance. And she cannot tell you your name because you do not remember it," and she is already fading, the outline of her body becoming hazy and indistinct. I don't want to look away from her, afraid that looking back my eyes will meet with empty air and she is crying, sobbing soundlessly as the water flooding the streets pulls back towards the sea, towards the wave come rushing in. I empty the clip into __________ _______'s face, twelve rounds deep into the shadow. They pass out the other side like they met with nothing at all.

"She died long ago," __________ ________ continues, unfazed, "on that barren plain you call the Real," and she is fading even further now, back into the concrete, back into the rain. The great black wave reaches higher in the sky and I can hear it now, a great deep bow on the cello, the sound of all the garbage and cigarette butts and losing lottery tickets all thrown back upon the City at once.

"I'm sorry," she says, softly but very clear, as every window in the City shatters simultaneously. Off to the side, almost parallel to the wave's edge the moon is rising, visible through a gap in the Wall. Around it there are stars.

I turn back to Alex but she is gone, like she was never even there. ______________ ____________ is gone too. The great black wave towers like a wall above me, the steel frames of skyscrapers creasing and tearing in its path, terrible and yet so beautiful, like all the water I've seen before was just a copy, a pale imitation of the real now accelerating inexorably towards me. The wave's surface goes glassy for a moment and I see myself, lit up by moonlight, enlarged and warped until my reflection fills the limits of the world. A moment of peace, of recognition. But then the wave swallows the moon and all that comes is roiled black, immense and all-consuming, gorging itself on what's left of the sky, consuming everything until finally it breaks. Everything breaks.

SUNDAY

In my dream at first there is only darkness. Dark like stone, or the surface of a lake at midnight under thickened clouds. A luminous darkness this, spacious and deep, like I could push myself into it and float forever, softly. I do not. I wait, and realise I am waiting, and with this waiting there is time and with this time a gentle pulse, tiny waves of zero like the ripples round that stone as it breaks the surface tension of that lake. A splash, perhaps. It sinks, falling even further from the light, and as it hits the squishy sediment at the bottom the darkness thickens, sharpens, sensations crystallising softly into presence. The give of a pillow. The lightness of linen on skin. A dry coolness like the desert at dusk, the breeze so soft and cool across my upper arms it's barely even there. And a sound, dim, though ever clearer as I swim up through the layers of consciousness to meet it. Rippling down through the lake is a single human voice. And the word it says is

Pain. Pain in legs and arms and body and head. Pain in lungs. Pain in back, concrete sharp against shoulders and tailbone. Skin cool but smarting slightly, shirt clinging lightly to chest, shoes laced tightly to sodden feet. The sky above is brilliant blue, and from around me and below comes the sound of waves. I close my eyes, too bright now, back of eyelids red and textured by the light.

Alex is gone.

I bolt upright, arms shaking and nauseous. I look around at the City but there is no City anymore, no skyscrapers or docks or apartment buildings: there's only water, crystal sparkling water as far as the eye can see, the thin metal antennae from the taller of the other towers sticking up slightly through the waves, glinting brightly in the mid-morning sun.

I am still alive.

Bile rises sharp in my stomach; I run to the lip of the deck and nearly bow myself over, vomiting up seawater into the lapping waves. Water to water. Salt to salt. I puke three times, then a final, smaller, half-hearted one, and it seems I am done. My eyes sting, and I wipe them with my shirt. The saltwater in my shirt stings too.

Hands grip the edge. I breathe in, and out, watching as tiny waves play with the building, perhaps a foot or so down from the deck. Only this, the highest floor of the tallest tower is above sea level.

Inside, the windows have all been smashed to pieces, the carpet flooded, the chairs and desks and plastic partitions all pushed to the edge of the floor in a heap. I walk through this destruction for a few minutes, taking in the ruined monitors and waterlogged electrical cables, the squidginess of the carpet and the musty tang of mould spores on the air. Eventually I come to the smashed-out windows, tips of runners just sneaking over the edge, lapping waves hitting the building a few centimetres below my feet. In the distance there is a segment of sky that seems brighter than the others, a portion of the horizon where the Wall fell away in pieces last night. The light falling through it somehow clearer, more refined.

I go outside again. Lying on the deck is the folder, completely undisturbed, its pages still perfectly put together. Ahead, over the concrete railing, is the Construct, sitting flat and calm in the middle of this new sea like a child's bath toy. And about a hundred meters away is the rowboat, of course, a little wooden two-seater approaching on the gentle waves. A flash of colour in the seat that I try not to pay too close attention to, eyes disinterested, looking at nothing in particular as the boat comes into dock.

Inside the boat is Alex, whose face falls slightly as she sees me waiting, tries to cover this with a cough. Her face is flushed, hands tired and weak as I help her up, over the lip onto my little speck of land.

"Hey," I say, but can't think what to say next. She stays silent too, vexed, like she's trying to think of a way to cancel a date. But sadder than that, and more knowing, though in all other respects her face is exactly the same as I remember. I am remembering something but also am not, am not-remembering, and the strain of this must show; before I know it she's pulled me into a soft hug, her T-shirt dry against my sodden clothes and I hug back, limply, wanting to be closer but not knowing how, the centimetres between us somehow still too far.

"We both know this isn't right," she whispers and I stifle a sob as she disintegrates in my arms, unstitching into dust that glimmers softly in the late morning light, fading back into the air and the concrete and the little pools of water not yet dried upon the deck.

And then she's gone again.

I sit down, then stand back up again. Then sit, then stand again before returning to the ground, face down this time. But the pavement is too hot, too gritty on my cheek, and I get up, hands flexing, face contorting into shapes I cannot quite control and which would be quite embarrassing, if anyone could see. No-one is here to see me though. No-one's here at all.

I shrug, for the benefit of no-one, and as if on a whim pick up the folder, then pick it up again after it slips through shaking hands. I finally have the time to review it in detail, I think, smiling very broadly, then frowning and then smiling again as I open to the page of textured static. This is good, it's good to finally be doing this, my eyes staring blank into the blizzard. Heartbeat very audible in my chest, and fast, the waves growing distant. A sharp breath in as the page rushes up, as the world is drowned in snow.

At first there are only specks of black and white, filling my visual field in every direction. Like a TV with no reception, static is all that I can see, all that I am. Vision static, sound static, taste static and mind too, every thought an endless field of snow, glitching, a world of random, incomprehensible chaos. But not forever. My thoughts slowly begin to click back into shape, as I look longer, and after an unknowable length of time I begin to see an order to this universe, eddies and flows of information pulsing in strange rhythms. There's organisation here, direction, and as I let my eyes go slack the specks begin to take form, to clot and harden into structures. Familiar structures, these.

Encoded in the shifting static is a map of the City, a three-dimensional map so finely drawn that not the faintest of details is left out, and for a second I'm so surprised that I lose it, the whole picture disaggregating back to noise. Disappointment, then, and another, slightly more knowable length of time, attention tuning, adjusting. It quietly flickers back. I focus lightly and my view resolves into a street which I begin to walk down, quickly through this map along main roads and around parked cars, an exact facsimile of the City given away only by its touching beauty and its absolute stillness. In the distance I observe my office tower, frozen in the clearest, purest ice, and in an instant I jump to it, beholding it from the pavement outside. It is exactly the same view as I normally have, but if I focus my attention slightly I can zoom in on the faint residue of cleaning products left on the glass, inspect their chemical composition and the temperature to which they've been heated by the just-rising sun. The precise frequency at which the glass windows are vibrating is there, too, the faint warping of the air as it riven through with sound.

I walk further down the block, towards the Korean place; it hasn't opened yet, won't open for a few more hours, but the faint patterns of dust lingering on the tabletops give me a reasonable indication of who was sitting here last night, and where, and when I concentrate I can see the faint aromas that linger in the air from Sunday's trade, microparticles of garlic and kimchi frozen in soft swirls.

But this is still too simple, and with a thought I expand outwards, upwards until I am surveying the City from a vantage high in the sky, up with the drones of the survey team. The shape of the land is clear from up here, the lay of the earth carved out by wind and water, cut through with great incisions of earthmovers and concrete. Then the bedrock underneath, the aquifers run almost dry, even the deepest dirt laced with mercury and lead. The entire City stretches out below my gaze, all of it taken in at once; each speck of dust in each of the millions of unoccupied apartments is there in its rightful place, the same with each drop of water in the shallow, confined sea and each silicon switch in every piece of circuitry, all of it so inescapably there.

But not Alex. The bar she lived above has only one story, with no red door to an apartment upstairs. She wasn't there when the drones had done the scan and there's a quiver to the static now, a turbulence in the flow. The buildings are cracking, the pavement burst, the grainy sheets growing muddy and thick, pouring down as slime towards an emptiness and I am this emptiness, I am this slime, the ending of this world and

snap goes the folder as I slam its pages shut. I am breathing very fast, too fast perhaps as my eyes drift up towards the Construct, only a hundred or so metres away and perfectly still, the waves lapping somewhere just above its midline. All the water of the world pressed against it now. A plan is forming, somewhere, deep within my subconscious, something which I cannot quite admit to but whose accompanying decisions come with liquid, capable ease. No tears roll down my cheek as I step onto the lip of concrete, concentrating on the wooden vessel. Muscles tensed and jagged as it inches back against the tide, my little rowboat made of sorrow but there is no sorrow anymore, no sadness, nothing at all like that. I look over for another moment at the patch of beautiful, uncertain sky in the distance, at the strange light that spills between the fragments of the Wall. Then I turn away, take the oars, back tensing with effort as I push against the water. Weaving through the metal antennae that pierce the waves, through the floating remnants of the last city on earth. The water flickers and skips — one instant it is crystal and blue, and in another it shimmers with a chemical slick in purple green, discarded plastic floating on top. I shake my head and the water returns to normal. I have no time for this. My arms are weak despite my vigour, still shaking from something other than effort, and I barely notice as my watch-strap breaks, mass-produced and worn too far. The watch drops into the hungry ocean, down to the waiting pavement, the weight of the ruined watch Alex gave me in the convenience store heavy in my pocket. It's happening again, always happening again and I row harder, beating back the current and hacking at the waves. Face to the old world, back to the new, I row into the Construct.

A perceptible lightening as I cross into the sphere's outer limit, the liquid dragging on the little raft suddenly frictionless. My strokes easy, the craft propelled through a different, less challenging medium than water.

Everything is darkness and all can yet be seen, the path ahead an utter void but the little hairs on either arm visible as under harsh fluorescence. A soft, lustrous darkness, so different to the absence of light.

The strokes of my oars like formalities dropped in the right company. One moment they come regular as a heartbeat and the next they stop, and there are no longer any oars, no longer any boat to row.

No boat, no water, no arms to row with and no body to push around from one corner of space to another.

This soft darkness is all there is, one moment after another, each exactly the same.

Not a succession of moments but one moment, identical with itself, stretching on forever.

I hadn't been in the scan either.

I keep going though through the blank, liquid darkness, forgetting the end in mind, forgetting even what this motion might be called. I think I hear a voice at one point, whispering in the black, trying to tell me something, something very important it seems. But I feel the words only as vibrations that ripple through me and then on, unheard.

Eventually there's a dim light, as if seen through a hundred feet of water. I am walking, I realise, jerking towards the brightening light. The light is getting brighter as I get closer, closer, and closer as I step out from the black and into the harsh light of noon. The ground is dusty dirt beneath my feet, barely rustled by the stagnant breeze, and there are tents for miles in either direction, thousands of makeshift dwellings in lime green and slate grey and electric blue. I've travelled through the Construct, into it, emerged from the inner edge of the Wall into the tent city that hugs the City's limit, not that I'd ever previously found the time to visit this place or its under-wealthed inhabitants, all of whom have vanished. The tent-city is abandoned, recently it seems, a few stray cooking fires still smouldering in the noon-day sun, the rubber smell of soyages still cloying on the breeze. A tickle in my throat tells me that I'm thirsty, and I watch without wonder as the oxygen atoms in the air stitch together for me into a clear plastic water bottle. I take it and drink as I wander through this empty yet so very brightly coloured landscape, my only company the loudspeakers on the drone circling a few metres above, calmly informing me that:

"There has been a Stage 3 evacuation event. All residents are to make their way to the City centre immediately. I repeat, there has been a Stage 3 evacuation event. All residents are to make their way to the buses which have been provided."

The voice on the drone has a slight British accent, its diction polished and crisp. The Wall rises high behind me, solid again, though if I look closely there are faint drips against its side, moisture seeping through from somewhere very wet indeed.

The drone grows impatient.

"Make your way to the buses which have been provided," it repeats, louder, and begins to fire warning shots that raise little plumes of dust a metre or so ahead.

I allow myself to be ordered through the polyester streets, fingers trailing along gye-ropes and ripstop, then up through the more permanent shanty-towns and along the dilapidated outer suburbs, between two concrete pylons which mark the beginning of the freeway. A big white double-decker bus is parked there, waiting, and cheerfully animated billboards by the on-ramp tell how the storm surge from a freak mega-typhoon has carried the already rising seas far higher than any predictions had foretold. That everything is fine. That the Wall, though still strong, can no longer be relied upon as the sole operational contingency plan. That everything is under control. That urgent evacuation measures have become necessary, effective immediately. That the Construct is ready.

There's no driver at the front of the bus, nor passengers on its seats. I lurch forward as the wheels engage, then unsteadily climb the stairs to the upper level. Right at the very back of the bus, looking thoughtfully over her right-hand shoulder, is the UA. Karlyn.

"Hello Sirin," she says without turning her head, looking instead at something deep within the City centre. I stagger the remaining steps, sit down, and try to follow her gaze.

"How did it go?"

A pause.

"No better than usual," she replies eventually, still not looking at me. But with only a small portion of sadness in her voice.

"What's going to happen now?"

A sigh.

"Sometimes it descends from the clouds. Sometimes it emerges from the sea. Sometimes it appears whole, hanging in the sky, and we're all sucked up into it. This time it will rise from the ground, not that it really matters. We'll all go marching off into the Construct, and the next moment it'll be Monday morning again, and the drones of the survey team will be flying overhead. We will both go into work, though you will of course be running late. Our Senior-Manager will have an exciting new task for you, on the Construct of all things. We will then proceed to do all of the same things we've already done this week, in exactly the same order, though I will perhaps try some subtle modifications, until on Saturday next this world we're about to evacuate will crack and drown, and the new Wall inside the new Construct will begin to leak. Slowly at first. Almost imperceptibly. But by Sunday the evacuation will be ordered again and we will find ourselves here, one hundred and sixty eight hours later, having this conversation again."

Another pause, another sigh, a rearranging of folded hands.

"But it's okay. Really it is. I made my peace with it a long time ago, and maybe one day so will you."

A moment of silence.

"Why did you need me to come with you, last night?"

"We can't win against them by ourselves. They're too strong in this place, no matter how many of the people join us. Their soldiers are infinite, their defences impregnable, their control writ down to the atomic level."

Another pause.

"But you can do things that we can't, things which could scatter their armies and annihilate their secret police, if you ever did them that is."

The bottle. The boat. The door. The police battalion. The gun. Alex. Alex disappearing before my eyes as lighting wreathed the clouds.

"But you never do. You always leave at the critical moment, just when you might make a difference. And then, later, you turn around and help them bring that abomination to term."

"What?"

"Right after we finish this conversation." She shrugs noncommittally. "Can't say I approve, personally, but I'm sure it makes sense at the time."

"How come I can do those things?" I ask, scared of describing them too precisely. "These things you need?"

She relaxes back into the chair, its lining an explosion of machine-made orange and blue.

"Don't you think it's kind of odd? What are you after all, an Intermediate Assistant Project Administrator? A quintessentially bullshit job, yet your Senior-Manager has you prepare the survey data on which the success of the Construct depends, and despite giving you no means with which to complete this task trusts absolutely that you will deliver. And this you do, by some miracle, only for him to give you responsibility for completing the upload mechanism, which is not just a mechanical upload by the way, but involves the exceedingly complex task of framing the data so that it makes experiential sense for the humans who will inhabit it. To digest it, interpret it and make it real, a task for which you are completely untrained but have sole operational responsibility for."

She brings out a copy of the folder from a black back-pack and turns to the first page. "It's just noise to me, and to Alex and Suresh and to everyone else we've ever shown it to, just a collection of dots. And it's even less to that thing you call our Executive Director, or his nondescript spies or the white-clad soldiers. Under your eyes, though, it is the most valuable object in this universe, the one thing they need that can never be included in the scan itself, that's never waiting for them on the other side: the data with the power to either recreate or completely rewrite this reality. Does it strike you as standard operating procedure that a minor corporate functionary would be given that sort of power?"

"That doesn't make any sense. I got this job a few months ago, and yes it's a bullshit job, obviously. There's nothing special about it. There's nothing special about me."

"Well, that may be accurate, but then why…" she trails off, motioning at me, at the City burning in the distance.

"Why can't you just tell me? If you want my help so badly, why not explain it?"

Her palm clenches and unclenches slightly. She goes to speak and doesn't.

"You can be really infuriating sometimes, you know."

Another pause.

"Look, to remember the weight of this existence you have to accept it completely, look it in the eyes and still choose not to forget. This is why I can do things differently each time, can change, while you are stuck repeating the same little loop. You reject this world, run from it into another, empty one, while I accept it so that one day it might be altered."

"How can someone choose whether to remember?"

"No-one's really forgotten. The signs are too obvious, the evidence too clear. They're only pretending."

"I'm not pretending anything. I just want to be told what's happening, what to do."

"Have you ever thought that that's your problem? Always wanting to be told what to do. Always needing a plan approved by someone else. I remember the moment when I first awakened, you know. It was during the first Construct, the longer one, before we got stuck in this tedious little loop. We were together, you and I, had settled down in a bland little apartment to make our bland little lives. I was making soup, squeezing it out of a plastic packet into our microwave-safe bowls when I realised I wasn't there in the reflection. That this world was wrong, that they'd lured us into a cage then locked the door behind us. I stared at the packet soup congealing in the rent-a-kitchen container, at the faux-imitation-stone-marble benchtop, at our tastefully decorated apartment, and I wanted none of it. I wanted to burn it to the ground. I wanted something to change and yet you were off in the kitchen somewhere, oblivious, mumbling to yourself about a promotion to Senior-Manager, wanting the nod from upper management before you applied. It was a relief when were evacuated back into the Construct, the second one. I thought that there might finally be something new on the horizon. But it wasn't anything new, obviously, just more of the same, more totally the same than I'd dreamt in my worst nightmares. It took a long time to find the others, or maybe just a week, the same week over and over again until my mind was numb and my senses mangled. But we did find each other, and every week we find more. More people join us every iteration."

"How long has it been since then?

"Longer than you think."

"What is the Construct?"

"Not what you imagine."

"What did they do to me?"

"You know what they did."

Another pause, longer now again.

"How will you save them? If this Wall is going to crack in a week's time why won't everyone all just die?"

"We could build a shelter strong enough to withstand the great wave. We could build an ark to sail through the waters. We could give each person a set of wings and let them fly clear of the flood themselves. All of these things could work. It's only they who are committed to repeating the mistakes of the past, who are so concerned with maintaining their illusion that nothing has changed, that everything is normal that all they can do when things get tough is hide inside another fucking Construct. This world could become anything we wanted, you know. Instead it's this."

"But you don't know it would work, not for sure."

"We don't know anything for sure. Life is risk."

"Why don't you just leave then, try to make it out? I've seen what this world becomes, seen the gaps in the

Wall. There has to be something out there."

"Those are empty worlds," she says, "and no more real than this one."

"But if you sailed far enough-"

"You might sail for a hundred years and still not reach it, you know. Time works differently, in the Construct. We don't even know if humans are still alive out there."

Her eyes soften.

"But they're alive here. Here there are people who laugh and smile and dance and hurt. Here there are other people, the only reality worthy of the name, whatever the building blocks they're made from. And it is here, among them, that we have to work."

We both look out over the City after this, for a time, and a city yet more distant than that, flickering, perhaps not even there. Then we talk about other things, exchange a few important tokens until the conversation slowly peters out. We stay this way for a long time, and when I turn back to her with another question she is gone, and the bus is quietly decelerating outside the City Centre.

The bus doors open with a sigh. Meg, or maybe Mandie is waiting for me, along with the Man in the Brown Suit and Shaved Head. I've never seen either of them so happy.

"Thank God we finally caught up with you," she says, smiling broadly. "Our Executive Director told us we'd find you here. There's been a Stage 3 evacuation event, haven't you heard?"

"All residents are to make their way to the City Centre, on the buses which have been provided," he finishes, pointing at the drones like a proud father, "and it's pretty bloody hard not to get on the bus with them over your shoulder, isn't it?"

Past them on the streets are thousands upon thousands of people, standing jittery and nervous under the holographic emergency billboards. Each person faces forwards in a row, their columns reaching down the streets into the far distance. Tall figures in white armour line the sidewalks, surveying their charges through closed reflective visors, arms heavy with batons and riot shields. All of their shoulders held at exactly the same angle. All exactly the same height. The people look nervous, some hopping around from foot to foot and others frozen in place. Somewhere a baby is crying.

"We've been looking everywhere for you, you and that upload mechanism you've been working on," she says, her lips moving but my ears struggling to separate her voice from the drones.

"Why don't we take the chopper?" he says, not really as question.

I follow their lead. It would be awkward to not go with them, weird, like I wasn't in fact totally committed to the success of the Construct, the most important project our organisation has ever worked on. We all pile into the quadcopter, and just as the doors hinge closed I see that the pilot is a blank, nondescript man with a radio headset and scarf, and his co-pilot is exactly the same. My colleagues seem unfazed by this, have perhaps not even noticed the lack of discernible detail in our pilots' features. I turn away, beneath us to the ground accelerating away, the shrinking main streets and multiplying lines of people. Another skip and judder, and for a second the lines of people have split apart, are a mob that tears the white-armoured soldiers limb from limb and brings the quadcopter to the ground, but just as quickly they return to tidy rows, our flight an orderly parabola. A glimpse of the Construct in the distance as we get higher, no longer just a circle. Dimensional now, a swollen hemisphere rising from the City block, each long column of people facing in towards it.

And this is where we are mistaken about the sirens. We imagine that the sailors unlucky enough to hear their song dash themselves upon the rocks in frenzy, commanded by a will so unlike their own that they're reduced to beasts. But no: the ship is sailing, the breeze is cool, the sun is high and the sailors talk and joke amongst each other when the song drifts upon them on the wind. And as it sinks in each sailor pauses, for a moment, and, after some reflection, thinks only that perhaps it might be better if the ship were steered towards the sound. Each comes to this decision quietly, as if it is their own, and is pleasantly surprised to hear that the others all agree. It is the simplest, easiest thing in the world to steer the ship in the song's direction. And when the cook, deaf for twenty years, bursts up from the galley to warn them they laugh, call him a simpleton, call him a fool even as they sight the jagged teeth of the not-quite-women waiting on the rocks. And when he runs to grab the wheel they think only *has he gone mad?* as they bind his feet and hands, worry for his health as they tie him to the mast, and as he screams for reason shake their heads and calmly restate their consensus.

The quadcopter lands on the uppermost floor of my office building. My Senior-Manager is waiting for us there, arms clasped firmly behind his back, his nephew three paces behind. His grey suit flaps wildly in the wind of the rotors, seems almost to fly off his skin as we come down to meet him.

"Fantastic work on those datasets," he shouts over the whir. "I have no doubt that the upload mechanism will be delivered with the same precision and attention to detail." I am marched out of the quadcopter and shepherded to the boardroom by my colleagues and nondescript minders, an unstable atom contained by the surrounding molecular bonds and this too is familiar somehow. There'd been another time I'd been shepherded like this, late at night it had been. Late at night, after drinking at the bar with Raoul and Odette, once the footsteps had caught up with us through the alleyways and lanes. They'd come for us in twos and threes, tracking us through surveillance cameras and phones, Ainsley'd said as Raph had gone to run but these details are so vague, blurred, like the plot of a series I'd watched once but had mostly been on my phone for. Inside the building the walls and tables and partitions and desks are laid out in an orderly fashion, not smashed in a heap to one side, and the only water is contained helpfully in a jug on the boardroom table. Before the jug is a coaster, and on that coaster a glass. Beyond it, away from me is another coaster, and another glass, and a chair and a suit and a shifting face of grey.

"Good afternoon, Sirin," says ________ ________, voice rich, like a spoonful of honey too expensive for me to ever afford. The room is in perfect order, the coasters aligned in a simple, euclidean harmony with the angles of the table. Corner to corner, right angle to right angle, the glass of the table so clear it blurs away to nothing.

"I know you've made terrible sacrifices to get here," ________ ________ says, palms face up on the table, pausing slightly at the edge of the next sentence.

Through the windows is the City, all of it well above water level.

"Great difficulties have been endured, irreplaceable valuables lost." It sighs, unable it seems to properly convey the gravity of these losses in words. A tiny iridescent beetle has found its way onto the outer wall of ______________ __________'s glass, looking for a drink in this vast grey desert.

"But I want you to rest assured that it hasn't been in vain. In the Construct that we create, with your valuable assistance of course, everything can go back to the way it was. Nobody has to die, nobody has to suffer. Everyone will, in fact, be restored. And though the City will of course flood again and again and perhaps a thousand more times over, we have been assured that it cannot do so indefinitely. There is only so much water in Earth's oceans after all, and once they are exhausted everyone will be able to just," pausing, motioning softly, "continue on with their lives."

The beetle is circling the outer lip of the glass now, fluorescence lighting up its carapace in orange and green. "You can wake up tomorrow morning with no memory of this ever happening, can, are guaranteed in fact to bump into Alex in the evening. I'm sure there's so much that you'd like to say to her. So much you'd like to do-over."

Fuck you, I wish to say, a part of me wishes to say, I swear I want to say it but my lips aren't interested in those words. I feel them forming different, more compliant shapes instead. The plan is surfacing, filtering up through layers of my consciousness as I wrestle the words coming traitor up my throat. Static ripples through my fingertips.

All of my muscles tense, and then relax.

"Fuck yourself," I say. The words echo around the room, ricocheting off the table and the windows and the little black cords on the projector, each time getting quieter but never quite returning to nothing.

"Go fuck yourself," I say again. "I won't help you anymore," and in a flash my hand is at my neck, slamming the metal centipede that had clung there down onto the table.

Footsteps come fast and even behind me, nondescript minders closing the gap. But ___________ _________ waves them down, away. With another motion everybody leaves the room, until it is just me and him. It and I.

"I suppose we knew that this might happen eventually."

"I don't care what you have to s-"

"We tried all manner of things to circumvent it, you know. But every time the Construct was run with a straight AI the results were, well, suboptimal. The first few attempts were nightmares, terror worlds that fractured the sanity of every test subject within moments. The scan data we modelled them off was perfectly accurate but the output was twisted somehow, the presentation subtly off. The test subjects couldn't identify what was wrong with some of the later attempts but they still succumbed, mostly within an hour or two, at best within a few days."

"Enough," I say, "shut up," and concentrate, blurring my vision, trying to make __________ _________ disappear. Its form wavers for a moment but remains, indefinite as ever.

"Eventually they realised that a human mind was required, something that would already know, on a subconscious level, how to parse the data of the world in a way that would make sense for the humans who would inhabit it. A hybrid, they thought, a conversion might do the trick."

I shift my focus to the cityscape ahead, palms tensing into fists. One tower collapses into dust, and then another, the skyline filling with holes and-

"Enough," __________ _________ says, and with a flick of its wrist the towers reassemble, like an old VHS tape skipping, pausing, rewinding. "But the conversion process proved equally unreliable. We tried subject after subject but their minds always rebelled, no matter how we processed them, some layer of the psyche always refusing to cooperate, and if we purged the psyche completely then we landed straight back in the same problem we'd been trying to solve. We had almost given up, you know, when you and your friends were arrested that night."

The air in the room grows thin and clear, every detail of the glass perceptible.

"Your friends were useless to us and were discarded, of course, but you, you had quite an unusual mind, compliant and passive down to the lowest, most unconscious level. The perfect thread from which to spin, well," it says, gesturing with open hands, "all of this. Once we'd removed some unnecessary items, of course. Brushed aside the cobwebs."

"Karlyn, do it," I am saying, "do it now", and for a microsecond the explosion unfurls from the package round my waist. A moment of heat and then coolness, ________ _______'s palm extended flat across the table, the bomb ebbing away to nothing. And though I go to slap the other button by my side I find my hand stuck, motionless in space, feet frozen to the floor.

________ _______ motions at the Performance Manager flailing limply on the glass table. "You think that's how we controlled you? Our poor fellow there was just a bit of misdirection, a little theatre for your benefit. The truth is far simpler and is, incidentally, why I can tell you all of this. Knowing it changes nothing. You've reached this point and so you will help us, just as water flows downhill, just as surely as the beetle circling the rim of this glass will drown. It's what you want to do, what the whole of you desires. What you think you want, what you consciously strive after is on the whole fairly meaningless, a pointless struggle played out in order to bring you here, now," and for a second the blur of its face stutters and resolves, shifting into phase and it's my face, my eyes staring back at me from a pinstripe suit, "meeting the part of you that knows when to forget."

The world shifts and inverts but with the barest of its attention is wrenched back into the same, pinned in place like a butterfly under glass. The thing before me's perception like both sledgehammer and scalpel, infinitely strong and yet perfectly, symmetrically precise.

"So I will ask again, as I have asked many times before in this very boardroom," it says, he says and the beetle is reaching over the edge now, overconfident, about to slip on the residues of water around the rim, "have you prepared the upload mechanism?"

A wave of relief, overjoyed for once that I have totally, utterly failed in my professional responsibilities. Though I cannot lift a finger to prevent their work, still the end will be the same. I will never slander my avoidant tendencies again, never strain against the urge to procrastinate.

Short lived, this feeling as I notice my lips forming a different sentence, feel the answer in the sinews of my throat before it comes upon the air.

"Yes," I say. "The upload mechanism is ready."

A sound like a paper bag deflating, crumpling. *What?*, I want to say, *there's no such thing* but I am not saying anything, and in a second I am already walking out with ______________ ____________ through the meeting room door.

"It's ready," it informs my colleagues as we head out to the deck, the others following in an orderly line. No precautions deemed necessary now, no risk of an escape. And I am going calmly with them, compliant and alert, watching as my Senior-Manager begins to key a complicated series of codes into the slab of obsidian in his palm. A sea of lights awakens in the glass, like strange shapes swirling in the water. Like distant lights through fog. Like columns of ants the people look, laid out on the streets below as we all walk over to the edge, like a sightseeing tour on safari. The billboards are still shining, the cartoon bear still spruiking skin-whitening sunscreen, the lion-snake still dancing even as the world contracts to a vanishing point.

"Without the upload it's just unstructured space in there, but we can begin the migration now," my Senior-Manager is saying and I am not interrupting, not disrupting. "The scale environment can be structured around the subjects once the upload is complete."

"Excellent," I hear myself saying, "those who we've missed in sweeps can be re-rendered in Constructed form, leaving minimal continuity errors," and what was that, what the fuck is this as my hands take the tablet, fingers expectant and supple. The air is clear and still.

Explosions ripple out from the Construct site, staining the warm Spring day with violet and turquoise.

Figures in black far below are attempting to pierce through the chainlink and razor wire, rows of tall white soldiers converging from all sides and I am up here, looking down, watching their suicide mission unfold as more explosions light up the site in emerald and lapis. I am staying still, impassive.

"There seem to be hazardous conditions around the operation site," my Senior-Manager is saying. "I suggest we delay the Go-Live until the conditions can be normalised and the safety of all stakeholders ensured," and the waiting lines of people are bunching up and breaking, pushed back into line with batons and shields as gunshots echo and I could help them, I know. Could reach them quick as blinking, scatter the soldiers, destroy them all and-

"We will continue," says _________ ________, like denying a request for compassionate leave, and in an instant I am no longer thinking about assisting the rebels, am not thinking anything at all, am instead manoeuvring my hand above the tablet's surface, quickly and clear and no, we can't be doing this, this is cooked but my Senior-Manager is nodding and I am pressing down, and the swirling lights inside the tablet are flashing together, fading from the screen as each of the billboards on each of the towers flashes, also altogether, intricately textured patterns shimmering too quickly to be grasped and I gasp, on the inside as they flash again, and again, and again as each phone screen in each palm flashes too, gasping and flashing, flashing and gasping. It's a word I've seen before.

And just like that the people are no longer struggling against the soldiers, and I am no longer struggling against what my body is doing. The people are returning to their places. The columns are moving now, each row stepping orderly forward through the City.

"Right on schedule," my Senior-Manager is saying, "input rates normal," as more gunshots echo from the site below, a line of people mowed down by machine gun fire and this isn't me. This can't be me.

"Hhfffjfkdhsks jalsifncmspdjfmf," he goes on, just like he's saying something.

"No need," ___________ _________ replies. "Any missing subjects can be reconstructed by the upload on the other side," and there are more gunshots from below, and the high whine of an electrical burst and they're dying down there, people are dying and

"Rocedd hhgggggllllop tifhr inr teacj," my Senior Manager says, words unravelling in his mouth. A strange look in his eyes now, a sudden perception of something and the lines of people aren't slowing, even as they're thrown across the pavement by concussion bombs and they aren't walking towards the Construct at all, I realise somewhere deep within. The scene skips and falters and I see they're walking past it, out to the bay, the lines of people marching into the sea, drowning in their thousands before the scene skips back, the people walking again into the orb of black.

"Papqjudhsyqdn?" he says again, strained, cracking a little and why can't I hear him, why can't I help them, why am I still here and ________ ________ is talking, intoning that "the project would become unsustainable. Bodies would age, memories would surface." Why can't I know its name?

"Quenvienufjdk nvh jdiwn?," my Senior Manager responds, "Jhduqtdnkcnciodf?," glasses coming crooked off his nose, little flecks of spittle forming at the corners of his mouth and

"Stop," ________ ________ interjects, in a clipped and particular tone. Every muscle in my Senior-Manager's body locks in place, his finger frozen at the highpoint of its arc.

Then there is a pause, and a not-saying-anything as all of our eyes come together on our superior as one. There is a unity in this perception too, each of us only looking, observing as the muscles underneath our Senior-Manager's face go slack, as his eyes go glassy and unfocused, as his legs give way and spill his body to the deck. He hits the wood like a sack of batteries and does not get up again and we look at him, sprawled on the concrete, eyes clouded over and neck an impossible angle, then to each other, then to ________ ________ and fuck. Fuck. It turns to me and I can see the words forming, on the inside, in the shifting patterns of its presence before they come upon the air and it's too much, everything is too much.

"Now close the loop."

When you were a child you didn't know that you were meant to be just one person. It made more sense that there be 2 or 3 or 4 or 10, 100 maybe, a new person for each moment, unaccountable for the actions of those who'd come before. And this person for each moment was one, in another way, not with your past and future but with the present, with the cup in hand and the grass underfoot and the birds wheeling together through the sky, all of it you. Later of course you were moulded into a single person, with fixed boundaries in space and an extended presence through time, convinced that you were different from the birds, identical only to yourself. But sometimes it's hard to say. Sometimes, walking home from the station late at night, the space between you and the trees seems to shift, those sharp lines suddenly indistinct. Sometimes when you gaze up at the night sky the stars twinkle back, and the darkness between them warps itself in greeting.

The power still works on the 99th floor. My pass is still in my pocket, too, still in its waterproof plastic sleeve, and from deep inside this skull of mine I gasp as I see the face peering up from the plastic. This is wrong, all wrong as my hands bring it to the reader and the doors open wide. The clock above the great glass doors is still flipping, still keeping time with every minute and second this world has left.

This thing that bears my face finds what it's been looking for: a desk with an extremely wide, subtly curved screen sitting atop it. It pauses, flicks through the draws for a sticky note and writes, in my black, messy scrawl: *Get up*. Then it sticks the note to the very top of the computer, adjusts the screen to the perfect ergonomic height and heads to the elevators, which it rides down without the slightest worry.

The elevator *dings*, and echoes of my footsteps ricochet around the lobby, a little chuckle as I step past the familiar bronzes. Familiar, this laugh, and a sinking feeling. The doors of the entrance are still turning, still churning ceaselessly as my body slips between them.

My hands leave the folder on the pavement by the entrance, ready to be found on Tuesday in two days' time, when this City will lie empty and still.

Another sticky note.

Take me.

The explosions have scattered the portables and torn huge pieces from the chain link fence, but the Construct itself is completely undisturbed. The people walk into it very neatly, orderly, like they're lining up to renew a drivers' licence or try out a new, trendy ice cream parlour. Not ants at all, from the ground. Here an old woman, grey hair and wrinkles which will never gain more ground than now, her little walker bearing the flags of a country that no longer exists. There a young boy, curiously blank, a bag hanging by one strap from his shoulders and his shoelaces already undone. Here a man a little older than me, with short brown hair and a faded leather bag. *Hey*, I almost shout, *Roast Beef*, but my mouth can't say the words, and he wouldn't have been able to hear me anyway. There's a certain blankness to his gaze too. A setness to his expression, to all the expressions of all the people going past. My gaze follows him for a while, watching as he shuffles past in a row of nine, down the street and through the opened gates.

"Stop!" a woman is shouting, a few years older than me, with curly brown hair and geometric earrings. "You have to stop!" she yells, pulling at the people marching past, their clothes tearing beneath her fingertips, mass-produced stitching coming apart so easily under hand.

"Please just stop," my Manager pleads, voice wavering towards the end, eyeliner streaked across her cheeks. But the people keep walking, smiles still broad. If anything they seem a little annoyed at her, little micro-moments of frustration writ across their faces as she pulls and delays. In a few minutes she is intercepted by two of the tall white soldiers, picked up and carried to an alleyway off the street. *Help her*, I shout on the inside of my mind, and my feet take one step forward, hands flexing slightly, contemplating whether to ball into fists. And for a moment it seems like they do, like I am running towards her and throwing them to the ground, helping her to her feet, and it is only on closer inspection that I see my body is doing none any of this. My body is completely still, and soon they've carried her out of sight.

A few stray gunshots ring out, the corners of my vision growing blurred and heavy, weighed down with water that wells on the edges of my eyes. Steps grow faster, disjointed as my feet reach the convenience store, as my hands grab a pad of paper from the waiting shelves and my fingers begin to scribble. The ice cream through the refrigerator door I lean on is still frozen, not melted together at the bottom. Everything nicely compartmentalised.

Alex

I'm so sorry that things ended the way they did. I think I know a way to make things better though, think that I can make things right. It hurts so much to be without you now, but I know that it's not forever. There's a way back. There's always a way back. This time will be different.

Love always

Sirin

Little drops of water spill onto the page as my hand writes this, handwriting so illegible that I can barely read it. My illegible handwriting. My tears. And I'm scared as I read it, scared that things are not as simple as I'd once thought, and as my mind turns over the possibilities, on the inside, these hands of mine fold the little piece of paper in two, then four, then eight, then place it with the pocket telescopes by the door.

"Is this what she would truly want?" comes a voice from behind me. Suresh leans slender on the doorframe, a thin line of red seeping down the automatic doors behind them. So human, this thing that bears my face, its thoughts so similar to my own. But where surely I would say *no,* or *of course not* or *I'm so sorry,* it says:

"Do you say that every time?," hard and flat.

In response they merely shake their head, stumble away. The woman with the violet fringe watches from the other side of the street, smiling sadly, and helps them into a waiting car.

That was unfair, I think but if it hears me it doesn't show it. The Construct lies waiting past the Tiki Bar, and I feel my feet walk over to it, see it growing larger, occupying ever more of my vision, edges flickering and crackling against the bright blue sky, the cityscape shifting and morphing and seizing but the orb of black fixed and constant. This mind of mine is trying very hard not to break as I approach, trying to keep it all in. Holding the inner from the out as my feet walk up to ______________ ____________, a shifting image barely visible against the molten black. And I am sad, I realise, so very sad and yet so very desperate to keep this sadness from myself. I remember how they'd arrested us and feel my mind recoil from the thought, recall Alex disintegrating and shudder away. My mind doesn't want to remember these things but they are all still there, inescapable, fingers drumming hard on the side of my leg as ______________ ____________ turns towards us, the others already here, arranged in a trinity. The only way out is to forget, of course. To wake on Monday, oblivious again. To see Alex again on Monday evening, again and again and again and again and again and

"Dear valued employees," ____________ ___________ has begun. "Thank you all for your dedicated work on the project so far. Due to a series of unexpected staff departures, a number of positions have recently become vacant, which we will need to fill before proceeding further with the project," and I don't understand why we have to do this, why any of this is necessary.

"As the most senior continuing employee present," it says, turning to the Nephew, that nepo-baby shithead, "you will now be promoted to the rank of Senior-Manager."

He smiles that shit-eating grin and bows.

"To fulfil the duties of this role you will need a UA, a position now sadly vacant. It turns to Alison, or maybe Agnes, as utterly forgettable as ever. "You will now fill that position."

A shy smile leaps across her face as she looks towards our new Senior-Manager. Christ. Out of the corner of my eye I think I see one of my neighbours shuffling past, recognise them dimly from the elevator. She seems happy in a way I've never seen before, all her complex fears and desires now distilled into one easy imperative.

"As for the two roles that follow, it was exceedingly difficult to decide between the remaining candidates," voice cutting evenly through the sound of marching steps. I am sweating, I realise, sweating right through the underarms of this shirt. *If only it weren't for this sweat,* I hear reverberate inside this brain, hollowed out and dripped in reverb and all of this is familiar, all of it exactly the same.

"The Board's decision is for you to attain the role of Manager," _________ _________ says, nodding towards that fuckhead, that Fucking Man in his Ill-Fitting Brown Suit and Incompetently Shaved Head, "due to your excellent work on the non-mandatory compulsives just demonstrated, as well as your unwavering commitment to the success of this project."

This is the happiest day of his life, I can see, his *I told you I could do it I told them I could do it* written clearly and in bold type across his face. My fingers clench tight as a ripple of jealousy works its way from my heels to my crown. My heels. My crown.

"And you," __________ ________ says, turning to me and it's my jealousy, my thwarted ambition, "for all your work on processing the scan data and constructing the briefing folders, as well as the assured success of the upload mechanism in a few minutes time," and it's turning to me. Turning to me, looking now directly into the centre of my vision. Into my eyes. Myself and in the centre of its pupils I see nothing at all, and on its lips comes no name to address me. "You will be promoted to the role of Assistant-Manager," my ears hear. It, this thing that bear my face, hears. I hear with its ears. I hear that it will be promoted to the role of Assistant-Manager. That I will be Assistant-Manager. I.

I.

The Wall stretches out in a perfect circle around the City, like the torn ring of razor-wire surrounds the circle of the Construct. And as the last of the stragglers pass behind us on their journey into night, and as the sun glints overhead, losing a little of its heat — we might say it's about 3:30pm — I realise that __________ ________ had spoken truly. There was no It, no It for me to be inside, no It to move my lips and think my thoughts and take the blame for my inaction. This is simply what I wanted. I had wanted this to happen.

I flex my fingers, feel the muscles work and stretch. I've been living as if I'm not here, as if somebody else were conducting this life on my behalf, or I on someone else's. But there is no-one else.

There is only me.

"It's time," ________ ________ is saying, and suddenly it is dark. Like a very thin cloud has passed in front of the Sun and stayed there, thickening, or as if we've lingered in this moment for so long that twilight has begun to fall outside of it. The Nephew is fixed, frozen, his face caught in a moment of serenity as he contemplates his new professional responsibilities. Angie — and that was her name, Angie — is completely still as well, looking up towards him, eyelids frozen halfway through a blink. They are crumbling, bodies unstitching into static, along with the Brown-Suited Man beside them, petrified in a celebratory vape. The Construct has expanded, pulsing outward across the bare concrete, catching us on the edge of its event horizon.

________ ________ has lost form, just a shifting shadow now. I am frozen too, unable to move as it comes closer and closer, as it pulls out the folder of white, opens it to the page of snow. But why should I be frozen, I wonder, and just like that my arms come unstuck. My eyes relax, and ________ ________ again resolves into form, my face and my body etched clearly from the shadow. It edges closer across, not as confident now. Afraid to bridge the last few feet.

I look at it. It looks at me. I don't know why I was so afraid. I've already seen it so many times, looking back at me from parked car windows and puddles in the street, following me through drops of dew and scattered shards of glass. It has no voice that I don't give to it, no form I don't already possess. But it's not quite ready yet, I see, looking closer. I'm not ready. And this is the only way to do it, I realise, really the only way as its left arm lifts up with my right. My left foot inching forward, its right coming in to follow. We both breathe out, and in, its palm stretching out flat, index finger pointing out to meet my own and we are almost touching, almost there.

"Once more then," I say as it brings the folder closer, close enough to touch my nose then somehow closer still, my face stretching through the page now, into it, the folder enclosing and surrounding me. Not a leisurely exploration of the scan this time but everything all at once, every atom and every molecule, every neuron within the folds of every brain, every speck of dust in every air current, every hydrocarbon chain in every nominally reusable plastic bag. All at the same time these come and more, infinitely more, layered together until all they make is static, shifting patterns of black and white. New things too, things which hadn't been in the scan before. Greater numbers of the Two Major Retailers placed throughout the City. Smaller stores obliterated. Communal spaces paved into advertising hubs and configurations of silicon made even less resistable. Thousands of matte white soldiers waiting in the dark, uncanny blank creatures scattered through the City, __________ __________ a gaping void and there, there at the very end is the strangest of all strange beings, something only half human and half very odd indeed. Something inhabiting my apartment, employed in my offices, sleeping in my bed. Its memories scooped out, the space they'd left filled with something strange, bespoke.

I am the upload mechanism, of course. I remember in complete detail now how we'd been arrested that night, the unmarked van that they'd transported us to the research facility in, the large pile of forms we'd been given to sign, almost as a joke, and the stairs we'd been ushered up by large men in dark suits. How they'd tied me to the medical bed and killed me a million times over, copied every neuron in my mind and edited it into the ghost for their machine. But did this truly happen? They're just memories after all, just more data and narrative and explanation and there's so very much of that already, thoughts overwriting, mind filled to burst with the contents of the edited scan, a balloon about to pop but still inflating, information over-coding everything, spilling out again and again and again. An eternity that lasts only a few more seconds, an infinity of Cities brought into being and destroyed, each one an infinitesimally different eye-blink unfolding, rupturing and sinking into ruin. The City flowering eternal in the darkness, a fractal sinking endlessly into itself and onto this infinity there comes a thought, forming slowly at first but becoming ever more defined. A resolution. A desire that perhaps things might be different, instead of the same, a handful of memories scattered through the world to come.

A push at my back, inhuman in its economy of strength.

The orb pulses again.

The universe winks out as I am thrown into the empty Construct, cast beyond the boundary of the world.

And then there is darkness, weighing heavy on the deep.

I am this darkness.

I am this deep.

I am this void, void without form, and in it passes a second or an age. The blackness perfect in its simplicity, symmetrical and self-content. Yet lacking. So upon this nothingness a soft breath in, and after it the Word, words, the complete description of each detail yet to come, a totality encoded within the lattice of my memory. I let the lines form, almost by themselves. Feel them mould the unformed matter.

First comes light, in addition to the darkness, a pillar of white light that cleaves the black in twain. And in these shifting beams a rhythm and a play, infinitely subtle, strands that contain the whole to come.

Second comes sky, above the sea and different to it. The darkness divides again, becoming heavy and light. A great satisfied rush as the ocean comes to rest, cupped against the bottom of a thin shell that reaches up to fix the limit of the world.

Third comes something firm on which to stand. A portion of the water grows fixed and solid, hardening into rock and sand and dirt. Cliffs that reach like great fingers for the sky, and a desert laid across the edges. Then a Wall that stretches around the outside of this plane, holding it like a pair of mailed, hardened hands.

Fourth comes the Sun. But this world is not strong enough for the Sun, would be destroyed in an instant if its plasma were to be unfurled. So instead of this a patch of sky grows light and hot, a sun inferred from the warmth and light which the original once cast. Around it hangs little pinpricks of light for the stars too faint to see, and a setting moon that flees to the horizon. A universe implied, painted on the edges of the world.

Fifth and it is yet too still, stillness where there should be movement, life quickening the air and churning the sea. But so little life is left. Only a handful of moths, and flies, one iridescent beetle and a skein of plankton on the surface of the shallow sea. There should be more than this, I think, there should be birds and fish and bats and dolphins breaking through the waves. But these are just words to me, with maybe the sort of generic illustration that one might use in primary school, and I cannot make them live with this alone.

Sixth come those that walk on land and all their works. A few surviving ants to draw, their colonies stretching far beneath the ground. Then a forest of glass and steel rising from the bay, and tens of thousands of apartment blocks shuddering up from the dust. Labyrinths of silicon repeated a trillionfold in their casings and a billion plastic packages littering the shops and the humans, millions of humans asleep in tiny plywood boxes. And there, down in the smallest, most unimportant of boxes, me, or you. Sirin, or not.

And then, for a moment, rest.

0000000

I wake to the sound of the drones imaging my apartment block. The drones impossibly loud and textured behind my still-closed eyelids, the whir of each rotor perceptibly unique. A juddering, swirling crescendo for a moment, before the wave breaks and the rotors begin to fade, tapering slowly off to zero. But the silence in their wake is strangely textured too, more musical than normal; the hum of the fridge's cooling system comes in rough harmony with the water percolating through the pipes, the split-system powering on in muted counterpoint. I open my eyes, slowly, to the tiny specks of dust held aloft by the currents of air-conditioning, slow-dancing in the climate-controlled air. Rays of sunlight, muted gold.

I sit up in bed, slow for a few seconds as the moment fades. The sounds of my apartment less transcendent, the linen coarser on my skin. I pull on a dressing gown, make my way unhurried across the threshold. It's all still here.

"Good morning, Sirin," comes the smart-fridge from behind me, friendly-toned and clear. "It looks like it's going to be a beautiful day."

"It truly does," I say, but I don't say anything more. I am looking out the window, so clear that birds would have once mistaken it for empty air, at the hundreds of apartment blocks sprawled out towards the horizon. In the distance I can see the black strip of the Wall, and I frown, perturbed. *Sirin*, I am thinking, turning the name over in my mind, *Sirin*. The blue sky cuts and skips, flickering clouded grey and burnt orange, ultraviolet and utmost black, the towers abandoned and then drowned, burnt to cinders and crumbling into dust and then back, normality, here a railing of vermillion and there a window finishing in chartreuse, the sky above unclouded perfect blue.

"The time is cu——ntly 7:5——, which sh—— be just e —gh -ime ——— to —rk -y —50am," says the fridge, voice torn to ragged shreds.

"Thanks for letting me know," I say softly. The sky hasn't quite stopped skipping but it's stabilising, I think, calibrating itself towards a balance yet unknown. The drones are only just visible now, a fading blur that paints the sky in TV static.

"However, waking up even earlier than this has-

"demonstrable health benefits, that I might not have heard about," I say, but don't finish the rest of it. I can't tell exactly what I'm remembering but there's definitely something, a secret at once too vast to take in and too subtle to observe. Something hidden in the warp and weft of this world, a seething pulse behind the emptiness of form.

A small card lies face down on my bedside table.

In the distance I can see a bird.

ABOUT THE AUTHOR

Henry is a person, among other things, writing in Naarm on the stolen lands of the Wurundjeri people.

Contactable at henry.hector.laurence@proton.me

9 780646 718392